The Recumbent
and
the Upright

*A Bicycle Adventure by
Two Retired and Unfit Cycle Enthusiasts,
That Grew Into a Ride Across the Continent*

by

Sheryl Van Fleet

PublishAmerica
Baltimore

ISBN: 1-60474-655-6
PUBLISHED BY PUBLISHAMERICA, LLLP
www.publishamerica.com
Baltimore

Printed in the United States of America

To my family:

*To Bryon, my husband—the love of my life-
who dreams the dreams and makes all things possible—*

*To our sons Andy and Tyler—who make all things fun—
and center our lives—*

*To their terrific wives Madri and Meghan
who are wonderfully supportive of everyone—*

*To the next generation that Kaylin Jean has begun—
she lights up our lives-*

and

*To my 94 year old mom, Millie Rosvall, who is the original,
"YOU CAN DO IT" mom!*

Contents

Introduction

Frontiers

"Frontiers are regions where people are up against the new, the different, the unexpected, the still-to-be-mastered, and the still to be understood."

—**Jack Schaefer** *(Author of the western classics Shane and Monte Walsh)*

Like many people, I have often thought I was born in the wrong generation. I wished I could have traveled west in a covered wagon, built a cabin in the woods and survived off the land. If I could have only been a part of the frontier, what an *adventure* that would have been.

As it happened, I was born in St. Louis, Missouri, which was at least the Gateway to the West, but was born too late to see the show. 1947 was at the end of WWII, not the beginning of Westward Ho! Sad but true. There would be no Oregon Trail in my life. No frontier towns with dirt streets and horses tied to hitching posts. But even as a young girl, I admired that time. In the 5th grade I was clueless enough to wear my Fanner 50 cap gun and holster to school, just for fun. I was uncommonly oblivious. I practiced twirling my beloved Fanner 50 in my right hand and learned to effortlessly, without looking, slide it into the holster just like Wyatt Erp. (Can you imagine what would happen today, in most schools, if some kid brought a Fanner 50 to class?) I watched all the westerns on TV and all the westerns I could see at the movies. I was especially sad to be growing up without a horse. My poor parents. I asked for a horse every Christmas and birthday, and they had to re-explain to me that it wouldn't fit in the backyard.

Then I grew up, stopped romanticizing about Bonanza, and Maverick, and Paladin and led a pretty normal life for a girl growing up in the 50's and 60's. Though my family did do a lot of "vacation" camping where we cooked over campfires, ate the fish we caught, and swam in lakes and streams, who are we kidding, that wasn't the FRONTIER!

However, as luck would have it, I hooked up with a guy that had a lot of the frontier in him. My husband Bryon has, ever since I have known him, been seeking out the regions where he was, **"…up against the new, the different, the unexpected, the still-to-be-mastered, and the still to be understood."**

Because of Bryon, we started our life together in the 1970's teaching in Australia, then New Zealand and finally in Japan. Because of him we saved our money and backpacked through the third world. We traveled through the likes of Russia, Thailand, Laos, Indonesia, Malaysia, Nepal, India, Pakistan, Afghanistan, Iran, Egypt, Ethiopia, Yemen, Kenya and Turkey. He was the driving force, the planner, the navigator. I was the trusty sidekick, and the partnership seemed to work for us pretty well.

Somehow, between then and now, we raised two sons, got old enough to retire, injured our backs and knees, put on weight, gathered other assorted health baggage, and frankly, it was looking like the big adventures were over. But then one day a few things fell together, like a snowball gathering itself into an avalanche and we found ourselves smack in the middle of a whole new **Frontier.**

This new frontier had wheels and spokes and pedals, and sort of bushwhacked us unexpectedly which was all the more sweet, because it came to us so late in life. We had been seduced by the bicycle, you see. Well into our mid-fifty's, we had found a new frontier to explore, and it became one of the big adventures of our lives.

This then is an Everyman's Adventure by two retired, overweight Oregonians with herniated discs, bad knees, high blood pressure and general lack of fitness, who managed to ride their bikes across the State of Oregon. They liked the adventure so much that they then tackled the whole continent. The following is that story.

Part One

Why Do This?
and
What Is This Thing?

Chapter One

"...Do Not Despair..."

"When I see an adult on a bicycle, I do not despair for the future of the human race."

—**H.G. Wells**

Why do people do the things they do? There is often no satisfying answer to that question. We have all heard the, "I did it because it was there," type explanation for why one tries to climb the likes of Mt. Everest, etc. But that's really not the whole answer. The answer is much longer and more involved and may not even be fully known to the person who did the odd deed which prompted the question, "Why?"

What made us think—at our age (55+) and in our condition (questionable at best)—that we could successfully ride our bikes all the way from New York to Oregon? What were we thinking? As our plane sliced through the air I thought about the fact that we really were tackling a big job, and we pretty much didn't know what we were doing. Having successfully crossed Oregon, in the summertime with pretty good weather, was a lot different from the vagaries of the weather we would be subjected to leaving the East Coast in April. It was hard for me to relax.

I worried about everything as we flew east. Would our bikes break down out in the middle of nowhere? Would our bodies break down? Would we have a serious accident? Would our bikes get stolen? Would we get lost from each other? Would we die of thirst out in the middle of nothingness in some scorching place? Would we ever be strong enough to cross the Rockies? The little voice in my head kept saying, "America is a very big country..."

To *real* cyclists, this whole story will seem like, "What's the big deal? Anyone who wants to, can ride their bikes across the country, why all the fuss?" But the truth is that we did not *know* if we could do it. The jury was out when it came to us, and there in crept the tension. So, if you *know* that you could ride your bike across the country, you should put this account back on the shelf. There won't be much of interest to you here, honestly. In other words if you are a real cyclist, DON'T READ THIS! But if you like riding a bike, and have had little thoughts now and then about taking a long bike ride, but have never done one, then you might read on a bit. Or, if you have given up riding an upright bike because of injuries, aches and pains, but would like to ride again if only you could, then you might keep reading for a while. If you are interested in recumbent bikes and curious about a grey haired novice crossing the country on one, and an overweight retired guy leading the way on his no-tech upright bike, you might keep reading, just for a lark.

Now, to get back to the question. As I began to put ink to paper, and think about all that lead to our late-in-life bicycle adventure unfolding, I found that I was trying to answer that *Why* question, even if it was just for myself. *How did it come to pass that we two unlikely people started out to cross the State of Oregon and then, improbably, the whole continent by bicycle?*

The answer, I think, is *sequences*.

Chapter Two

Sequence Begins:
Alaska and the Last Chance Bike

Life is full of—*one thing that leads to another*. Much of life isn't planned, it just happens. Some of the biggest things happen from just being in the right place at the right time, or one thing happening after another to propel us on a trajectory in life. We all know this, and the sequences that led to our bicycle odyssey were no exception. We wouldn't have cycled across the country if we hadn't first cycled across the state; we wouldn't have cycled the state, if we hadn't accidentally run across the chance to do *Bike New York*; we wouldn't have done *Bike New York* if we hadn't bought a recumbent bicycle; and we wouldn't have bought the recumbent if we hadn't gone to Alaska...SEQUENCES.

When my husband Bryon retired from teaching high school science, he was ready for his long dreamed of Alaska trip. He had welded, bolted, sawed, hammered, chained and reinforced our used 1988 class C motor home, so that it could carry a fold-a-boat on one side, and designed and built a box for the back that would hold the fold-a-boat's seats, motor, and related gear. The last thing he concocted was a bike rack that sat above the boat motor's box.

Bryon had always liked riding his bike, but had never done much in terms of long rides. He had dreams though, when it came to long rides. His dream was to someday ride his bike across the U.S. He wanted to ride from East to West—the direction the country had been settled. The reason on this trip to Alaska, however, in taking his bicycle, was that he would have it as a back up, in case the motor home broke down, so that we wouldn't be stranded. (No cell phones then.) He could ride off for help which I guess, thinking about it now, would have sort of left me stranded out there.

I had always enjoyed riding my bike too, but had never taken any long rides, just used it for outings here and there with the family. Sadly, I had had to give up bicycles altogether (along with my hand-thrown pottery business) about 15 years earlier when I was diagnosed with a herniated disc. It was just too painful to ride more than even a block. Since I was pretty much reconciled to not riding anymore, I had volunteered to be the motor home backup support for Bryon's cross country bike trip dream, should it one day come to pass. I thought that would work.

But then came Alaska.

As we drove up the Al Can Highway, fishing exotic off-the-beaten-track waters (ala fold-a-boat), fly fishing rivers, and gawking all the while at Alaska's peaks and valleys, we also saw something unexpected: amazing numbers of bicyclists riding all over the state. I was surprised. Alaska didn't seem to me like it was an easy state to cycle, and yet we kept coming across people who were going tremendous distances, with heavy loads, tackling BIG climbs, on all sorts of bicycles. Many people pulled trailers behind their bikes with heavy loads, and were camping no less. Notably some riders had really odd looking bikes which rode low to the ground and sported a reclining seat with a back rest. Their feet stretched way out in front of them as they pedaled away. I had never seen such bikes. They looked agreeably offbeat, and enticingly comfortable.

Most mornings and evenings, Bryon would go for a spin on his bike and when he got back he would tell me about what he had seen. Hmm…I think I was getting jealous. I'll be honest; I *know* I was getting jealous. I wanted to share those rides. But, because of my back, I couldn't. *Or could I?* It made me wonder about all those strange looking, low riding, *recline-o-bikes*. I wondered how a person with a bad back might feel riding one of those things.

So it came to pass that when we encountered someone on one of these strange contraptions, I would yell, "Stop!" and fling myself out of the RV, race over to them and start grilling.

Recumbents. I soon learned they were riding what were called *recumbent bikes,* and almost everybody using one had a specific reason. Most people had given up on upright bikes because of aches and pains: carpal tunnel, bad backs, sore bums, stiff necks, you name it. Hmmmmm…

The *recumbent* began shaping up in my mind as *the last chance bike* for the riding wounded. I came to the belief that if I was ever going to ride a bike again, it was going to be on one of these new fangled contraptions. Thus, the hunt was born for a recumbent bicycle that would work for my particular back problem. As we turned for home after Fairbanks, we looked in bike shops in Alaska, Washington and Oregon. Very few shops, in those days, had recumbents on display and fewer still felt they could let you take one out for a test ride. I knew I would need at least a short test ride to be sure the thing wouldn't hurt my back. I did manage to try out a few bikes, swerving around wildly and scattering the nice bike shop people into running for safety. But the first critical thing I learned was the importance of the angle of the seat back. If it was too reclined, it hurt my back. The back of the seat needed to be almost straight up for me. So the seat back had to be adjustable, or had to be just the right angle to begin with. That, at least was good to know. And that was really all I knew by the time we got back to Klamath Falls, Oregon. That—and the fact that I was going to find a recumbent somewhere.

Chapter Three

Sequence Unfolds:
Recumbent Love Affair Begins...

A local bike shop had some entry level recumbents for sale. They also had a loaner video about recumbents. That video along with my test ride on one of their bikes convinced me. I could ride a bicycle again! The seat was big and soft and comfortable, the back was adjustable, as was the distance from the seat to the pedals, and after a few minutes I could see that I could get used to the thing and feel in control of it. The bike fit me just right and so did the price. Though the $400.00-$500.00 range seemed like a lot to pay for a bike, it was not a lot to pay for a recumbent bike. This was an entry level recumbent price. It's now several years since we purchased that "bent" (short for recumbent) and I just looked it up on the internet today, out of curiosity. It is now selling for under $550.00. There were a few other entry level recumbents, for sale at the time, but I couldn't ride some of them because the seat backs wouldn't adjust straight up enough for my back.

We bought the bike and immediately I was a kid again. After 15 years of bikelessness, I was once again a kid on a bike, and falling in love with riding the recumbent. That old feeling of getting exercise the fun way, of the wind in my face, seeing the landscape unfold slowly, sensing the environment; hearing, smelling, feeling in a way you can never do from a car. *Sweet seduction* was this recumbent.

So now that I had a recumbent, what next? We started out riding around the Klamath Basin, where we live. It's a good place for recreational day rides. You can map out a route without too many hills, for 10, 20, 40 or more miles. From our house we could ride to the bike path and along it to Olene and return to our house for a distance of 10 miles, almost all of which was on the flat and on a paved bike path, away from cars. We could also go from our house and out and around the airport, on rural roads with very little traffic for about a 20 mile loop. There's a restaurant, in a little community about midway on a 30 mile round trip from our house, which made a great lunch stop. For many of the rides, the hills were few and mild. If you wanted a longer ride, you could map out a route to take you around the basin, on rural roads, for most of the day. There were hills all around us in the Klamath Basin, but you could ride all day and not really have to slog up them, unless you wanted to. We did some of these rides (the shorter ones) and the new recumbent did well. I could not believe how much fun it was to ride a bike again.

Bryon, who LOVES to travel, started planning a motor home trip across the states. We were to meet friends in Florida and join them for a Spring Break Cruise. With both our bikes on the back of the motor home, we had a blast.

Everywhere we went; there was always something to do because we had our bikes with us. Washington D.C was a memorable ride, and then we finally arrived in New York.

(*This was in May 2001 and the World Trade Towers were still standing in NY, but would stand for less than four more months.*)

As luck would have it, Bryon amazingly had managed to discover a campground in New Jersey, the Liberty Harbor Marina and RV Park, that was just across the Hudson River from the World Trade Center. I was stunned at the location. Who would think that you could find a campground almost within a stones throw of the World Trade Center in New York City?

As we settled into our campsite, we noticed that just about every vehicle pulling into the campground had a bicycle or two along. *Unusual...*And not just a bike or two, but trailers full of bikes, pickup trucks packed with bikes, bikes on every motor home. There were bicycles everywhere, more and more bikes. What in the world? We thought, *Gee, East Coast people must really love to ride bikes.*

As we sat in our lawn chairs pondering all these bikes, an older fellow cranked by asking us if we were, "...doing *Bike New York?*"

Uh, what's he talking about? "No, we're just going to see some plays, and take in some sights." We had never heard of this *Bike New York* thing.

The old guy then proceeded to tell us about how great *Bike New York* was. He brought out maps. "They close down all these streets to traffic, through all 5 boroughs. There will be 30,000 bicyclists, it's awesome; you just have to do it!" he commanded.

We questioned, "How long a ride is it?"

His answer was, "42 miles."

I became very quiet, and said haltingly, "42 miles?" In my head I was shouting, "**42 MILES!**"

The greatest distance that I had previously ridden my recumbent was 20 miles, from our home and around the Klamath Falls airport and back. I spent the rest of that day on the couch. Could I even do 42 miles? My husband and I huddled. Bryon was sure he could do it. The question was: *Could I do it*? Hmmm, this had the smell of an adventure. *Was I going to let myself miss it?*

Now, as we discussed *Bike New York*, I felt nature calling in a way that it has a habit of doing when I get anxious about stuff. I excused myself, took stock of my adventure reserves, and when I came back I had decided. *I can do this*! My husband, *El Navigator,* got out the maps and plotted our route the next day to the *Bike New York* headquarters in Manhattan. It was 100 degrees that day, but we biked through all the city traffic, signed up and biked back to our campground.

Bryon is much better at maps and directions than I am, and it follows naturally, that if he knows where we are going, he leads our team. That is just fine with me. But the *lead dog*, has a different take on the ride, than the rest of the team. The *lead dog* is in charge, making decisions, being responsible for the result, and experiencing everything with more immediacy and impact, than the rest of the team, which would be—me. Bryon LOVED biking through Manhattan. It was a real rush for him to follow the unwritten bicycle codes of this most bustling of urban cities. The *codes* appeared to allow cyclists to liberally bend the traffic rules. It was a liberating experience for him. But I was just trying to keep up, and trying not to get run over or lost in the withering heat. Anyway, although I thought it was neat to have made it across Manhattan and back alive, he was nearly giddy with how much fun it had been to bicycle the place. As with so many things in life, the guy who takes the lead may have the most responsibilities, but also he reaps the greatest rewards.

Chapter Four

Sequence Continues:
Bike New York

How do you get ready for a 42 mile bike ride? When you are a novice you have so many questions. How long will it take? What do you take in terms of spare tires and tubes, and tools? How much water do you take and what else should you bring? What do cyclists eat, anyway? What if you just get too exhausted and can't make it to the end? What do you do about bathrooms? Questions swirled.

We packed everything we had on hand, that we thought we might need, and then tried to get some sleep. We were told the riders would all be allowed to take their bikes on the Path Train from New Jersey to the start of the ride in Manhattan, but we wondered about all that we weren't told about?

Bryon set his alarm to wake us up hours in advance of the start of the ride, so that we would be sure to catch the Path Train early enough to get to the World Trade Center on time.

(Note—The Path Train was destroyed on 9/11 along with the Towers and it finally just reopened while I have been writing these pages.)

It was quite cold in the morning when we joined the quirky cycling crowd. The day before had been a scorcher, but this day was going to be different. Everyone was excited. There was a young family near us in camp, and they were all ready to ride. The mom didn't think she could make it all 42 miles, but wasn't worried. She had come on this trip with her family for many years, and she had never made it to the end of the ride. She would go as far as she could and enjoy however far she got. I tried to find out how she would manage to rejoin her family if she couldn't make it to the end of the ride, but we were following the quickening stream of people-powered-transport as it worked its way toward the subway entrance to the Path Train, picking up more folks at each juncture, and I lost track of her. It was a struggle hefting and huffing our bikes and gear down stairs and escalators, around tight corners, and through the crowds. All the folks with upright bikes managed to hike them up over the turnstiles pretty easily, but for me with my unwieldy recumbent it was a challenge. Everyone was in a jovial mood though and people were quick to be of help.

When we reached our platform and the first train rolled in it was PACKED with riders and bikes. The doors opened, but there was no room in any of the cars. Bryon and I exchanged glances and raised eyebrows, thinking, *how many trains will come through before we can get on one*? We surveyed our options but there was no way on earth of turning our bikes around in this crush of humans and machines to try and make it back the way we had come. We were committed. The ride was supposed to begin at 8:00am, and we sure didn't want to miss the start. The old salts though, the veterans of previous *Bike New Yorks*, reassured us doubters that there would be extra transport and it wouldn't be long until we were on one. But trains came and went, with no room for the likes of us. Then, at last, when we were starting to give up hope, a train arrived with enough room for a bunch of us to get on. Whew, *we were on our way*. In no time at all we went from New Jersey to New York and were released, a colorful tidal-like flotsam of bikes, bobbing about, right under the World Trade Center, on Broadway. It was a sight that just took my breath away.

30,000 Riders wait for the start of Bike New York 2001

This was unexpected, to say the least. We knew that there would be a lot of people, but we had never been in a big ride and were amazed at the scene. As far as the eye could see there was this ocean of bikes and riders. There was every conceivable color of clothing and bikes, a staggering array of different kinds of bikes, and endless rider configurations on the bikes. There were upright bikes, recumbents, tandems, three wheelers, four wheelers, bikes pulling trailers full of people, unicycles, and who knows what else. There were people of all ages. It was all there. And it was all energized.

With so many tall buildings on Broadway, the morning sun couldn't reach us, and it was a bracingly crisp, cold morning. Standing there in the shade and starting to shiver, (we had no warm clothes, just shorts and short sleeve shirts) I noticed some people walking by with steaming cups of coffee. *Aha! That's the ticket!* The one and only coffee shop open in the area, on this Sunday, was not far from us. The line was long, but once through the door it was warm and cozy. Working my way back to Bryon with hot donuts and coffee, I just laughed out loud at our good fortune. Here we were in a great adventure that we hadn't even known existed. Sipping our coffee, we happily took in the sights and sounds and waited for the starting gun. At 8:00 the ride was supposed to begin, but nothing happened. We all just kept standing there. By 8:30 we were starting to shiver again. All the rookies were wondering, *What's going on? Why doesn't this thing get going?* People with radios reported that the ride had started on time, but with this huge crowd it would take awhile to get the whole thing rolling. And so it did. We finally began moving at 8:45.

With 30,000 bicycles trying to get rolling we thought, *look out!* We were all just too close together. It was CRAZY. People and bikes were gnashing together, and clanging off of each other and off of curbs and other objects. People and bikes were hitting the pavement in pile ups. We managed to stay alert and kept out of trouble, until the crowd began to thin out. Finally there was some tiny bit of room to breathe, and we could relax a little and soak up the event. (It was certainly a good thing that *Bike New York* was a *ride* and not a *race*. If these 30,000 people had all been trying to win the start of a race, what carnage might have occurred. In fact the organizers, aware of this, had pacers in the front of the *ride* to keep people from trying to turn the thing into a *race*.) We finally reached the starting line where Mayor Guiliani was officiating. He waved as we passed and we realized that we were really doing this thing, and it was going to be a splendid day, as it was in fact among the most beautifully clear days they had had for the event.

On we rode. It was wondrous, riding up Broadway, with no vehicular traffic, as opposed to the day before when we were weaving and dodging vehicles. It had become a different place entirely.

As we approached Central Park, the breathing room got much greater as the crowd began to stretch out further along the route. Feeling euphoric, we peddled on through Central Park. We had survived the slow motion, cramped and tense start of the ride and were now gliding along and really enjoying riding through this wooded wonderland. Before we left the park though, in front of us, one rider clipped another rider's tire sending them both somersaulting and skidding along the asphalt, reminding us to pay attention.

On we rode. But too soon the morning's coffee had gone through us and that was when we realized that the biggest problem of the day was likely to be the paltry number of portable outhouses arranged along the route. The waits were long, but the spirits of the crowd were so high, that even the waiting couldn't keep 'em grumpy for long. As we waited in line, some smart-alecs with stop watches started yelling out times for the harried people inside. When someone finished their deeds, and opened the port-a-potty door in record time, a great cheer would go up, like with Olympic crowds when a great score gets returned by all the judges. "25 seconds," the time keeper yelled. "YEEEEEEY," the crowd roared! But, if you were slow to reopen the door you got loudly reprimanded by the crowd. "2 minutes and 10 seconds" brought a chorus of "BOOOOO!"

Competitive eliminations! This was clearly no ordinary event for our twosome from Oregon. On we cranked.

As we rode through Harlem, my thoughts raced ahead of me. I was obsessed with the idea that we might cycle too slowly and be the last two people over the finish line, or that someone might even make us stop and turn around, because we were too far behind the allotted time. We had heard that if you didn't get to one of the bridges by a given hour, you wouldn't be allowed to continue, because they would, at some point stop blocking off the bridges for the cyclists, and start letting just motor vehicles go across again. I was afraid to stop and afraid to slow down. There were rest areas and food stops here and there along the route, almost all of which we passed up, as I was afraid to slow our momentum.

On we pedaled, through Queens and then Brooklyn. The miles just kept ticking off, and at last it became evident that nature was calling again, so we headed to one of the rest areas/refreshment zones. What a scene. We were along the waterfront now, and tired people were lying in the grass, on the dirt, and wherever they could find a place to stretch out in the sun, relaxing, sleeping, and digesting. Not us. I was so afraid that if I dared to really rest, I would never get up and going again. I knew I was getting tired, but as long as we kept with the crowd, and kept moving, there was all this energy to feed off. So on and on we rode.

As we rode south along the banks of the East River the air was crystal clear and the afternoon sun lit up the Manhattan sites in all their glory. The UN, The Empire State Building, The Brooklyn Bridge, and finally the Twin Towers all were proudly demanding attention. For a couple of gumdrops from rural Oregon this was pretty heady stuff.

All went well and we kept ticking off the miles until we hit the approach to the Verrazano Narrows Bridge. Then everything stopped. It took forever for the 30,000 riders to inch our way through the neighborhood and onto the bridge. Maybe there was a construction bottleneck, or something. People were getting a bit fed up, but at last we were pumping up the final incline and then rolling over the bridge and on toward the park at the end of the ride on Staten Island. The last incline was a bugger for me, but we knew we had almost made it, so we just kept pumping along, slowly for sure, but making progress.

Then, it dawned on us, *we've done it!* As we rolled off the bridge, it looked to us that we were finishing the ride pretty much in the middle of the pack. What a relief. We were pleased with that, even proud of ourselves. We hadn't been last. In the park, stretched out on the grass, soaking in the sun, and listening to live music, we let ourselves finally relax. Oh my, it felt good to doze off in that sun.

It was a ride we will never forget.

After pulling ourselves out of our reverie on the grass, we bought assorted *Bike New York* hats and shirts and then realized that the sun was going down, we had eaten every scrap of food stuff that we carried and we were HUNGRY. It was time to ride the next little stretch to the Staten Island Ferry that would take us back to downtown Manhattan. The ferry's main deck was filling up chock a block with a tired but still cheerful and colorful contingent of people and bikes and the boat was situated in just such a way that, looking down the length of the deck, you could see the World Trade Towers, as though intentionally framed by the opening at the back of the boat. It was a fitting end to the ride, just beautiful in the evening light.

Rolling off the ferry, we headed through downtown, finding a spicy Thai meal in one of New York's many ethnic restaurants. As we ate and relaxed we started to add up the miles we had ridden and figured out that with the miles from New Jersey to the starting place, the miles of Bike New York itself, the mileage we rode until we finally found a restaurant, and then the distance back to our campground, we had done about 50 miles all told. For us, that was quite a day. And riding through the nearly deserted streets of Manhattan that Sunday evening, Bryon was enjoying the whole experience so much, that he started to let his mind entertain the possibility of us doing a much longer ride, a multi day ride, maybe…

We were hooked. *Bike New York* did it to us. Who would have thought that we would have enjoyed this event so much? It had been a blast.

Chapter Five

If We Can Do This, You Can Too!

In the summer after we got home from the *Bike New York* trip, Bryon and I were making preparations to drive to Kelso, Washington for a wedding. Kelso is just a few miles north of the Oregon border. Interestingly, Klamath Falls is really just a few short miles north of the California border. As we discussed attending the wedding, Bryon threw up a trial balloon. With his eyes twinkling and brows raised high he asked, "What would you think about the idea of cycling to the wedding?"

"You mean ride our bikes all the way to Kelso, Washington?" I asked, trying to think this through and talk at the same time. "That seems like a pretty long way to ride the bikes." (pause) "For us I mean." (pause) "I don't know." (pause) "How far is it?"

"Well, I think it would be close to 400 miles," he said looking carefully at my reaction.

400 miles. 400 miles. 400 miles. I kept repeating *400 miles* to myself as though repeating it over and over might make it seem like a smaller number of miles. But that didn't help much and it still seemed like **400 MILES.** The longest distance that I had ever ridden my bike was the 50 miles we rode during Bike New York. *I don't think I can ride my bike 50 miles a day, day after day.* I wondered what Bryon was thinking?

"Well, we have time, time we have," he said. "We don't have to be at the bookstore. The ladies are running it just fine without us." That was a fact. The ladies that run our store, the Basin Book Trader, are just fantastically competent, and we don't have to be there much. More and more, we are just their support personnel. "I think we could ride to Kelso with almost no trouble at all, if we give ourselves enough time," he speculated.

Hmm, I wondered how far I could ride each day, day after day. I had no idea. 50 miles seemed too far to expect, one day after another. "How far do you think we need to try and make each day?" I didn't know what his answer would be, but I could tell that I was beginning to warm to the idea of this ride.

El Navigator would look at the maps...

Logistics/Route

What route might we take? Bryon wrote away to the Oregon Department of Transportation for a copy of the Oregon Bicycling Guide Map. Some states have better, more detailed and informative maps than others, and Oregon's appeared to right up there with the best of them. Kudos to ODOT. So, what does a cyclist need to know from a map? The one we used (1999 edition) told us where we would be allowed to ride our bikes on the I-5 freeway, and where bikes were not allowed on it. The city inserts were color coded for: bicycle lanes, shoulders, through streets, and traffic volumes. Separated paths were also depicted. The larger map of the state highways and county roads was even more specific, including caution areas to help the cyclist know about narrow roads and roads with poor visibility or high truck volumes. The map also showed bicycle repair facilities, and campgrounds, as well as such things as some of the prevailing summer wind directions. But one of the critical pieces of information for us was the degree and direction of slope to the hills. We were such rookie riders (still are), that we were very concerned about our abilities to climb the hills. Any experienced cyclist knows that this sort of information will be on a good map, but it was news to us, a revelation, as to just how helpful such maps could be.

After studying possible routes, Bryon reported back with his plan. "We'll take it easy. The first day we'll just go to Melitas (about 30 miles), then Chemult (45 miles), Lapine (35 miles), Bend (30 miles) and then Black Butte (30 miles). There will also be two 50+ mile days, heading to and going up the Willamette Valley but the hardest one will be going over the Cascade Mountains at Santiam Pass. The Pass is a two arrow climb (the toughest are three arrows on the map). The rest of the days will be in the 25 to 30 miles a day range, or less. We'll have some short days, and a couple days to rest in Washington, before we ride to Vancouver, to catch Amtrak back to Klamath. The whole trip will take about two weeks. What do you think?"

Wow, we would be riding almost the whole state, from near the southern border with California to across the northern border into Washington...Now that would be something. We had talked a little about doing an overnight or multi-day ride some time. But I hadn't really given any thought to riding across the entire state.

"Hey, if we started out riding from Tulelake (California), then we will have crossed the whole state on this trip." I was clearly getting pumped.

"Yeeees," Bryon said slowly, "Is that something you want to do, start in Tulelake?"

I didn't know why that held so much appeal, but it did, and I was getting into this whole idea. "I think it would be really neat to ride across the whole state. What an adventure. It's a great idea. I'm game if you are."

That settled it; we would ride our bikes to the wedding, in Kelso. The day or two before leaving to start heading north, we would ride south to the California boarder and back home again, just so the trip would be all the way across the state. It didn't matter if our first layover day was in Klamath Falls, did it?

Together, we have driven the roads of Oregon for almost 35 years now, more if you count college daze. Bryon can almost be your personal geological roadside guide to the state, while I, on the other hand, can't. He remembered the roads and passes and many of the difficulties we would face. He chose a good route for us. We would go up the eastern side of the Cascade Mountains to Bend, Oregon, then head to Sisters and up and over Santiam Pass, to the Willamette Valley. We would stop off in Oregon City to see my mom, and then ride across the hills that abound in the Portland area to see our son Andy, in Beaverton, followed by a ride up the Columbia River to Washington. That was the plan.

Equipment/Technology/Clothes? Foodstuffs?

What should we take along on such a trip? Do we take camping gear? Do we just plan to stay in motels? Do we have to make reservations if we stay in motels? It didn't take us long to decide we didn't want to carry camping gear. This ride was going to be enough of a stretch for us as it was, and we were determined to travel as lightly as possible. So, motels it would be. Bryon spent hour upon hour on the internet, looking at how many motels would be in any likely stopping spot. If it looked like we needed reservations, he lined those up. If it looked like we would have some choices and wouldn't get stuck without a room, we would just wing it.

We put together extra tubes, tube repair stuff, and a few basic tools. Made sure we had good working speedometers, and water bottles. For bags we each got some soft cased, padded, zippered bags. I actually used a small fabric icebox, which I pronounced to be my bike bag. We then spray painted the back side of all this stuff with bright orange paint to help our visibility. This had the added affect of making our bags look pretty shoddy, and less attractive to would-be thieves. I had an oversized waist pack that I strapped on the back of the bike above my ice box, and Bryon had a handlebar pack. We took little flashlights, minimum toiletries, undies, a few quick dry shirts, extra shorts, sandals, socks, rain jacket, travel clothes line, and books to read. That was about it. Oh, and a helmet, of course. We hoped we had thought of most of what we would need. We kept telling ourselves that we weren't going to be bicycling in Mongolia, and we could just go to a store and buy whatever else we needed.

Our good biking friends, Mike Reynolds and Pam Traina, told us about a product called *GU (energy gel)*. We had never used the stuff. But they convinced us that it really helped when you *hit the wall* and had no energy left. We bought a bunch of *GU*, and other *GU*-like stuff, as well as various energy bars. And believe it or not, I even bought a 6 pack of prune juice, just to be on the safe side.

Oh, there was one more item that got added after we learned about them—arm warmers. We didn't know such things existed until we took a bike ride with Mike and Pam one day to see Crazy Horse in South Dakota. Our big mistake for the trip across Oregon was that we didn't buy leg warmers too, but the weather was supposed to be HOT, and we figured we wouldn't need them…

Training?

We kept *thinking* about doing some training rides. We actually did a few 20 mile rides, in the weeks before we were to leave. We even did 20 miles two days in a row, once. But that was about it. I kept thinking I should get more dedicated, and make sure I could actually do some longer miles, day after day. But we had lots of other things we also needed to do, and the days just drifted by, getting closer and closer to *take off* day. I did vow, though, to TRY to ride my bike to the store or to run errands, etc., whenever I could arrange to do so.

One day I decided to ride my recumbent to a doctor appointment. It was a good 45 minute ride to get there, with no stopping. Sitting and waiting at the doctor's office, I watched quite a storm blowing in, with skies darkening, and temperatures dropping. *Oh great (*I thought*) I am going to freeze my tootsies off riding home in this weather.*

The appointment over, I went outside and started to unlock my bike just as the thunder began to roar. Then came the rain. I extracted my new flimsy yellow rain jacket, from a bag on the bike, and raced back into the waiting room, to put it on. *A lovely, warm, 70° day can sure get cold in a hurry in Klamath.*

Klamath Falls is situated at over 4,000 feet, and the weather changes on a whim. It was doing that as I stood looking out the window, cursing my luck, and trying to hug myself out of newly sprouting goose bumps. I wondered, *how long will it take for this storm to pass*? Then it occurred to me, in an epiphany, *this is an opportunity to grab hold of.*

How can I be standing here feeling sorry for myself, wimping-out, thinking about letting the storm pass? Bad weather is going to happen to me, sometimes, when I am out riding. Maybe there will be shelter handy and maybe there won't. I should just go ride this storm, and stop standing here like a coward. (But then again, what about getting electrocuted by lightning. What's the chance of that?)

Anyway, I began to think of the storm as an opportunity. If I was out cycling on the open road, and this storm hit, what would I do? I don't think I would stop, get off my bike and just stand there in the rain and cold, with my body temperature dropping by the minute. I think I would just keep pedaling.

That decided it; I went out into the rain and started to ride. *Be careful*, I told myself. *The streets are wet, it's kind of dark, and motorists might not see you in the rain and gloom…*

My new little raincoat had me worried. It appeared to be made out of thin, fragile, yellow vinyl tablecloth type stuff with gauze backing. I doubted it would survive a light wind, let alone a potential thunderstorm. It was suppose to keep me dry and yet let my body breathe. As I rode along I was a bit amazed that it did both. I stayed dry under it, but my legs, shoes, socks and shorts got soaked. Even so, I felt fairly comfortable as I pedaled along. The exercise helped keep me warm, and with my upper body dry and warm enough, I actually felt kinda cozy. My hands were the exception and I made a mental note to buy some gloves for the trip.

We were getting close to departure day now.

Chapter Six

The Oregon Ride

Day One: Klamath Falls to Melitas

The moment had arrived. It was a beautiful July day, and our few belongings were packed into the small bags we had attached to our bikes. Inside my bags, everything was in zip lock baggies, in case it rained. I had had to sit on each bag to get the air out, which took awhile, but the result was that all my stuff fit in the bags, and it was all pretty much waterproof.

It seemed strange to head off on a 400 mile trip so quietly; Just the gentle sound of two moving bicycles. As we rolled the bikes down our driveway, and turned left onto Watson Street, we caught each other's glance and wondered out loud, "Are we nuts?"

The bikes picked up speed going down the hill and the ride had begun. It reminded me of the feeling I had when Bryon and I, in the early to mid 1970's, put backpacks on and went off to see the world. We had started out packing our suitcases, and going to work, as teachers, in Australia, and then New Zealand. We ended those overseas working years in Japan and saved up all the money we could, to head off with newly purchased backpacks, to travel around the world.

When we put those backpacks on, everything changed. We left behind the easy travel of cars and well-planned, functional and punctual mass transportation. We started to travel by shoe leather and whatever local transport we might find. We backpacked the third world on a shoestring budget, learning much about patience, discomfort and illness. And though we left ease and speed of travel behind, we replaced them with a kind of freedom that is hard to describe. I feel this sense of freedom, to this day, whenever I set out to walk a great distance, or ride my bike. And it is not just freedom; it is much more than that. You see so much more, hear so much more, feel so much more, and you understand so much more, when you walk through a place, than when you drive through it. When you backpack through countries, you learn about them more intimately than when you take cruise ships along those same countries' coasts, or fly into the tourist spots. I believe that our country wouldn't have gone to wars in either Viet Nam or Iraq, if our leaders had back packed those countries as kids.

Anyway, as we began our trip across Oregon, leaving our neighborhood and quietly rolling toward the South 6th Street artery that pulses through Klamath Falls, that sense of freedom was sitting on my shoulder, whistling in my ear.

But even whistling freedom has its limits, and some of the charm of the moment drained away as I realized my mileage meter (or *bike computer*) wasn't working. This was annoying, as we had spent hours, the day before, on the bike path, trying to set it correctly through trial and error. The directions that came with the thing were so bad that we gave up on them. I thought we had gotten it right, but I was wrong. Bryon took a few minutes to tinker with the thing and got it working again. I don't know why it mattered to me, how fast we were going, or how far we had come, but it did.

We made it as far as Haggelstien Park, (near the half way point for the day) and stopped there to use the john and rest. Resting is a different affair, when you are bike riding. In a car, you can pull over, drop the seat back, and have a snooze. We didn't even have a towel we could spread out on the grass to lie on. So we stretched our legs for a bit, I worked on the numbness that had started to inhabit my toes, and then went to the john. When I came out into the sun, there was Bryon, his helmet still on, lying on his back on top of a picnic table, in the shade. He was asleep. He looked so restful, that I tried the same thing at another table, but with typically different results.

First of all, I tried stretching out with my helmet off, which turned out to be really uncomfortable on a hard wooden table. Since I had no pillow type substance, I put the helmet back on. Whoever would have thought that trying to nap with your helmet on would be more comfortable than with it off? But nature's relentless pursuit to annoy started to inch my way. I began noticing that ants were crawling up the table legs and onto my skin. *Oh, Great.* Someone must have spilled something sweet. Anyway, I could tell there would be no nap for me, though I did get some rest lying there brushing the ants off. Life was reducing itself to basics. I looked to my right and Bryon was still peacefully asleep.

After *Naps-R-Us* woke up we started to think about getting going again, but we were very surprised that we both were feeling so drained of energy.

For cryin' out loud, we hadn't gone so far that we should be feeling this tired. *How in the world can we expect to cross the whole state if we bonk after riding just a few miles from our house?* Digging into our bags we pulled out the highly touted *GU* and other *GU* type stuff, ripped off the top of the packets and squeezed the contents into our mouths. The *GU* had 100 calories, 25 grams of carbs, and 3 grams of sugars. The other substance was supposed to be less of a boost, but better than the *GU* in the flavor department. Bryon's vanilla bean squirt seemed to go down OK, but my apple crisp whatever was a real gagger. No wonder the directions said to, "...follow with a few mouthfuls of water." We gave the stuff a few minutes to take effect and, I'll be darned, it was magic. When we left the park we had our energy back.

As we pedaled along Klamath Lake, the largest body of water in the state of Oregon, I was really too busy being aware of the traffic to fully enjoy the beauty of the lake, which is considerable. *Stay focused, stay alert, and stay alive.*

As we continued northward, along the Williamson River, we were enjoying a stretch of mild downhill, savoring the sensation of not having to pedal hard, when abruptly Bryon slammed on his brakes, pulled over and screeched to a gravel spewing stop. His heart was racing. Turned out a strap that held his sandals atop his back bag had broken and the sandals had come swinging down, still attached to another strap, like a pendulum, smashing into his spokes with a force that set his chest a pounding. He was lucky the sandals didn't wedge in the spokes.

After 4½ hours of riding, we rolled up to the Melitas Motel. No major mishaps and we were still chipper with each other. After washing our riding clothes in the bathroom sink, we showered and headed out to find a cold beer. Nestled into the bar, we were treated to the Melitas Happy Hour, which consisted of little pull tab things that said: *Full Price, Half Price*, or *Pay 25 Cents*. Guess what, we *Paid Full Price* for each beer. Imagine the odds of that happening.

Day Two: Melitas to Chemult

It was really hot when we went to bed. No cross breeze, no air conditioner, just an oscillating fan, which alternated between blowing on Bryon, leaving me in a sweat, to blowing on me, and leaving Bryon sweltering. I thought I would be so tired that I would sleep like a log. Maybe the problem was that we ate a large meal, later in the evening than usual. But, *oh my goodness*, that was a pleasant surprise of a dinner. This little rural restaurant just happened to specialize in prime rib dinners complete with sweet potatoes and other trimmings. What a feast! After having been on the Atkins diet for a couple of years I think my body went into some kind of shocked state. Sleep came hard.

We were both awake at 5:30 am and ready for breakfast at 6:00. Two cups of coffee helped me to focus on the fact that Spring Creek Hill was going to be our morning challenge. The only three arrow climb on our route, Spring Creek Hill was looming tall in my mind. Any real cyclist would not have given the thing a second thought, but last night I did. I didn't want to risk knee injury, by pushing too hard. That could end the trip. I wanted to ride the whole hill, if possible, and not burn out and end up on foot, pushing my bike. My plan was to pedal at a reasonable pace (pretty much fall over speed), not straining the knees, and to stop and rest when I could.

As we commenced to climbing at our snail's pace, Bryon found the "shoulder bounty" of a jettisoned bungee cord (just the right length to secure his sandals to his bag) and a dime, so the morning was proving profitable, and we reached the top of the hill to boot.

Around mile 21 for the day at Sand Creek, feeling hot and tired, we bought ice creams and stretched out under the shade of some pine trees. This looked more idyllic than it turned out to be. I began to see this pattern developing, of thinking I'll get some rest, only to be foiled again. Bryon stretched out on the pine needles. He looked comfortable but have you ever tried to take a nap on pine needles, whilst wearing shorts and a short sleeved shirt? Pine needles are nasty little inventions; they are sharp and prick you a thousand times, no matter how still you try to be. They leave little pine needle impressions and stab points all over your skin. Then there are also the tiny biting critters that infest the pine needle sub culture, adding their contribution to your *rest break*. So, we didn't linger too long there in Sand Creek.

After 39 miles, we reached Junction 138, and lunch time. It was the hottest part of the day, and in the air conditioned restaurant we commenced to try and read the entire *Oregonian*. It felt very good to give our 55+ years old knees a rest. (I keep mentioning our knees, because they are what I believe are our weakest links. I am reminded of some Klamath friends who set out to cross the USA by bicycle from Klamath Falls one recent summer, and made it only to Burns, Oregon before the oldest rider's knees packed it in.)

So far, though, so good. It occurred to us, as we drank our third cup of coffee that no matter what happened, we were no longer just *day trippers*. We had completed an overnight bike ride, at the least, but the question yet to be answered was; could we pull the whole trip off? Anything could still happen. We weren't cocky.

Then we ran across *Butterfly Man*. Riding up Highway 97, a silver car kept passing us. It would get a ways ahead of us, just far enough that we couldn't figure out what the driver was doing, then it would stop for awhile, and as we got closer, it would take off again. This was odd behavior. *Does this guy know us or something?* It was a little unnerving. After a few episodes of this stop and start driving, a guy dressed like *Indiana Jones,* sprang out of the car and went tearing across the sagebrush, leaping through the air with the biggest butterfly net we had ever seen. He was comical, darting this way and that, stumbling about as he raced out through the brush. We decided as we drew near his car, that this would be a good resting place, and pulled out our water bottles to sip whilst enjoying the antics of *Butterfly Indiana*. This friendly bloke, we soon learned, turned out to be an academic from California, who was due in Corvallis, Oregon for some scientific, butterfly gala gathering. Not much for idle chit chat, he asked only to know where he would find the best butterfly collecting on the way to Corvallis. No one had ever asked us that question before and Bryon cast about for something helpful to fling the guy. Before he could respond, though, we were all startled by a huge explosion down the road.

Looking down the road, we saw one of those big rig trucks with multiple tires, headed our way. One of its inner back tires was flopping and thumping and shooting off tire chunk projectiles with great mass and velocity, all over the road and shoulder. None of the pieces hit us, and the driver was able to control the vehicle and managed to pull off the road after a bit. That was riveting.

But it gave *Butterfly Man* narry a pause. He was all business, waiting impatiently for the nitty gritty on the prime real-estate for butterflies. Bryon did his best with ideas and we talked *Butterfly Man* into taking a photo of us in action, riding the bikes. We rode up the road a ways, turned around and rode back toward him, so he could take the picture. There is a lot in this picture.

Sheryl's recumbent and Bryon's upright hybrid on Hwy 97

First of all, when I got the photo developed I thought, *what the heck are we doing riding the wrong way on highway 97?* Then I remembered why, and the whole episode with *Butterfly Man* and the exploding tire replayed in my head. Another aspect of this picture is that it shows what a lot of our trip looked like, going up 97; good shoulders much of the way and pine trees, lots of pine trees, mile after mile of pine trees. The last thing of note is that the picture could be titled: *Mutt and Jeff Go Bicycling*, or *Man and Small Child Ride Up Hwy 97*, because that is kind of what it looks like. Also it points out one of the reasons that Bryon doesn't like the idea of riding a recumbent. He likes the better visibility you have riding an upright bike. He feels he can see better, and that car and truck drivers can see him better than they can see me. The picture is a pretty good visualization of that argument. Those points are true, but I wouldn't have even been in the picture, or along on the trip at all, if it hadn't been for the recumbent. Taking all things into account, we almost always ride with Bryon up in front of me. That way, traffic can see him, and he can see what is going on up ahead, better than I. (We rarely ride side by side, it's too dangerous.) Also, people driving by often think that we are a kid and his/her dad pedaling up the road. Drivers tend to give kids a wider birth and are less aggressive toward them, which is a nice bonus.

As we said our goodbyes to *Butterfly Man* and headed on toward Chemult, I started thinking about that exploding tire back there. Yesterday Bryon had the pendulum swinging sandals episode, and today we could have been nailed by exploding tire projectiles. Sometimes BIG TRUCKS go by really fast, and the wind created could blow you around enough to cause an accident. There is also always the threat of drunks and just inattentive drivers in general. There seems no end to dangerous possibilities. You can never be too alert when riding a bicycle.

Day Three: Chemult to LaPine

On the way to LaPine, we hit another milestone. Our little speedometers clicked over to 100 miles. Pulling to the side of the road, we raised our water bottles in a toast. *100 miles! We're about ¼ of the way to Kelso!* We were getting there, albeit at our snail's pace. As we drank our luke warm water and chatted, the conversation rolled around to our friend Mike Reynolds and one of his most extraordinary rides. He rode all the way across the entire state of Oregon in one, I repeat *ONE* day. He rode 400 miles in 24 hours! It is almost unbelievable, but Mike did it! His rear-end was turned to hamburger in the process though, and it is one heck of a story. We also thought of all the cyclists we know who have ridden 100 miles (a century) in one day. There we were, after 2 plus days and we had only just finally hit 100 miles. Nevertheless we were pleased as punch. This was not a competition, it was an adventure and we had made it to the 100 mile point. *Hooray*!

We rode 35.9 miles to LaPine and it was by far and away the easiest day of the trip; we weren't even tired. This amazed us. Could it be that we are riding ourselves into shape? We felt we could have gone another 30 miles. But once again the concern of pressing our luck and putting our knees at risk, won out. We still had Santiam Pass ahead of us and wanted to be uninjured for that. The old maxim of youth, *No pain, no gain*, had flown out the window and been replaced with, *No pain, no pain*.

Pam Traina had given us a dinner recommendation, so we were off to try the *LaPine Hunan Chinese Restaurant*. We bought an *Oregonian* on the way there, placed our orders and started to browse the paper. On the sports page we read that Tour de France riders averaged close to 30 mph on segments that were 140 miles long. I was in disbelief. I just couldn't imagine, even on the flat, *averaging* close to 30 miles an hour. *How much fun it would be to see the tour, especially in the mountains.* Those guys are inhuman. Dinner arrived, was good, and also met the touring cyclist's main criteria, which is volume. We ate and ate and ate, but there was still food left. Finally we threw in the towel and asked for the check. The obligatory fortune cookies, of course, then appeared. Opening my cookie, I was skeptical. I never get a *fortune*. Never. Ask my husband. His fortunes say things like, "You will have the opportunity to expand your business, don't be timid." Mine say things like, "Even though the sun shines, it may not be warm." I always whine, "That's not a fortune, why don't I EVER get a FORTUNE?" But this time, as I suspiciously extracted the little strip of printed words, I was taken aback by what I had received, "Now is a good time to explore." Thank you Chinese typist, or whoever, for this great little omen. It *is* time to explore. It is *our* time to explore. We are exploring Oregon, by bicycle. We are in our mid 50's and we are going to git while the gittin's good. Now *is* our time to explore. I took that to mean that this ride was somehow sanctioned by the great fortune cookie in the sky, and no ills would come to us.

Day Four: LaPine to Bend

We thought yesterday had been an easy day, but it couldn't come close to how easy this day had seemed. We figured it was about 26 miles to the out skirts of Bend and we got there in 3 hours. That was almost 9 miles and hour, our personal best for this trip. Secretly, I hoped one day that we would comfortably find that we were doing 10 mph. If we could do 10 mph, hour after hour, we could go 80 miles in a day. We could cover a lot of terrain that way. Once again, the road was not very hilly, and the hours just seemed to fly by. We got to Bend in time to poke around the Outlet Stores, ride to the rafting supply store to buy more straps (no mater what you do, you always need more straps) and stock up on 40-30-30 bars at Albertsons. We had lunch and then rolled into the Motel (with a pool!) by 1:30 in the afternoon. We felt so good that we toyed, seriously, with just skipping the Bend stop, and heading off for our next destination of Black Butte. But it was really hot, and we wanted time to enjoy Black Butte (Resort) in the daytime. So we stayed in Bend, but the idea of starting to extend the miles each day was tickling itself into a thought, and maybe we will do that, as we head up the valley, but *after* Santiam Pass.

The road to Bend had an impressive *lavascape* section. We stopped at one particularly robust stretch showing extensive remains of volcanic activity. While we marveled at the landscape, drank water, and took some photos, a car stopped near us. A young boy got out of the car and scrambled up the lava rock hills, shouting, "Wow! Lava rocks! Look at this one! Oh no, look at *this* one!" He came running back to the car with his precious specimens, eyes wide with excitement. Then this enthusiastic, bright eyed example of the future of our nation rejoined his family. As I watched them drive away, I thought about how this cycling was transforming us into wide eyed, enthusiastic kids again too. It is a real gift to find new interests in life as the years go by. As we shoved off, I was very grateful for this trip and for my husband, my kids, indeed my whole family. A strong sense of wellbeing rode with me into downtown Bend, at least for awhile, until the road started to deteriorate.

Bend, Oregon is a mixed success story. The area is just a gorgeous chunk of geology with the beautiful and muscular Mt. Bachelor volcano as the centerpiece. Great winter sports abound, and the snow stays longer than most places, so a lot of Olympic Winter Sports training comes to Bend. There is a river for rafting and fishing, and there is hunting as well. Golf courses are in great abundance. Outdoor lovers have been flocking to the area the past few decades and the place has been struggling mightily to keep up with all the growth. There are always lots of streets torn up, undergoing some change or another, and lots of construction. Congestion problems get to the choking point, and then they design some new roads and bypasses to ease the bottlenecks. The changes work for a while and then the place gets stuffed up again. Nevertheless, people continue to flock to Bend to live and to play.

No matter how beautiful the area, Bend proved to be no fun at all to bike through. The traffic was heavy and we kept to the shoulder which was really rough to ride on. *Rattle, rattle, rattle*…Everything on my bike was chattering away, threatening to disassemble. It is a lot of physical work riding on rough roads, and a lot more stressful too. And after all the open spaces we had been riding through, this was a new ball game. To top it off, the last 10 miles into Bend looked like a missile range for exploding tires and incoming bungee cords (among the top road bounty we see, along with fast food rubbish and beverage containers). There were heaps of new distractions coming at us from all sides.

At one point I wasn't paying proper attention to the road, drifted off the abrupt edge of the shoulder and careened around on the red cinder gravel, at about 12 mph. And then, to make matters worse, I found myself looking too long at the pretty mound of flowers, in a divider in the middle of the road, which was neatly planted and groomed to spell out *BEND*. Once again I found myself swerving around, spewing cinder gravel all about.

We didn't want to squander our night in the city, and miss the chance for some entertainment and a much needed break in our routine. So, after dinner, off we pedaled to the movies, successfully making our way across town, down toward the river, and to the movie theater complex. But once we got there we realized we had a new decision to make.

My bike was starting to draw attention everywhere we went. There just weren't many recumbents around and people were very curious about them, especially kids. The bike drew lots of attention to itself, maybe too much attention. After we locked both the bikes to the bike stands outside the theater we stood there looking at my bike and wondering if it would still be there when we got out of the movies. Bryon's hybrid Trek was several years old, and we didn't think it would be a prime target for a thief. But my bike looked pretty tempting…. We hemmed and hawed. One minute we were sure no one would steal it, then the next minute we were convinced someone would be attracted enough to the thing to risk trying to nab it. In the end our solution was to unbolt the seat, which made the bike seem much less racy, and also made it look terribly uncomfortable. The seat, with the back attached, is not a small item, but I just hefted it into the theater, like it was a perfectly normal thing to do, and took it to the movies with us. No one seemed to raise an eyebrow. I wonder now, in our post 9-11 era, if they would let you drag something that large into a movie theater with you? (Doubtful.)

Day Five: Bend to Black Butte

The shoulder was smoother riding out of Bend than it had been riding in, but the best thing of all was the amazing scenery we pedaled through. Heading toward Sisters, we followed the most gorgeous string of mountains that you can imagine—a spectacular setting. There was a turnout about 8 miles out of Bend, where people stopped to take photos, and used to stop and read the interpretive signs. But, alas, the vandalized sign post had a note on it that read, *There are no official interpretive signs here because some miscreant ripped them off—TWICE!* However, the writer of this note was kind enough to also point out that we could see, from this spot: Broken Top, Mt. Bachelor, Three Sisters, Black Crater Butte, Three Finger Jack, Black Butte, and Mt. Jefferson. (At least that was what I scribbled in my notes, but there was no *official* sign to go by.) This ride to Sisters was enchanted and rated a clear 10 in my book.

We passed the House of Rocks Museum, complete with a red station wagon in the front yard with a rock nearly the same size as the vehicle crushingly perched on its top, as well as a bulldozer sized rock on top of the porch roof of the house.

We couldn't resist taking a closer look at all this *rockage*. The museum/shop was quite a tidy little place to poke around, and the thunder eggs display was decidedly cool. As we started to leave, the lady who owned the property reminded us that the place was for sale, in case we hadn't seen the sign. When that news didn't bring much in the way of comment from us, she asked if we had found anything we wanted to buy. We explained that we were riding bikes and couldn't add any more bulk or weight to the bikes. She thought a bit and then suggested, "Maybe you could come back later, in a truck, and haul a load home?" We said we would give that some thought, and made our getaway.

The town of Sisters got its name from the three impressive Cascade Mountain peaks that preside over the town. A pamphlet informed us that Faith, Hope and Charity make up the Three Sisters. Whether that was true or not, I couldn't say, but the Sisters area has been a crossroads for as long as people can remember, with four major Native American trails intersecting there. Today it has a bit of a Disney type Old West feel to it, but it is a great little community. We go there every year, to the Sisters Folk Festival, which is so good, that I won't say any more about it, because it is already too hard to get tickets and accommodation for the event.

41

When we headed out of Sisters toward Black Butte, the terrain started to change markedly, and in a way that I did not appreciate. I dubbed it *knuckle hill country*. I hated biking it. Imagine pedaling up and down giant knuckles. It's really hard work and for all the effort you don't gain much distance on the ground. Seems like wasted effort, up and down, up and down, up and down. We were getting tired of this and stopped near a pine tree to rest. As we started to think about sitting down in the shade we saw the usual suspects: ants and other creepy crawlies, prickly needles…and then we saw the sign on the tree: *WARNING! This area has been treated with a noxious herbicide…*

Oh Great. I had just read an article in a local newspaper about, what was it, Hogweed? Hogweed from Russia, I think. Anyway, if you came in contact with it, the article said, you would swell up and be left with ugly black scars. Is that what the noxious herbicide was trying to kill? We may not only be contaminated now, with *noxious herbicides*, but we might be on the way to growing *ugly black scars…*

What was to come next? There were no ends to the possibilities.

Thankfully, Black Butte would be next, and we were looking forward to getting there. Black Butte is a destination resort, with bike trails, swimming pools, ponds/lakes, golf courses and tennis courts. We were feeling very grubby and sticky (and were no doubt stinky) as we rode up to the reception building. I had on my *Bike New York* cycling shirt and Bryon had on his many colored Motocross/Nascar/Wrestling Mania shirt. He got this shirt in Klamath because he couldn't find anything else in town that had the bright colors he wanted, along with the quick dry feature we needed, but we never really knew what the shirt was all about. All we knew was that it stood out. I am sure it stood out a whole lot in the reception area of the dignified Black Butte Resort. Looking at the two of us oddly, the girl at the desk checked us in and told Bryon we were in Condo #8. As Bryon reached for the keys, she hesitated and then said slowly, as if talking to a child, "That's between #7 and #9."

Squinting at the lady, Bryon took the keys and as we walked out he grumbled to me, "I must look pretty dumb in this shirt…do you think?"

Neither of us much like wearing these brightly colored shirts when we are off the bikes. But they seem worth wearing, to get that extra bit of visibility, when we are on the bikes. So we'll keep on wearing the things, I guess, even if people feel they need to talk slower to us, and point out the obvious, with great care.

Black Butte is an interesting place. The condo/room we had was nice, and had the feel of an older resort, just a bit outdated, perhaps "vintage" would be a better term. This kind of endeared it to us; it had character. But the lodge and the restaurant were most decidedly upscale. We had reservations for dinner at 7:00 pm. My riding shorts were just lightweight, very short running shorts, hardly appropriate for an upscale dining room. My other shorts were old, thin cotton, faded navy blue gym shorts. But they were a little longer than the running shorts, so they got the nod. I selected one of the 2 camp shirts I bought about 15 years ago, and my ensemble was complete. The dinner turned out great and no one even seemed to stare at us. The restaurant at Black Butte Ranch overlooked one of the premier settings in all of Oregon. We gazed out over meadows, a lake, amazing mountains, trees, horses on the range and cattle grazing. It was beautiful. But there was something else that was interesting about the place. The binder supplied with our room, told us that what made this place different from other resorts was that, "…no developer remains to control any part of it. It is owned and managed by the people who purchased home sites. Each of them owns an individual and equal share of everything within the Ranch boundaries. As far as is known, there is no other resort of its size and structure totally owned and managed by its (property) owners." The Ranch had 1830 acres with 1185 out of 1252 home sites completed. Mt. Jefferson, Three Fingered Jack, Mt Washington, The Three Sisters, and Broken Top watched over the Black Butte Ranch. It also had 2 championship golf courses. Quite a place.

Day Six: Black Butte to Santiam Pass to Detroit Lake
We went to bed early, because we wanted to get an early start in the morning. It was to be a 50 mile day with the Santiam Pass near the start.

Waking up at 5:30 am, we were showered, dressed and drinking coffee by 6:00 am. Glued to the TV weather channel and the Oregon Department of Transportation camera that was showing live conditions on the pass, we froze as we saw that it was raining hard. Each time a vehicle drove into the camera's range, we could see huge waves of water coming off the tires. Trucks were worse, like tsunamis. Good grief, it looked miserable. It was a dark grey day and looked dangerous as well. In that kind of weather, drivers might not notice two cyclists on the edge of the road. Anyway, who would think that cyclists would be out in *that* weather? When big trucks went by, the wake they threw up would have been well over our heads. It made me shiver just watching the scene on television. It did not look like fun.

We switched channels and found some local weather people. They kept repeating that it would rain in the morning, with clearing in the afternoon, but we felt we needed to leave early to beat the traffic. The shoulder was so miniscule, that we wanted to avoid all the traffic we could. Also, we had no idea how long it would take us to get over such a steep grade, which lasted for so many miles. We didn't want to wait till the afternoon.

We tossed around options:

Leave immediately and ride up to the summit in the rain, get sloshed by cars and trucks, and get freezing wet (the temperature on top was 45° with winds gusting to 30mph).

Wait and see if the weather gets better.

If we didn't go immediately, what were our options?

Because of a car show in Sisters the Black Butte Ranch was full for the coming night. No room for us.

All the motels in Sisters were also full, and we weren't even assured a room, if we went all the way back to Bend.

If we managed to get a room somewhere for the night, there was no guarantee that the weather would be any better tomorrow.

If we stuck around til later in the day, and hoped the weather would change but it didn't, we would have no place to stay.

(We channel surfed for another half hour. It looked like the temperature had gone up to 46° and winds down to 13mph. That was an improvement. But the next surfing session produced a temp of 45° and the winds freshening to 30mph again! *Oh woe.* Next, the local station said the snow level could get as low as 5,000 feet. *What*? *How could this be*? The last time I looked, it was summer, and now we were getting snow forecasts! The pass is at 4,800 feet. We were both bummed out.)

We could call a Taxi and go over the mountain to
Detroit lake, but how would we get both bikes
(especially my recumbent) in a taxi?
We could try and hitch hike with every truck headed up the pass...

Undecided still, and somewhat emotionally drained, we both stretched out on the bed and closed our eyes. We were surprised to find that we actually drifted off into a fitful little snooze. When we woke up, we were glued once again to the ODOT camera. It looked like less of a wake was being spewed up by the vehicles. We drank some more coffee and watched a bit longer. It looked like the rain was lessening and there was even *less* wake being sprayed. It was almost 8:30 am when we finally decided to go for the pass. We put on all the warm, dry stuff we had and donned our rain coats, but we were wearing shorts and there was nothing to be done about that. We hurriedly checked the room, thought we had packed everything, and away we went.

It was cold outside. We cut a mile off the trip by cutting through the woods and overlanding through the pine trees to the main road. After hitting the pavement, we began to climb. That warmed us up. We stopped for a break and I discovered that in the rush to leave, I had forgotten to fill my water bottles. Each bottle was about half full. Bryon thought he had more than he needed and would share his with me. We kept going. After about an hour, off came the rain coat, gloves and arm warmers. We kept pedaling and wondering what the weather would be like on the top. *Up, up, up, slowly, but up.*

We were really working hard (by our standards), breathing hard, sweating and pumping our hearts out. We felt like cyclists. Then, without warning we heard behind us the deflating words, "On your left," cheerfully trumpeted. A wafer thin guy on a wafer thin bike zoomed past us, effortlessly, and raced up to the summit. It wasn't long until he had attained that, and was happily descending from this early morning joy ride, while we continued to grunt and strain our way toward the top. *Gad zooks we are easy to pass.*

After a long while, Bryon said, "Hey, we've gone 10 miles!" Almost, as though that was a cue, it started to rain on us and a chill set in. At the next pull out we donned the raincoats again, and noticed the traffic was getting heavier. There was, as I have repeatedly said, not much of a shoulder, and it was cold, and it was steep. I wished I had a device to measure the degree of slope, a grade-o-meter or something? I also wished I had a thermometer to check the temperature. It was hard going and at one point I was going so slow that I hit 2 miles per hour and nearly fell over.

You see lots of *road bounty* when you bicycle. When you are going as slow as I was, you have time to think about the residue you see. Off to the side of me, up on a low, red gravel shelf I saw a CD in its case. *How and why did it end up there?* Did some driver or passenger get so sick and tired of *that CD* that they couldn't bear to have it in the car one more minute, and just heaved it out the window? But before they heaved it, they took the time to put it back in the case? A few feet later, I saw an almost intact aluminum crutch. Let's see, what scenario could have put that crutch where it was. There was NO place for a vehicle to have stopped along there.

45

Maybe something like this happened: *Two addle brained, chin stubbled, beer guzzling guys, on a dare, stole a car and drove up to Santiam Pass. While looking for a can of beer that they had dropped on the floor, one guy slurred out, "Hey dude, look at this, I found a crutch back here on the floor (burp). What say we javelin it out the window, see how far it will go, maybe aim at something?*

A few revolutions of my wheel later, I saw the crutch's arm padding and then the rubber tip. Going so slow, and with so much time to think, I played out a few other crutch scenarios in my mind before pedaling past a good looking Rubbermaid ice box, and one after the other, a string of Rubbermaid mugs and plates. A picnic gone wrong?

For a few miles we kept gaining on a blue pickup truck that was in front of us. There was a tarp covering some furniture in the bed of the truck. The people driving the truck kept stopping to try and get the tarp to stay put. Sometimes we would pass them and I could see that they were using bungee cords to secure the load. I was starting to gain an appreciation for the failure rate of bungee cords on the open road. They seem to not work very well, under a wide range of conditions, and are especially suspect in the wind. The last time we passed the blue truck, they were applying what might have been their last bungee cord to the unruly tarp. They then passed us with the tarp already starting to flap menacingly. It was not long before we saw a new, bright red bungee cord lying in the road. We never saw the truck again, but I'll bet their furniture was a little soggy when they finished their trip...

Finally, we attained the summit. WE MADE IT! For us this was a huge moment. Spiritedly, high five-ing, we shared a congratulatory kiss, took a couple of photographs in front of the summit sign, and then, as though on cue once again, it began to rain, just a bit at first, but then in earnest. We had been stopped at the summit for long enough that all the warmth our bodies had generated getting there, had left. I was *soooooo* cold, standing there in the rain, that I couldn't get my fingers to unzip my bag, fish around for my arm warmers, and get them on. I barely managed to tug and curse my gloves onto my hands. Not only was it cold and wet, but the shoulder on the road was now truly nonexistent. We shoved off and down the hill we went. Wooooooooosh! I was tensely coiled, cold as ice, and trying to stay out of the red cinder gravel, dodging the growing numbers of potholes, and trying to keep from dumping. The traffic was busy and noisy and I rode well behind Bryon so I could see the road ahead and any problems that might arise. Also, if he should have to suddenly maneuver, or hit the brakes, I didn't want to be running into him. We flew down that road. EEEEEEEEEEEEEYAAAAAAAAA! It was the longest and fastest descent of our short careers.

Whew! Made it to the summit!

Bryon, though aware of the traffic and road conditions, was having the time of his life. When no cars were in front or behind, he was giddily weaving back and forth on the road, like a little kid, yelling, "Yee Haw!" over and over. He was enjoying this downhill for all he was worth. As I watched him I had the recurring sense that, it seems to me, males have a genetic playfulness that exceeds that of most females. I believe they often have an enhanced capacity to *enjoy the moment.*

The restaurant at Marion Forks, blessedly, came into view, and we pulled over. *Whew.* We had been so adrenalin pumped and focused, that we didn't fully realize just how cold we had become. As we started to relax a bit, but sitting there in our damp shorts, we began to shiver involuntarily, waiting for hot coffee to arrive. Bryon added another shirt layer, and I went back out to my bike and grabbed the arm warmers. I wore the arm warmers, under my raincoat, all through lunch, but never really felt warm. (Why for pitty sakes hadn't I bought leg warmers too?) We were lucky though, because after lunch and about 10 refills of hot coffee later, the sky cleared, the sun came out and we actually felt comfortable riding along the beautiful Santiam River and into Detroit Lake.

Once ensconced in a motel room, I showered while Bryon took a nap. Then the couch, ratty, short and clumpy though it was, cast its spell. I sank down into it for just a second and promptly was out like a light for an hour. After that, feeling refreshed, we pedaled into town for a most appreciated dinner. Quite a day.

Day Seven: Detroit Lake to Sublimity

Last night at dinner, we saw a group of people wearing long pants that zipped off into shorts. What a bonzer idea. That was exactly what we needed. We had thought this trip would be in the balmy 70's and 80's. *Guess again.* It was cloudy and cool this morning (I made another mental note to remember to get a thermometer.) and it sure would have been nice to have had long pants to wear last night. I'm going to start looking for a pair of those zip-off pants. I also wished, once again, that I had thought to buy leg warmers to go along with my arm warmers (Duh…what was I thinking?)

This morning, while having breakfast and looking out of the window, we watched a large contingent of cyclists gathering. Among them were the usual uprights, two tandems, and one recumbent with a windshield and a red stretchable fabric *cab* that covered the rider entirely, except for a slit in the middle that his head poked up through, making him look like he was in an enormous cocoon. *Cocoon man* looked pretty bizarre, but when you thought about it, his setup was just great for the kind of weather you get in the valley, from whence he had come. He was protected from the rain, a major irritant for cyclists in the Willamette Valley, and he was also pretty wind dynamic, I'm guessing. I thought, *we have just seen the future of bicycling* and it is legions of cocoons on wheels, slicing through the rain. But, who knows?

Just a ways down the road, sitting in Mills City, we were trying to get warm, and dry, once again, sipping coffee and hoping the rain that started a few miles back, would subside (No cocoons for us, yet). Thank goodness we were not still at (burr) 4,000 to 5,000 feet. We were also getting our heartbeats back to normal after what happened in Gates.

In Gates (a wee community along the highway) we were pedaling a very slight downhill section at maybe 17 mph, just starting to go by a restaurant's driveway, when right behind me there was a sudden loud CRASH! *A car crash*, I thought. Gently applying my brakes and turning my head to see, I caught sight of a motorcycle, on its side, screeching along the asphalt sliding right at me. Bits and pieces were flying off the machine and the road was grinding up what was left of it. If I had braked harder, I think the mess would have hit me. But I was trying to stay on the shoulder and out of the gravel, and braking slowly, so the wreckage never reached me. I came to a stop maybe 20 feet from where the disintegrating motorcycle finally settled. The rider was all in thick leather protective clothing, and it was a good thing, as he was rolling sideways and scraping down the driveway toward the restaurant. By the time we came to a complete stop, several cars had also stopped and people were assisting the stunned and disoriented rider.

Bryon's heart was beating as fast as mine as we had been riding pretty close together and when he heard the crash, he thought it was me getting hit by a car. We stood there, as the rain pelted us (quickly lowering our body temperatures) and decided there wasn't much we could do to be of help. The motorcycle rider was up now and walking and his cycle, what was left of it, was being moved off the road. The rain was not letting up, so with physical and mental shivers we commenced to head on down the road looking to find some warmth and shelter. That is one of the things about bicycling—you can't control stuff. Wind, rain, snow, cold, heat, all of it is ready to pounce, and all you can do is keep riding until you reach something that will provide relief. If there is no place to go to get out of the weather, you just ride on....

As we sat in the coffee shop that had thankfully appeared on our route, we were aware that what had happened in Gates may have used another one of our *nine lives*. Some people in a car behind the motorcyclist said the guy was going down the road and appeared to just fall over. I knew there was some gravel there, on the road, and I wondered if he had started to turn into the driveway when he hit the gravel. Gravel is such a huge problem for bicyclists and motorcyclists. I also remembered seeing some pieces of wood along the shoulder, and wondered if they might have been involved. The road is a place of life and death. There is so much life inside all the vehicles moving up and down the road, but there is always the reminder of how easily life can turn into death, alongside the road. That morning I had seen more than enough road kill: 2 bucks, 1 doe, a coyote, a possum, a raccoon, a bird and a porcupine. I was glad I didn't have a dead motorcycle rider to add to the total, or a dead me.

After a BLT and a milkshake at lunch, the rain let up and all our wet clothes began to dry out as we pedaled along. *Ahhhh...the simple pleasures.* It felt so good just to be dry. But it wasn't long before we were reminded once again that the Willamette Valley is green for a reason—and that reason is spelled R-A-I-N. The rain was settling in for what looked like—the rest of the day. At 2 pm we found the only motel in Sublimity. It had a room big enough for our bikes, and an indoor pool, a hot tub, and an inexpensive laundromat. All of this was too good to pass up. Last night's room in Detroit Lake was not a room you wanted to spend time in, cramped, not very clean, old and smelly, the couch had seen better days and the bed was so-so. But this room was very spacious, pleasant and clean. A place that was easy to comfortably while away a rainy afternoon.

As I pedaled along today, I thought a lot about how things had changed for us. There was a time, in our travels of old, when that room at Detroit Lake would have been a wonderful luxury. After all, we had our own bathroom, plenty of hot water, and the place had a heater. Things were certainly not like that in the third world countries we traveled through many years ago. One night in Yabello, in Ethiopia, the only place to stay in the village was a room with just a dirt floor, no electricity, and two very short beds. Instead of mattresses, each bed frame had long pieces of inner tubes nailed on and woven together to form a kind of bed/hammock. Those two *beds* were the only furniture in the room, and there was not even a sink, let alone a shower and a toilet. Of course the bed was way to short for Bryon, it was even too short for me. When the lady proprietor showed us to the room, she gave us a rusted coffee can with some water in it. That water, it turned out, was the sum total we would get for washing and drinking, for that night and the next morning. We learned that the water truck came through the village only once a day and that that tin can of water was our allotment. I have often thought of that room and those people in that town. It has put many of life's inconveniences in perspective. That Bryon and I have the money and time, now, to do something as frivolous as this bike ride stands in stark contrast to the lives so many people are living around the world. Tonight we can afford this luxury motel in Oregon, where we can swim in an indoor heated pool, and relax in a hot tub. We can read and write by lights near our bed as we sit on clean white sheets. We can have a hot shower whenever we want. Not like In Calcutta, India, during the monsoons, when we came across a family living in a concrete drainage pipe, in a pool of mud.

On an incongruous note, today we hit our fastest bike speeds yet. Bryon's computer registered 41 mph and I got up to 36 mph! He can do a better tuck than I can do on this recumbent, and gets going a lot faster. He doesn't seem to mind waiting for me to catch up and I am not sure I even want to go 41 mph. I do have a version of a tuck I do on my recumbent though, that sort of turns me into a tweezer, and I have to be very careful when I do it. If my hands aren't right out to the end of the handle bars, the bike gets unstable when going fast.

I am sure that everyone who has ever ridden a bicycle any distance will know what I am talking about next. The man at our motel desk assured us that there was a restaurant, "Just up the hill." We looked to where he was pointing and *up the hill,* looked pretty close. So when it came time to go to dinner, we felt we didn't have far to go. It was still raining, but not too hard, and we decided that for such a *short* ride, we wouldn't bother with helmets, and shoes, etc. Silly us. We put on our sandals (our shoes were still wet) and donned our raincoats for the *short* trip. Off we went, and went, and went, and went, up and up and up and up. This was one more example of how you need to get specific with non-bicycle riders, about distances. Ten minutes by car, say for example like—UP a HILL—can be a long, long ride on a bike. The good news was that I was pumping slowly enough that I was able to avoid the *mud line* the unfendered tire throws up the back of my clothes. Finally, soggily arriving at our destination, we shook off our raincoats before entering the restaurant, and sat down to a nice meal, except for the fact that we looked out the window at ever increasing rain

The rain got heavier and heavier. It was coming down the hardest we had seen on the whole trip. *Maybe it will let up before we leave*? Maybe…But it didn't let up. We lingered. Still, no let up. At last we suited up, as best we could, but we had no riding glasses with us, and a couple of miles in heavy rain can soak you pretty fast. Without glasses, it was very hard to see, especially going fast, downhill. Passing cars were sloshing us liberally. When we finally got to our room, I noticed my raincoat was streaked with road scum up the back and across the shoulders and even the collar was a mess. I touched my hair and drew my hand away to find there were chunks of wet dirt/mud/gravel all over it. I probed the back of my head and when I pulled my hand away, it looked like I had just wiped it on the road! I had never ridden without my helmet in the rain before, YUK!

(Oh, yes. Speaking of biking in the rain, we are very sensitive to doing all we can do to keep from creating any bicycle related mess in our hotel rooms. We don't want motel folks to see cyclists as problems. We make a point to NOT wipe the chain marks off our legs with hotel wash cloths, and we are very careful not to scratch any surfaces of the room or furniture with the bikes, or leave muddy tire tracks, etc., on the carpets. We like being allowed to bring the bikes into our room. It is so much safer that way. And we don't want that to change. Our hope is that all cyclists take lots of care in their motel rooms, too!)

That night in Sublimity we celebrated our earlier attainment of the Santiam Pass Summit as well as the fact that we had added up our miles to date. We had ridden our bikes over 271 miles, averaging better than 40 miles a day. Though this would be laughable to accomplished *cyclists,* it was quite satisfying to us, even sublime.

Day Eight: Sublimity to Canby

I want to die in my sleep like my grandfather. Not screaming and yelling like the passengers in his car.

Emo Phillips (web site: home.att.net/)

Sleep, or rather the lack of it, seems to be more and more an item for observation and conversation, as the years roll on. It becomes just one more thing to discuss that makes young people roll their eyes and dread talking to old people. Mark Twain may have gotten it right, *"Well enough for old folks to rise early, because they have done so many mean things all their lives they can't sleep anyhow."* Personally, I've noted that sleepless nights have often been associated with some of my more recent stupidity attacks, so Twain rings true.

But, *Ahhhh,* last night was my best night's sleep of the trip. The older I get, the more surprised I am when I wake up in the morning and realize I have slept all night long, and never had to get up once, or turn on the light to read. Last night brought nine hours of uninterrupted sleep. Bliss.

Wide awake, but straining and contorting from bed to peer out the foggy window at the morning, the outside looked cold and clammy. The roads were wet, and the grey morning appeared to be misting and spitting on Sublimity. A chill was drifting in from the open window and I hunkered down, pulling up the covers, reluctant to get out of my warm bed and close the window.

We did eventually tear ourselves away from this cozy room and turned the bicycles, once again, northward. The Cascade Highway from Sublimity to the town of Silverton was a beauty, with rich rolling farm hills. The only negative was the road had almost no shoulder. The positive was that there was very light traffic. Up and down we rode, up and down through the heaving, landscape. The good news was that during the *downs* we gathered enough momentum to carry us nearly to the top of the *ups.* Nevertheless, there was a lot of work to this terrain and I couldn't help but think about how daunting this section would have been for us at the start of this trip. However, we had learned that pumping uphill was not something to even think about, it just became a part of the trip, not very noteworthy anymore. Also, beautiful scenery makes pedaling easier.

If the farm soil around the area could be compared to food, I thought it would be the richest raspberry chocolate that exists in the world, or maybe the deepest, darkest, creamiest cup of hot chocolate imaginable. While thinking those thoughts I became aware of my growling stomach and a glance at my watch confirmed that it was nearly lunchtime. We rode by the Oregon Gardens and we could see just enough from the road to make us want to go check it out. I have heard it is just gorgeous and have wanted to see it, but I'm sorry to say, I have never driven off the freeway and pursued the place. As we pedaled by it, I watched as car after car pulled in and paid the entrance fee, and I wished we had the time to visit too. It had turned into a beautiful July day.

The road was newly surfaced, there was a substantial and well marked bike lane, and everything about the approach to Silverton spoke of pride. We dropped down a little hill and there were flowers everywhere, and a gloriously clean public restroom awaiting us, near a chattering little stream. We sat on a bench overlooking the stream and noticed there were some restaurants with decks out along the moving water. We made our way to them and had a wonderful open air lunch, on a deck, enjoying the stream and the lively colors of flowers in boxes all around us. *Lovely.* Silverton was a gem of a little community. As we attacked our lunch, I found myself eating every morsel on the plate. No garnish was safe. (I actually licked the plate.) This seemed to be another common theme on this trip. I don't feel like I am loosing weight with all the exercise, sadly, but at least I can eat stuff I haven't allowed myself to eat in years, and I don't think I am gaining any weight. That's something.

As we pedaled along toward Woodburn, I lost sight of Bryon. But, *oh my*, he was gone. I wondered if he had disappeared when I started singing aloud some of the Chipmunks songs "...gee I want a hoola hoop, I can hardly stand the wait, please Christmas don't be late." The only other time he got way ahead of me was yesterday in the rain when I started singing, to the tune of *Where Have All the Flowers Gone:* "Where has all the sunshine gone..." I was having a grrrreat time inserting variations on that theme when he began to pull away, muttering something about being glad we weren't on a tandem.

It seemed the soil in this area could grow anything. There were all kinds of grasses, lots of corn, hops, grapes, berries, squash, onions, and who knows what. Fields were ablaze with all kinds and colors of flowers, not to mention Christmas tree farms and I can't even remember it all. Take that rich soil, and all that valley rain and warmth and you have a gardener's dream come true.

Day Nine: Canby to Oregon City

When I woke up on day nine, my stomach was doing its now customary Bike Rider Growl. In my old life, before we started this trip, I tried really hard not to eat anything before about ten in the morning, and then I would only have, say, 4 almonds and splash of yogurt. But not now. After devouring breakfast, we once again commenced to ride.

Yesterday had only been another 37 mile day, but it had been tiring enough for me. I knew that Oregon City had lots of hills, and I was happy to wait for them. But, as we headed toward Oregon City, I realized the terrain was even hillier than I had remembered. It was just nine or ten miles to Oregon City, but we got a really good workout. Whew! The good news though, was that the countryside was gorgeous, and I hardly complained at all. Beautiful vistas greeted us around each turn, over each hill, and we couldn't count all the charming dales. This is horse country. People are crazy about horses around here and you can see why. What a beautiful place to hop on your pony and ride.

As we pedaled into my mom's place in Oregon City, I noted we had gone 314.5 miles since we left home. Sounded like time to celebrate. We put together a chicken with all the trimmings dinner, complete with dessert, to help celebrate those miles with Mom, friends and relatives. (I just have to tell you this about my mom: at 94 years old, she still drives a car, walks to the grocery store several times a week, and carries the purchases home in plastic bags—one for each hand. She is amazing and never ceases to inspire me!)

Day Ten: Oregon City to Beaverton

Our oldest son was working on his Master's Degree and living in Beaverton, so that was our destination. We got as far as West Linn and innocently decided to take Skyline Drive toward Beaverton. Holy-Moley, those hills were diabolical. We huffed and puffed, gasped and wheezed and got off and walked the bikes, more than a few times. Talk about aerobics! The truth is that each day has its own share of the unexpected. I wondered, when we decided to do this trip, if spending all those hours, just pedaling a bicycle, would get boring. But I can honestly say that I haven't been bored once the entire time. The traffic and road conditions have been focusing, and when they were not too demanding, the scenery has been engaging. And it has been fun to have the time to just let the brain have a chance to let go and ramble around. Sometimes I would have such entertaining conversations with myself that I would forgot to keep track of Bryon and be surprised to see him almost out of sight. It has not been boring at all.

Today was our most urban ride. Traffic, traffic, traffic. Bryon had never gotten around to buying bicycle shorts, and he was starting to covet the thought of some extra padding. We spotted a bicycle shop and he bought a pair of loose fitting but padded bike shorts. He only rode in them a short while before we arrived at Andy's place, and he was having a hard time getting use to how weird they felt. It was great to see Andy. He gave us a tour of the area including his graduate school, Pacific University, and charmed us as he always does with the newest stories of his life. Adult kids are sooooo much fun.

Day Eleven: Beaverton to Longview, WA.

Cornelius Pass loomed ahead of us—impending doom. After a quick cup of coffee with Andy, the three of us bustled off to our different lives and said our good byes. On a street corner, pausing long enough to wolf down a couple 40-30-30 bars, we stood shrouded in the grey morning, while traffic whizzed all around, *cough, wheeze, gag*. Urban life. The car, once a symbol of such freedom, is now choking our health with traffic jams in big cities across the globe taking more and more a toll on our lives, and metropolitan Oregon was looking like no exception.

We had borrowed Andy's car, yesterday to take a look at Cornelius Pass and surrounds. A local bike shop employee we talked to had put the fear of this pass in us. "You definitely do not want to bike *up* Cornelius Pass Road!" he said in no uncertain terms. His details of heavy traffic, narrow road, lots of large trucks, no shoulder, no turnouts, no guard rails, abrupt curves and drop offs, had us worried. As we drove the car around, we decided on a route that got us onto the Cornelius Pass Road, but after the summit. So we wouldn't be biking *up* the road, but rather *down* it. We figured that, with some luck, we could manage the descent, going as fast as we could muster.

We headed up the alternative route (Old Cornelius Pass Road?) and found it to be a tough push, but a much less dangerous road. "Hey Bryon, I'm making about 22 pedal rotations, for each .01 miles." No response from Bryon. I don't think he was counting his pedal rotations. "I'm only going 2 miles an hour." Still no response from him, but he was starting to pull away from me on the climb, and I didn't feel like shouting. Settling in for the duration, I busied myself with counting the pedal rotations, observing the mph, and trying not to fall over. It took a long time to reach the top, and survey our next challenge, the descent.

We vowed to keep a careful lookout behind us, as well as in front. Our biggest fear was of two trucks passing by each other on the narrow road, forcing lowly bike riders over the cliff, which was as you might guess, on our side of the road. We tried to pick a *no traffic moment* to begin plummeting down the hill. Pedaling like a bat out of hell, it wasn't long before I yelled to Bryon, "Truck back!" and since he could see a truck up front as well, we both hit the gravel on the side of the road and sought out the widest part of the iddy biddy gravel edge. The two trucks passed each other and us, by just a hair's breadth. Yikes! It was hard to predict the traffic, because of all the curves, twists and turns; there was not much time to see trouble coming. We repeated these heart pounding dodges into the gravel, more than a few times, trying to stay perched upright, and not end over ending over a cliff, when at last we hit Highway 30 and with great relief waved goodbye to the infamous Cornelius Pass Road. We now peddled up the much more bike friendly Highway 30 and would remain on it until we turned onto *The Lewis and Clark Bridge* and crossed the mighty Columbia River into Longview, Washington.

We had heard some unnerving things about this bridge, in terms of cycling. In fact, it was taking on such mythic proportions in our discussions that we referred to it just as *The Bridge* whenever it came up in conversation.

Weather reports said that rain was coming. So our plan was to ride as far as possible and get as close to our final destination of Kelso, Washington as we could manage to get, before the rain hit, or our energy failed. Crossing *The Bridge,* though, was on our minds big time.

After who knows how long, we were within sight of the out-of-commission Trojan Nuclear Power Plant. As we stopped near the side of the road looking at the sign for the Power Plant's Park, I felt exhausted. This wasn't just exercise induced fatigue; it also had an emotional component. The whole Cornelius Pass encounter had taken a toll. We took the bike path through the park toward some picnic tables and trees. The park was sort of minimally kept up, but good enough to provide a place for two tired cyclists to split a Power Bar and a packet of GU, chocolate and vanilla bean delights.

As we munched, Bryon staked claim to a picnic table in the shade and I stretched out in the grass. This time, even the bugs that came to call, didn't irritate. Sweet rest.

Back on the road, Carole's Place appeared on our radar; the kind of mom and pop affair that held out hope for a good lunch. We locked our bikes up in front of the place and settled in for cycling's bonus reward of guilt free calories. As we studied the menu, two enthusiastic guys with bike helmets on their arms came in and sat down next to us. For cyclists, especially multi-day touring ones, bicycles in front of a restaurant are like moths to a flame. "We saw your bikes out front, who's riding the recumbent? How do you like it? How are recumbents on climbs? How far have you come? Where are you going? Did you go over Cornelius Pass Road?" They began to interrogate.

We countered with, "What will *The Bridge* crossing be like?" As we babbled on at each other, it became apparent that these two guys were the authentic thing. They planned to do 100 miles a day, and were camping each night, heading to Eugene, Oregon where they would meet friends and family members and establish a base camp from which the whole swarm of them would explore the area.

After animated swapping of information and stories, we all headed out to the bikes. This was the first time we had seen their bikes. They were camping all right! One guy had somehow managed to attach two large plastic laundry detergent buckets complete with lids, to the rear of his bike. At least they would keep his sleeping bag and such dry, which is a good thing in the Willamette Valley, but the buckets made his whole arrangement look— well—low budget. We thought we had won *that competition*, but those buckets gave the Eugene bound pilgrims a likely first place. They were loaded down with all this camping gear, and still they were going 100 miles a day. Impressive. There was not an ounce of fat on their bodies, even though they ate with great abandon. I thought, just balancing on those bikes would be a challenge, let alone pedaling any distance. They had our respect. As they rode away with bucket-man's heels just barely missing smacking the buckets on each revolution, I thought my bike looked airily light. When I got on and started to pedal, my bike was almost light enough to fly.

Getting back to our trip, though, we were learning from everyone we asked, bucket cyclists to policemen, that we really didn't want to try and ride up *The Bridge*. They warned us, *Just wait till you see the thing, there is no shoulder, heavy traffic, big trucks, and when you look up the on-ramp at the ascent, you will understand.* Hmm…What to do?

Pedaling north once again we finally caught sight of the Lewis and Clark Bridge. Now, if I had been in a car, I probably wouldn't even have noticed that the bridge had this arch to it, but on a bicycle, that is the overriding thing you see. "Did you bring an oxygen mask," I asked Bryon, who was scanning every vehicle that went by, close to flagging down a truck to take us and our bikes across. We were sorely tempted to do just that, but we had come this whole way on our own power, and this close to the finish we both hated to bail out. There was no way for us to ride *UP* this ramp, as we would tie up traffic for eons at the speeds we climb inclines and there would be no room for people to pass us (we didn't fancy triggering some road rage incident). We noticed, though, that there was a shoulder on the approach to the bridge, so we decided to pedal as far as we could on that shoulder, and when the bridge began and the shoulder ended, we would hug the rail for all we were worth, and walk our bikes to the crest of the bridge. It seemed a bit dicey, with all the heavy traffic. But it didn't seem totally insane. Anyway, away we went. Hugging the rail so closely that we kept grinding our knuckles into it, we pushed on as traffic hurtled past us. It was a tight squeeze, and it was hard to keep from letting my eyes wander over and look down to the water below, which I did more times than I would care to admit, and each time the drop-away view lurched my stomach.

Finally, continuing to push our bikes, we crested the bridge all in one piece, and started looking for a break in traffic so that we could hop on, push off, and launch our bikes into the traffic. A break appeared, and pedaling once again, for all we were worth, we filled the lane, side by side this time, and raced down that bridge lickety-split.

Relieved, we rode on with grins stretching from ear to ear. We had crossed into Washington. We had done it; we had bicycled across the state of Oregon. We were pretty pleased with ourselves just then. For sure—it had been every bit of the adventure I had thought it might be.

After pedaling off for happy hour supplies, we pulled, dragged and hefted our bikes up to our 2nd floor room. Toasting our ride with newly purchased Brandy and Seven, we settled in to enjoy the moment and add up the miles. I paused on the adding, though, when Bryon queried, "Just before we turned onto *The Bridge*, did you notice the sign to Astoria?"

I had. "You know I wondered what crossed your mind when you saw it, because my feelings about that sign had surprised me." The sign had said that it was 48 miles to Astoria, which is a city that isn't right on the Oregon coast, but very close to it.

We both began to laugh and together said, "I'll bet we were thinking the same thing…" There had been a lot of good laughs on this trip. We had both enjoyed the trip so much, that we were sorry to be nearing the end of it. I guess I had imagined being tired of the whole deal by the time we reached the border, and ready to have it end. But the urge to keep on going to Astoria and then down the Coast Highway, had hit us both, independently. We had obligations back in Klamath, and we couldn't just keep going, on and on and on, but it was a testimony to the fun we had had, that we thought the idea sounded good.

Meanwhile, I got back to totaling up the miles. From our house in Klamath Falls, Oregon to Longview, Washington, we had ridden 394.30 miles. But the day before we left home, we rode from the California boarder to Klamath Falls, and that 16 miles brought the total mileage for the trip to over 400 miles. *Cheers*! We toasted the miles with smiles!

This trip had been a real lesson in *one step at a time* achievement. The thought of riding a bike 400 miles, was overwhelming to me, at the start of the trip. But riding 30 to 50 miles on any given day was imaginable. Sequences had built on one another to get us to this point in time: The Alaska trip had led us to look into recumbent bikes, then the Bike New York ride had wetted our appetites for this adventure, and finally here we were, a couple of retired Oregonians—still overweight, still with bad backs and worrisome knees, high blood pressure and the rest—but we had just had one heck of an adventure. The bottom line though is that had Bryon not dreamed of long distance rides, and been willing to do all the planning and navigation, the trip would never have happened, and had I not bought the recumbent bike, I wouldn't have been along on the ride. So, one last toast, *To Bryon and to The Recumbent Bicycle.*

Day Twelve Plus—Kelso, Washington and the Return Journey

In the morning we headed to Kelso, retrieved the "wedding clothes" we had sent to the hotel before we left Klamath, enjoyed the wedding festivities and the time off to relax, but the bike ride was not over for us. We still had to ride from Kelso to Vancouver, Washington in order to catch the Amtrak Train back to Klamath Falls.

We knew this would be about a 45 mile ride and we ended up riding the first 8 miles on Interstate 5, which was a first for us. We had been avoiding the Interstate, but it seemed the best option for us at this point. The shoulder was wide and we opted to ride as far to the right on it as we could safely get.

We couldn't hug the right edge as much as we would have liked though, due to all the debris deposited there; mostly big chunks of bark that had been liberated by the wind from logging truck cargos, and various sizes and concentrations of gravel and rocks that had worked their way to the right edge of the road. These minefields we dodged, as the heavy traffic loudly blasted by us. This was energizing, to say the least. We found ourselves doing 15 to 17 mph the whole 8 miles, as opposed to our normal loopy speed of 9-10 mph. Since we were right down along the Columbia River, we didn't have hills to pull, and that also helped the pace. But finally we left the noisy Interstate and began to make our way cross country to Vancouver. Immediately we were into hilly terrain. UP and down, UP and down, UP, UP, UP and down. This stretch was a workout. My knees had gotten stronger during the course of this trip, and they were quietly doing their job, but now my calves were complaining. By the time we reached Vancouver my left calf was in a solid cramp. This wasn't unbearable, but it sure made walking painful. And it made me wonder about my fitness level. There had been a lot of hills today, and this had been one of the hottest days of the trip. Maybe it was the combination of heat and hard continuous work, that had caused the cramps. (The right leg was doing its best to cramp up too.) But I also suspected that my fitness level still just left a lot to be desired. I tried to drink heaps of liquids, thinking that might help. Anyway, we hadn't eaten very much during the day and hunger was gnawing as I limped away with Bryon to find a restaurant. (Oh, how I am going to miss this freedom to eat whatever I want when this trip is over.) We ran across a little hole in the wall eatery, run by an Israeli family. They served us pickled cabbage, potato salad and a spicy salsa or chutney type dish that we forked onto some flat bread, and hoped that was how we were suppose to eat the stuff. Who knows? Next came lamb kabobs for Bryon and a charcoal grilled chicken with mushroom dish for me that was soaking in a carrot and veggie sauce, kind of like a stew, with a piece of flat bread underneath it all. Delicious! Ahhhhhh, food tastes so good when you are really hungry. It was a fitting end-of-the-ride meal, but, we could have done without the screeching mid-eastern music. I think we had stumbled across some pretty authentic Israeli cooking, the waiter certainly had the demeanor of a mid-eastern "service provider."

The next morning we rode to the train station and bought Amtrak's Bike Boxes, which of course, our bikes wouldn't fit in. After spending about half an hour taking my bike partially apart and loosening up Bryon's so we could twist it this way and that, we finally got both bikes in their boxes. Couldn't fit the seat from my bike in the box though, try as we might, so I decided I would carry it on the train with me. We spent another half hour in the washrooms, trying to degrease our hands, clothes, shoes, and even faces, from all the gunk we had collected in the "boxing" process. We shoved a bunch of our dirty clothes, and other stuff we wouldn't need on the train, into the boxes and hoped that would help pad the bikes a little. Then, after generously taping up the boxes, we sent them on their way. It made me nervous to have my bike out of my sight. I worried about it, and hoped it would survive the train trip and the baggage room.

On the train, in about 7 hours, we covered the distance that it had taken us over a week to cover on our bicycles. Train travel is good, and we enjoyed the trip, but it wasn't even close to being as interesting as the bicycle ride had been. We sat comfortably now, in the air conditioned Scenic View Car as we thundered past landmarks from our ride. What took us a day to ride on our bikes, took us less than an hour to pass through on Amtrak. Gone was the numbing cold on Santiam Pass, heavy rains in Sublimity, and sweating to ride in thirsty 90 + temperatures. All of that had been replaced with plentiful food and cold drinks at our finger tips. I have no doubt that we appreciated the comforts of the train more than any one else that day. But we missed the adventure of the ride and we found ourselves already thinking about where we might go next, on the bikes...

Part Two

What Are Recumbents Anyway?

Recumbents

What? You're still reading? What a kick! You may want to skip this next section though, especially if you are not too interested to read in more detail about recumbent bikes. (The next chapter is the ride across the continent.) But for those of you that are interested, here are my two-bits on what I have learned regarding recumbents:

Recumbent bikes are a lot like used book stores in that the differences among them are endless. Before Bryon and I opened our second hand book store in Klamath Falls, we traveled all over the Pacific Northwest looking at used book stores. The variation on the book store theme was endless. Some stores sold only soft back books, others only hard backs. Some paid cash for books and some only gave trade credit. Some actually even sold books by the pound! The variations were boggling. So we asked ourselves, *which stores do we like and why*? We began to see that some policies produced stores we wouldn't want to own, while other policies helped create a store that we would be proud to own. And so it is with Recumbent Bikes.

Recumbents also come in never ending numbers of variations on a theme. So the potential buyer needs to figure out what he or she wants. But before we take a closer look at that, let's take a minute and discuss what a recumbent is.

The dictionary tells us that *recumbent* means: *lying down, reclining, leaning, etc.* That pretty much is a recumbent bike in a nutshell. It is a bicycle that allows you to recline, in a comfortable sitting/reclining position, with a backrest, while pedaling. The many ways that bike makers have translated this concept into metal and rubber though, is where things have gotten really interesting. Recumbents have been around just about as long as have upright bikes, and interestingly, in the 1930's a recumbent even won the race to determine the fastest bicycle in existence. But later that result was disputed because the winner wasn't on a traditional upright bike. There is prejudice and politics in everything, eh? But in the last few years recumbent bikes have exploded onto the biking scene. There are so many out there that I am quite confident that any one who wants to ride one, will be able to find one that works for them. But here are some questions that one might ask:

Why Would Anyone Want to Ride a Recumbent?

For most people, the answer is that it is a bike of last resort. They liked to ride bikes, but had to give up on riding uprights, due to one or more of a host of reasons. For me it was a bad back (herniated disc). For someone else it was carpal tunnel, and for another it was a neck injury, or shoulder or elbow problems. Some people just couldn't ride long distances day after day on an upright. Sore butt did them in. For some folks it was complications of prostate pressure that drove them off the upright. Most people that have come to the recumbent, have come not so much because they loved the idea of riding one, but because they loved the idea of riding a bike, and the recumbent made that possible again. What they didn't realize at first was just how much fun the recumbent would make of the overall experience of riding a bicycle. If my bad back miraculously cured itself, and I could ride an upright again, I don't think I would want to. I would stay with my recumbent. It is just so comfortable, and so much fun to ride. And then there are those who are drawn to the pleasing style, aerodynamics, and novelty of a recumbent. Even if they can ride an upright bike, there are those that also enjoy the chance to ride a recumbent for a change, or to ride only a recumbent.

Are Recumbents Less Safe than Upright Bikes?

Recumbents seat the rider closer to the ground than uprights. In that way, it is harder for traffic to see the rider, and harder for the rider to see over the traffic. But let's face it, bike riding is a dangerous sport, and there is no substitute for being focused on the road and diligently careful every moment. I wear bright yellow and orange clothing and I usually have a bag on the back of the bike that is either bright yellow or orange. This makes me pretty hard to miss. Also, keep in mind that the upright rider is bending over in order to hold his handlebars, and has to strain his neck to look straight ahead, so often is spending too much time looking too long at the road just in front of him. Have you heard the story of a rider who looked up and saw that the shoulder ahead was clear, then looked down and concentrated on the road just in front of him? BAM—he ran into a car that had pulled over on the shoulder and stopped just after the rider had looked back down. Head over heels he went— flying/bouncing over and off of the car he hit. This wouldn't happen to a recumbent rider, who is always sitting comfortably, looking straight ahead so that he sees more of the road and the traffic unfolding ahead of him.

Also, especially if you have a LWB (long wheelbase) recumbent, you will not go flying over the handlebars as upright riders are prone to do. This is a major benefit of the long wheelbase recumbent, and may be true of other recumbents as well.

Can You Ride Them As Fast As You Ride Your Upright?

Yes and no. It is hard to say. A recumbent can be faster going downhill, it can be faster into a head wind, it can be faster on the flat. The recumbent rider is just less in the wind, more aerodynamic than someone on an upright. But some recumbent designs are more aerodynamic than others. When I ride downhill, without pedaling, behind my husband who rides a hybrid Trek upright, I catch up and pass him on one of my recumbent bikes, but I fall behind him when riding the other one. It is my understanding that the fastest race times clocked are by recumbents. But it is my experience that I fall behind on the uphills, and whether that is the bike or the rider's fault, I honestly can't say. (Other recumbent riders I've talked to have also experienced *hill lag,* so it's not just me.)

Is It Hard to Get Used to Riding a Recumbent?

No. The recumbent feels different, for sure. But in just a couple of minutes you get use to it. Within 15 minutes of just riding around in circles or figure eights, most people will feel quite at ease on one. The turning radius is different, and you have to get used to the handlebars coming so close to your body in a sharp turn, but it is not hard to get used to recumbents.

What Are the Disadvantages of Having a Recumbent?

Most recumbent styles are longer than upright bikes. The longer the bike the less sharp a turn you can make. Also, the length of the bike may make them fit awkwardly on some bike racks. They don't fit easily in the bike boxes you get from trains or airplanes. They are a little more unwieldy when you have to pick them up (to go upstairs, etc.) especially when loaded for touring. See also the comments under the *Safety* questions. For big city riding, they are not as maneuverable or as visible as uprights in traffic. Also, you can't put your whole body weight directly over the pedals, as you can when you stand up on an upright and pump away with all that help from gravity. But you do get some pretty good leverage by using your back rest, back and legs on a recumbent. Lastly, I do have a problem with my toes going numb. When that happens I get off and walk around a little bit, and that seems to do the trick. (It helps to wear shoes with room enough to easily move your toes around.)

What Are the Advantages of Riding a Recumbent?

The number one advantage to a recumbent is that it allows you to ride a bike again, even if you can no longer ride an upright. I think that is the main reason people flock to them. But there are lots of advantages that you don't realize, until you have ridden one for awhile. The comfort factor is of course HUGE. And even if you can still ride an upright—after riding a recumbent for a while, you may never go back to your old bike. There is just no comparison. I have absolutely no back pain, no seat pain, no neck pain, no shoulder pain, in short NO PAIN at all riding my recumbent. (The seat is just so comfortable! This is a point that I can't yell loud enough about! There is no seat pain! Many an upright bike trip has been cut short by seat pain and it is non-existent with a recumbent, or at least with any of my recumbents.)

Another plus is that the upright seat back allows me to go grocery shopping, etc., and just tie the plastic bags on the back of the seat. My husband and I actually ran across a good sale on books one day while we were out riding and I managed to tie about 50 books, in plastic bags, to the seat back. Also, esthetically, recumbents can be very pleasing to the eye, with graceful and classic lines. The long wheelbase that I ride looks beautifully well proportioned. I just love the look of it. I chose a recumbent that fit me in such a way that I can sit on the seat, my back against the backrest, with my feet resting comfortably on the ground. I feel very safe on this bike, as I can easily touch the ground anytime I might want to, without having to get off of the seat.

Also, I have a personal "knee" story. When I was 40 years old and in New Zealand, Bryon volunteered to stay with our 7 and 9 year old boys, so that I could Freedom Walk (that means you carry all your own gear and food yourself) the Milford Trek. This is one of the world's most beautiful walks, and it does go up and over a pass of substance, and even snow. I didn't know I had knee problems until that hike. On the way down, I was in tears much of the way, walking backwards to lessen the pain. After we got home, I couldn't even walk up on the hill behind our house without excruciating pain when I tried to come back down. I kept trying, time and time again, hoping that my knees would have gotten better. No luck.

But, after I started riding a recumbent exercise bike and then a recumbent bicycle, my knees were night and day better. I can now hike up the hill behind my house, and walk back down with NO PAIN. The only thing that I changed in my life was that I started riding and exercising on recumbents. If my back had been good enough to allow me to exercise on upright bikes, I might well have experienced similar knee results. I will never know. But the recumbent allowed me to work out in such a way, that my knees found new life. This was an unexpected and VERY pleasant result of my involvement with recumbent bicycles.

Why Are There So Many Different Kinds of Recumbents?

I think recumbent makers are problem solvers. Different people have different needs, different physical and/or technical problems require different solutions. There seem to be as many varieties of recumbents out there as there are manufacturers, and designers, and problems to solve. At first it can seem overwhelming to figure out what you want or need, or will work best for you. And there is no shortage of information on the internet about the different "kinds" of recumbents. So look through it all, the more you know the better! But there is no substitute for going for a trial ride! What follows is just a quick overview that might help get you started.

Three Recumbent Wheelbase Styles

The recumbent I ride is a LWB (Long Wheelbase), so it is a good place to start:

I especially like this long wheelbase. It allows me to sit close enough to the ground to easily put my feet on the pavement. It is a very stable feeling. The back of the seat on my model is very easy to adjust to get the best angle for my back. The biggest problems with long wheelbases are the ones I have mentioned; they don't always fit where you want them to fit, the turning radius is not as tight as with shorter wheelbases, and you sit lower and so are a little less visible in traffic.

Long Wheelbase –
Notice the front tire is smaller than the rear

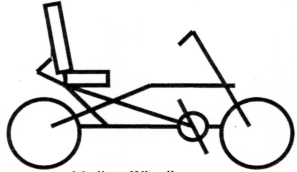

Medium Wheelbase –
Notice the seat sits back over and above the back wheel

Short Wheelbase –
Notice the pedals are above the front wheel

The medium wheelbase has its own pluses and minuses:
The turning radius is better, but you are generally sitting higher (above the rear tire), and on the one I tried, I couldn't reach the ground easily with my feet while sitting back onto the seat and into the backrest.

The short wheel base also has advantages and disadvantages:
I recently purchased a Bike SatRDay (from Bike Friday in Eugene, Oregon). It not only is a short wheelbase but it folds up and can be made to fit in a suitcase for air travel. I love it and have found it to be stable. This style of bike is less of a problem to transport, and is similar in length to that of an upright. It is more maneuverable than the longer recumbents, but also may feel less stable, especially at higher speeds. The pedals are up in front of the front tire, and this means the rider is usually angled back in such a way that seeing the road right in front of the front tire is more difficult.

So, it all depends on what you personally need in a bike. There are also many variations on the above three types of bikes. An option that is available on many recumbents is to have either OSS (over the seat steering) or USS (under the seat steering). The bikes above are all over the seat steering, which means your hands will be on the handlebars, somewhere above the level of the seat. If you have arm issues, and having your hands up all the time is a problem, you may want to try under the seat steering.

Under the Seat Steering, Three Wheelers, & Recumbent Tandems:
And to confuse you even more there are also three-wheel recumbents available. I have a friend who just test rode one of those with USS (under the seat steering), and she was very impressed with the stability of the bike and the relief she got for her shoulders with the under the seat steering. And to make your head swim even more, there are tandem recumbents as well. I could go on and on, but I think you get the picture. There is no substitute for research and test rides though. So get to know people who have recumbents, and talk to them, test ride their bikes, if they fit you, and test drive bikes from the bike shops. I wish you could rent recumbents to test ride, but I have tried all over the USA and Canada to do that, and I have only once come close. In Vancouver, Canada I found a bike shop that had hybrid recumbents for rent. They weren't anywhere near as comfortable as a full fledged recumbent (the seat is smaller and the seat "back" much smaller) but I was able to ride around a park for a couple of hours with the thing. I would have only lasted a couple of minutes on an upright.

Lastly, some recumbents will fit almost any length of leg, as they have a lot of room for adjusting the seat back and forth. Some recumbents have very adjustable seatbacks, too, so that you can change the angle of the recline. The first recumbent I bought, and rode across Oregon, was an entry level bike, which was very adjustable. I was able to figure out just what I needed in terms of all those adjustments. That helped me a GREAT DEAL later on when I decided to get a more customized bike, with less "wiggle room."

Well, that's a start. Have fun researching, looking and testing, and especially—have fun riding.

Part Three

The Ride

(Crossing the Continent)

Chapter One

New Bike—New Plans

"Get a bicycle. You will not regret it if you live."

—**Mark Twain**

OK, here we go. You are about to launch into the minutia and trivia of a long distance bike ride, if you're sure that's what you want to do. I wrote this whole thing up because I wanted to remember the trip all the way from the mundane to the spectacular aspects of it. I could tell as the months and years rolled by; I was risking losing the details: texture, flavor, insights, thoughts and emotions to the dust bin of my suspect memory. So one day I just got out all the notes, journal entries and emails home to begin the process of writing this story up. It occurred to me that there might be a few other people who have thought about riding a bike across their state or across the country, but had never given it any really serious consideration, and that perhaps one or two of such folks might stumble across this account and be interested to read it. So, here it is. But once again let me reiterate that this will be pretty old hat stuff to most cyclists. Anyway if you do keep reading, for whatever reason that might be, please skim away.

By the end of our ride across Oregon, in August of 2001, I was having a lot of trouble keeping my bicycle chain from bouncing off. I was uncoordinated wrestling the chain back into place and managed to get grease all over me—smeared just about everywhere. At first I had a few handy wipes in little individual packets that helped keep the mess at bay, but as time went by, more and more chain wrestling, meant more and more grease. When you wash out your clothes by hand each day, it is very hard to get all the grease out. My clothes, looking grayer everyday, were matching my mood, which was also darkening. The frequency of my bellowing, "...lost a chain..." increased (as did my bad expletives) so markedly that I had to buy an entire plastic can of handy wipes, which I took to carrying in the water bottle holder on my handlebars. Finally, on the last day of our Oregon ride, the shifting mechanisms began to go too. They looked to be falling apart.

When we got back to Klamath, the bike was still on warranty so the bike shop replaced the shifters and tried to come up with a solution for the chain throwing problem, but I came to the conclusion that this entry level recumbent was great for day rides and what not, but might not be the bike I wanted for really long, unassisted, trips. I was slow to admit this to myself, though.

Finally, after talking once again to our gurus, Mike and Pam, about long rides and having a bike that could take the abuse, I decided I really did need to buy a new one. I knew exactly what I wanted then and bit the bullet, buying a semi-customized higher end bike. This particular bike came in at least three sizes of frames, maybe more. I had to get just the right size for me, because there wasn't a lot of wiggle room to adjust the seat. (I would never have known so clearly what I needed in a recumbent, though, if I hadn't started out with that first, highly adjustable entry level one.) As it turned out, I bit the bullet pretty hard, as this bike cost four times what the first bike had cost. $2,000.00— Yikes! I just hoped I had chosen a reliable bike. I knew it was comfortable. And it certainly was beautiful. It was an Easy Racer, bright cherry red and I was in love with it. Talk about feeling like a kid. This was among the "funnest" purchases of my life. (My first car, a red VW Bug, would have to get the nod for the "absolute most funnest," though.) Anyway, this bike was terrific.

By then we had formally cast caution to the wind and decided to actually try and ride our bikes all the way across the country. We were amazed that we had decided to try and do this. We were almost afraid to tell anyone. Bryon got down to seriously researching the trip, and I couldn't begin to tell you the amount of hours he spent on the internet, pouring over maps, talking to other cyclists, and reading books. All of his work produced a route across the country that allowed us to start out with as few hills as possible, in areas where we could find lodging. The hope was that if we could slowly ride into shape as we crossed the country, we would be able to make it across the Rockies when we finally got to them. He reserved lodging for the start of the trip, and put together printouts with addresses and telephone numbers for any likely place we might need to spend the night during much of the ride. It was an awesome amount of work.

To top it all off, neither of us knew much about bike repair, and this made us nervous. We were sure to have difficulties and breakdowns on a really long trip. As it turned out there was a place in Ashland, Oregon, just over the hill from Klamath Falls (about 1 ½ hours from us) that taught bicycle repair. You could get certified through them to be a bicycle repairman. Our friends Barbara and Carlyle Stout are Peace Corps veterans and adventurers who live in Ashland. They like to ride bikes and Barbara had heard about this school and had been interested in learning something about the care and repair of their fleet of bikes. With four kids, the Stouts had a fleet of bikes. Anyway, she and Bryon decided they would take an intensive weeklong class. They were to bring a bike that they would tear apart, during the course, and put it back together before the class ended. It wasn't a cheap class, but seemed like good insurance. It made us feel a bit more secure about daring to plan a really long ride. The class had some absolutely serious cyclists, mostly very technically oriented people and one guy who basically worked as a dentist (no formal dental training) in the Amazon and rode his bike all over rough, remote terrain, sans roads, and needed to have repair skills. (And here I thought riding across the country on paved roads would be an adventure...) What an amazing fellow, living such an awesome, off the wall life.

There are many ways to go about organizing an unassisted bike trip across the country. Logistically, it seemed the easiest way would be to carry all our camping gear, and just plan on making this a camping trip. There would be no need to map out lodging, and we could always cook if there were no restaurants when we needed them. Hmm, we SCRAPED that idea fast. It was NOT for us. First of all, we needed to go as light as we possibly could. Even if we bought the most state of the art, lightweight gear, we would still be into a mountain of stuff to carry on our bike frames, or heaven forbid, in a trailer. *NO, NO, NO, NO! Get a grip.* This trip was going to stretch our endurance to capacity as it was, and we didn't need to be hauling *any* extra stuff. Also, 60 to 70 nights of sleeping on the ground, after full days of constant exercise, didn't sound, well—very refreshing. Not young, supple, and brimming with excess strength any more, we heeded the little voices of reality that kept chanting, *No Camping!* Mike and Pam also made the point that, from their experience, we should decide if we are camping or moteling, and then do one or the other, but not both. Otherwise, they counseled, we would just end up mad at ourselves for hauling a heap of camping gear all the way across the country and then hardly ever using it. So we made the choice; motels it would be.

While Bryon was ensconced in a myriad of preparations, I was helping out with the bookstore, and trying to see to all the stuff you need to organize in your life when you are going to be gone for over 2 months. Then one evening Bryon sat me down and wanted to *talk*. He had been stewing about something, I could tell. He wanted a heart to heart talk. As it turned out, he was really worried about how careful I would be on this trip. Bike riding is so dangerous, and the more you ride the more opportunities you have for making mistakes, or for someone else to make mistakes and the results could be deadly. We talked a long time about the dangers out there. And they weren't just dangers to me, but dangers to both of us. I ride behind Bryon most of the time and there have been times when I have been too close behind and inattentive and have almost caused him to crash. I promised to ride back further and pay better attention. Also, it is easy for the guy in the rear to just follow the guy in front, even when the traffic makes that a stupid thing to do. I swore to always be careful and not just follow him like a little lamb, but to keep alert and make my own decisions. On down slopes when we get to moving fast, I vowed to give him enough of a lead that I wouldn't be crowding him. The basic theme that we were orchestrating was one of being sure that the guy behind had enough time to respond to anything that might happen up in front of him. It was a very good talk for us to have. Especially it was good for me, since I am usually the guy behind.

We sat for a long time talking about safety issues and about other things like what we would do if we got lost from each other. What had brought all this to a head was that we had both read a bicycle book, a true adventure story about a young couple who rode their bikes around the world. What really caught our attention was that the heroine of the story survived the whole, incredible trip, and then after they had returned home to their everyday life and work, she was riding to work one day on her bike and she was struck by a car and killed. It left a knot in both our stomachs. We are very close. If one of us got seriously hurt or dear God, killed on this trip, it would be absolutely devastating. We would no doubt blame ourselves for the other person's plight and our lives would be a mess. So this talk was a must for us and a good wake-up call for anyone heading out on a long bike ride.

Chapter Two

The Route

"You're going the wrong way!"

Just About Everyone

There are a couple of reasons why we chose to go across the country from East to West. First and foremost, as I said before, was that Bryon had always dreamed of going in the direction that the country had been initially settled. He wanted the slowly unfolding experience of seeing the country, as the settlers had. Certainly it wouldn't have the same hardships and dangers and exhilaration the settlers would have had, but it would have *some* of those things. Also, we knew it would take us longer than most riders to cross the country and we planned to be home around the 4th of July. So, in order to give us enough time to cross the country, if we had decided to take the West to East route, we would have had to leave Oregon so early that we would quite possibly have found ourselves on snowy roads, and fighting nasty snowy weather conditions from Oregon on. We were planning to start riding in April, and just for example, it has been known to snow in June here in Klamath Falls, Oregon. Also, a West to East crossing would mean a much earlier crossing of the Rocky Mountains which presented us with two problems. The earlier we went over the mountains, the more snow we would face, and frankly, we didn't care to face any snow at all, anywhere. Also, the Rockies would hit us like a brick wall so early in the trip, and we doubted we would have "ridden ourselves into shape" enough to successfully make it up and over them, without disintegrating. And finally, for us there was an emotional aspect of *going home* that would come with a crossing from New York to Oregon. We would always feel that we were getting closer and closer to *home* and we thought that would be a psychological advantage, an added motivational tool in our bag. So we came to be committed to crossing the country from East to West.

Now, crossing the country from East to West on bicycles was met by almost one and all with the same comment, "You're going the wrong way!" It seems that everyone is an expert on the prevailing wind patterns of the country, and they were just sure we would never get across the country in time, if we went East to West. They couldn't believe that we would decide to go in the WRONG direction, AGAINST THE WIND. At first we tried to go through ALL the reasons that we chose this entirely WRONG direction, but that got tiring, as we had so many reasons, and we were telling them to so many *wind experts.* Finally, we adopted the strategy that when people advised us, "You're going the wrong way!" we just said, "Yeah, we know." (All this wind controversy did prompt Bryon, though, to keep track of the direction of the wind as we went along, and each day he recorded whether the wind was for us, against us, or uncommitted.)

Bryon spent a lot of time researching our route. You can purchase various bike route maps and information packages, to help you cross the country, from various sources on the web and magazines. Bryon did end up with some Bike America Maps, I think. A lot of these mapped cycle routes though, were really tough to ride because they took you to all the most beautiful places, which tend also to often be the most grueling terrains to cycle. What he eventually designed for us was a route that probably no one else has ever exactly taken. For one thing, he kept us next to rivers and along canals where the terrain would hopefully avoid some hills. And although we were so obviously, "Going the wrong way," at least the *wrong way* was pretty straight west. There was one substantial variation from that straight line west, though, and that was at the start of the trip. We had read and heard a lot about the legends and horrors of cycling Pennsylvania (hills, hills, hills…) and decided to avoid as much of it as we could. Also, there appeared to be a road that stayed close to the Hudson River which would make for a pretty ride, and hopefully, avoid some of the hills of Upstate New York. Our plan was to touch base with the coast of New York and then ride straight north to the Albany area, before taking a sharp dogleg west. We would only have to cross the tippy top of the infamously grueling Pennsylvania.

With the route chalked in Bryon started making the plans. The plane tickets, hotel in New York City, Broadway tickets, etc., needed to be snagged. Our calendar of non-bike related activities was starting to fill up, and we wanted to be sure we left a few weeks open before our departure date, in order to have some time to pack up our bike bags and to do some training rides, with all of our gear packed. Since we were starting out in the Spring (April) and would be riding up to and maybe after the 4th of July we would have to pack cold, hot and rainy weather clothes. Our bags would be heavier than they were for the Oregon Ride, and we wanted to have plenty of time to get use to the extra weight and awkwardness of it all. Also, we wanted to not be rushed, to stay healthy and to have time to ride into shape a little bit before we headed off. It would also take us some time, we figured, to pack up the bikes well enough to survive plane travel. This all seemed like a good plan. Plans are not reality though, and like an Ian Tyson song so succinctly put it, "…wishin' don't make it so…"

Stuff happens.

Through no fault of our own we ended up on a 3 week Panama Canal boat trip that included stops in South and Central America, and only arrived back in Oregon a whisper before we had to catch our plane to New York. (Poor us, you say?) It's a long story, but we got bumped off one tour due to overbooking so they put us on a much longer tour, and didn't charge us any extra. A one week trip became a three week odyssey, with just a couple of days breathing room between Panama and the start of the bike ride across the country. But it was a fantastic opportunity to see some of South and Central America, at a great price and we just couldn't pass it up.

That trip was incredible. But the bad news was that along the way, somewhere, I caught that cruise ship virus. (Norwalk?) I didn't just catch it, I must have rolled around in it, and wore it for a few days. A whopper and a doosey. It laid me low. I couldn't shake it.

I got off the boat with this raging virus and returned to Klamath with only a couple of days to get everything organized and packed for the bike trip. But instead of packing, I was sick in bed, shivering with a fever, and coughing up a storm. To add to it, my back was acting up again, and who knew where that might lead. Here we were, about to leave in a couple of days for the most continuously hard physical work we had ever tackled in our lives. Even if we had had time to do some training rides, I was too sick to even think about it.

I was sorely tempted to try and change the plane reservations, to just sleep the days away and try to get well, but that was going to foul up a lot of other things. We had a bunch of nonrefundable plans. The drum was rolling. I would just have to rest on the plane...

Gut it up Van Fleet, came that internal voice, and somehow, we got everything done. The hardest job for me was trying to get my new and longer recumbent to fit in the old Amtrak train bike box, and get it secured in such a way that it would survive the baggage handlers. Have I mentioned that I love this bike? I spent most of one whole precious day taking the bike apart so that it would fit in the box in pieces, bubble wrapping all the pieces, taping them to each other and to the frame and then taping this spidery mass in turn to my bike bags, and other odd bits, in such a way that everything in the box was secured to everything else in the box.

It was April 21, 2002 when our friends, Mike and Patty Reeder, dropped us off at the Medford, Oregon Airport and we commenced the battle to board a plane, ala post 9-11. The first indication of what was to come was in the form of a gigantic sign that dominated the little airport as we attempted to pass into the secure area: *No dynamite, large power tools, bull whips or cattle prods* were allowed. Also *num-chucks and Korean fighting sticks* were similarly excluded. (Who thought this list up?) The first skirmish came when the random search lady began to wand me. The wand turned out to be sensitive to my zip off pant legs, and also beeped wildly on the bike lock key that I had forgotten I had secreted in a compartment of my wallet. This was problematic as I had told her with great assurance that I had no keys, making wand lady more than a bit suspicious. She made sure to be extra thorough! Good thing we allowed plenty of time.

Chapter Three

New York

April 21, 2002.

I had been so busy and/or sick in the days and weeks leading up to The Ride, that I had had no opportunity to have Mr. Doubt or Miss Lack of Confidence sneak up on me. But as I buckled my seat belt on and settled into the flight, I could hardly believe that we were actually doing this. What had possessed us to think this was a good idea? As retired, overweight, over aged, under fit, inexperienced at cycling, and medically questionable, what were we thinking? I looked at my husband, in the seat next to me, as we flew out of Medford, Oregon on our way to New York. He looked confident. I however was working myself up into hyperventilating with self-doubt. *Breath in, s-l-o-w-l-y, breath out s-l-o-w-l-y.* I looked around at the other people on the plane who it seemed, were all reading the latest John Grisham novel, and looking very relaxed, sitting there in their normal clothing.

I on the other hand, was wearing recently purchased alien clothing. The pants had zip off legs, which were not of the quality of design or material (I'm too cheap for my own good) to foster much comfort. Neither the pants, nor the shorts they made into, felt good: binding where I wanted loose and loose where I needed fit. My shoe selection was similarly problematic. They weren't really stiff enough to be good soles for cycling and they were too stiff for walking comfortably, but since they would do "double duty" they got the nod. I was too cheap to buy special "cycling" shoes (when will I ever learn?) and these shoes *seemed* like they would work. Unfortunately I did not try them on after plunging them into a bucket of water at GI Joe's, before paying for them, which would have saved me lots of discomfort later on.

As our plane sliced through the air, a stewardess began asking people what they wanted to drink. This sounded promising. "Red wine?" I asked. Sure enough, red wine I got. The tension began to ease. I could feel my shoulders starting to relax, and that was a good thing. Keeping my back relaxed has been a big key to living with a herniated disc.

Bryon had fallen asleep in the seat next to me. Wide awake, I sipped my wine and was once again in wonder at his ability to so easily fall asleep. He has this amazing capacity to drift-off, under almost any situation. Sleep eluded me as the red wine began triggering a heat wave, and my mind was just too busy. What was going to happen to us, to our bikes and our crazy plan?

Once again, if there are any *real cyclists* still reading this story, I am not sure why you persist. But thanks for staying with me this far—you gluttons for punishment.

The aptly dubbed *Red Eye* flight got us into New York's Kennedy Airport at 5:30am. Worn out already, we shuffled off in search of our bikes. Bryon worried aloud, as he glanced around, "Where in the world, at this big *International* Airport, are we going to find some place to put our bikes back together? There's no room anywhere where we can settle down in peace. I've been worried about this for months."

Grumpy, tired, and scruffy looking after the *Red Eye*, we wandered around and finally found the big door where the oversized baggage got drug through. Our hearts were in our throats as the bikes took forever to appear. While I obsessed, *Please be in good shape*, the boxes finally got shoved through the door, and appeared only a little the worse for wear. Whew. One small step taken on the road to Oregon.

We are not very mechanically oriented people, and after sitting up in an airplane all night, we felt even less so. Thinking we could be in for a stressful assembly process, we lugged the heavy boxes around for awhile, realizing that there just wasn't going to be any place inside the airport where we could spread out and get to work. With no other clear choice, we trudged from one exit to the next. Luck was with us! Just a few feet from one exit some construction guys were building a new security office under an overpass. Boy, were we happy to see them. A friendlier bunch of guys you couldn't ask for.

Bryon painted the scene in an email home, *"Youse guys can build dem bikes right here!"* They took us under their wings (and under their roof). *"Where youse guys going?"* When we told them, they were just stunned to disbelief that the fat guy and the white haired lady were planning to ride to Oregon. *"You're kidding, right? AWWWH, I don't believe it! Really?"*

These good natured, big hearted guys started us off with a great feeling about the people of New York City. We already had friends. Soon, though, they went about their business and left us to go about ours. Blessedly, we got the bikes put back together with only a few bits left over. (*Hmmm, oh well, hope they weren't real important bits.*) We loaded up the bikes with all our bags and as we headed toward the street, as if scripted, it began to POUR. Ooooops! Hmm—what a great time for a coffee break, eh?

Reassembling the bikes at JFK

Coffee time kind of drug on and the rain just kept on pouring. At first we were so darned relieved to have the bikes ready to go, that we didn't mind the delay, even a little bit. The coffee escalated into muffins and more coffee, and after about sixty minutes of this the rain slowed to a light drizzle. It was time to go for it.

Leaving Kennedy Airport had us thoroughly puzzled as we snaked around and around trying to find a non-freeway exit. The rain picked up. We snaked around some more and the rain picked up some more. *Where are the snorkels when you need them?* Nearly inhaling rain, we asked every one we could find, but no one knew how we could get out of the airport without having to get on a freeway. Bryon put it like this*; They all wrinkled their brows and said, "Axe those guys over there." So we axed everybody in sight, rode hither and dither in circles, over bridges, through construction sites, and 4.7 miles later we finally "exscaped" the airport maze.*

Even though it continued to rain lightly on us, as we headed away, we were soon totally enjoying the ride, as we soaked in the sights and sounds of

New York by bike. The townhouses and dogwoods in bloom lined our way, making a great start for our ride. We were in very good spirits as Bryon navigated us to the 59th Street, Queensborough Bridge, and into Manhattan. About the time I started bellowing out *Feelin' Groovy* and other Simon and Garfunkle tunes, right there in the middle of the bridge, in the rain, my bike commenced to sound like I had reverted to childhood and put a playing card to the spokes with a clothes pin. Rat-a-tat-a-tat-a-tat! *What the heck?* We stopped in the drizzle and Bryon gave it his best shot at diagnosis and repair, but no luck. So I Rat-a-tat-a-tat-a-tat-a-tated away as we rode. Each Rat-a-tat went through my soul. *Please let this be a minor problem.* We had only just begun this trip, and I wondered, *Could this be caused by one of those leftover bits I found laying around, after I put the bike together?* That was not exactly a good thought and the rat-a-tats were not a good omen. Feeling a little sick to my stomach, I managed to cacophonate along. The neighborhoods we had been enjoying, gave way to downtown Manhattan, and the traffic got busier and more demanding. It was with great relief that we found our hotel at last. I had a moment of deflation though, when the clerk informed us that our room was on the 24th floor. He looked at my bike and said, "We have an elevator, but I don't know about that bike...it may not fit." Oh great, just what I didn't want to hear. I stood there waiting for the elevator, imagining my self in the stairwell on about the 16th floor, dragging my bike ever upward, when the elevator bell sounded. As the elevator opened I got worried even more. It was just a small box of a thing, and there was no way my long recumbent was going to fit. I was verging on whining when we realized there was plenty of room if we stood the bike up straight in the air, on its back wheel. Voilá! *Beam me up Scotty*!

We were revved-up as we wedged the bikes into our postage stamp sized room, "How did your rain gear do? Mine did really well!" We had been riding in the drizzle for over 18 miles and that gave us a pretty good feel for our degree of waterproofness. The only things that got really wet were **my** shoes. They were lead heavy with water, whereas Bryon's felt quite light and were just a titch damp. My shoes weighed about 5 pounds each. With all the wet stuff we had in the room, I figured the shoes might never dry out. That's when I spotted the hair dryer and pressed it into service. It was doing a fine job of blowing hot air into my shoe, and I rigged up a way to keep it going without having to hold on to it. That worked great until the thing shut off suddenly. I thought I had burned it out for sure. It felt really HOT. *Hmmm, not good, could probably short something out and burn this whole hotel down.* But then, after cooling for a spell, it came back on, and I just kept the thing blowing away (except for the periodic, built-in shut downs that kept happening). We found a phone number for the closest bike repair place and made an appointment for the morning. I told myself not to worry about it, but go on and enjoy Manhattan. I would worry in the morning. We got all the wet riding clothes hung up, until our tiny little room looked like a spider's house on washing day, a virtual web of hanging clothes and gear crisscrossing the tiny room on thin twine.

In the morning we walked my bike to the bike shop, and those clever folks diagnosed and fixed the problem by 10am. (I recall that it was an easy problem to correct, but I didn't manage to put the cause in my journal, and for the life of me, I can't remember it now. You would think that I could remember…but you would be thinking wrong.) The mechanics put everything aside to help us, as they understood what a pickle we were in. (We had to get this bike fixed.) But I was unnerved to have a *breakdown* so soon in the trip and with such a brand new bike.

The rat-a-tat sound was gone as we rode toward Ground Zero to pay our respects to all those who suffered in the 9-11 tragedy. Emotions spilled over as we toured the site, felt the weight of what had happened there and viewed some of the temporary memorials that locals had erected. Our hearts went out to all involved. We stood a long while in remembrance and respect, before heading on. The air at the construction site was still bad. I commenced to coughing almost immediately. Not completely over the Panama cough, this pollution did me in, I just couldn't stop coughing, and as I watched the workers going about their work, I wondered about *their* health. That air just couldn't be good for them either. I could not stop coughing, as we pedaled away.

We decided to ride out for a look at the Statue of Liberty. It seemed only fitting to see her again after having been to Ground Zero. A lot of the water frontage in Manhattan had, over the years, been opened up to walking and bike riding and when we pedaled to a vantage point and gazed out to sea at the Statue of Liberty, we realized that we were right then—as far east as we would be on this bicycle trip. From this point on we would be headed north to Albany, NY and then WEST, WEST, WEST, ever WESTWARD!

We rode the bike path *home* along the Hudson River, pedaling by a huge sporting complex built dock-like out in the river. It was neat to get to ride some of the great network of bike and walking trails around Manhattan, but on the way back to the hotel, a new rubbing/scraping sound took up residence in my bike. *OH, for crying out loud, what's next*?

Back to the bike shop. This time a shimmed derailleur had slipped down and was rubbing. This too was easy to remedy, but my fear was that this $2,000.00 bicycle was going to need too much tweaking. Bryon's $150.00 bike hadn't had a problem.

New York was a blast. We stood in line one night to see the Daily Show with Jon Stewart, and just barely made it, being among the last of the line allowed in. We **love** the Daily Show, and it was well worth the wait. The warm up comedian that came out at the start though, zeroed right in on us. The entire audience was dressed in black and there we sat in our brightly colored fleeces, "And you two, where are you from, cuz I sure as heck can tell your not from around here!"

We were having so much fun in NY we stayed an extra day. The research library on 42nd street was a don't miss at that particular time. We saw one of the original Gutenberg Bibles, a first edition of Poe's *Tamerlane*, an original Honus Wagner baseball card, and all kinds of neat stuff. We also snagged half price tickets to Les Mis and ended up near the front row, with great seats. But of course, all we had to wear was, you guessed it, our lovely red and orange fleece vests. This time I added my construction-yellow, paper-like rain coat to my—oh so fashionable—bright orange fleece. Bryon selected his provocative red fleece (surprise?) and we were all the rage as we stuck out there, sitting amongst the tuxedos and furs, like two plump gum drops, oddly dropped on the scene.

Aftah the *theatah* we went to a Brazilian Restaurant and noticed that they put *gum drop people* way in the back, where newly arriving customers couldn't see us.

April 24th we headed out of Manhattan, through Central Park and tried to find our way to a bike trail along the river. But that was going to entail a lot of back tracking, so we bagged it and dragged the bikes (fully loaded for 2 months touring), our pulses racing whilst huffing and puffing, up a bunch of stairs and then a bunch more stairs, till we lined ourselves up with a bike path and the George Washington Bridge. Crossing the Hudson River on a gorgeous New York day, was a great way to start to our journey.

We were headed north toward Albany, New York, on this dry, sunny day, but the weather report said rains were on the way, so we decided to take advantage of this day. We exited the main roads, and wandered down along the river through one beautiful little village after another. We were still just a stones throw from NYC, and this was no doubt, really pricey real estate. We were glad we took advantage of that beautiful day, because the weather was to be not often so wonderful to us on the road ahead.

The Weather Changes

Farther down the road, we woke up early one morning to the Weather Channel prediction of rain, rain, rain, which when coupled with cold, cold, cold, prompted us to get going fast so we could put some miles in before the sky opened up. That meant no taking showers for us, no time to spare. We wolfed down the motel continental breakfast, grabbed some coffee, saddled up and hit the road. Good thing we did, because by noon the rains began in earnest. The temperature was in the low to mid 40's, and we were cold and turning blue. When to call it quits, that is the question? Today the answer was, *call it quits now*, which is what we did. (But we always second guessed ourselves. Maybe it would fine-up and we would have been wimps, to quit so early? We held that prospect up against the other side of the coin that if we stayed out and got freezing cold, ending up sick in bed, what would we have gained?)

After eating as many pounds of Chinese food as we could pound down, in one more nondescript little Chinese take-out/sit-in restaurant, we waddled out into the rain, and back to the motel. Nothing was drying in our room with **no heat**, and almost everything we owned was wet. It was 60° in the room and though we tried to get the management to share our concern, the heater remained broken. Between the temperature and the humidity, we tried to fight off an emerging grim mood. We each put on a couple pair of socks, including neoprene rain socks, our long johns, fleece vests and I even added my raincoat. We still weren't warm and we weren't even *outside*. Bryon periodically got up and started waving his wet shirt around like a crazy man. I thought, *Why not?* Maybe it would start a little molecular chain reaction, and with molecules colliding around, maybe stuff would dry quicker? As I sat watching the human drying machine, I started to sneeze, and that spot in my throat started to feel dry and a little sore, again. Dr. Bryon prescribed Echinacea to boost the immune system. I added lots of hot drinking water from the tap, which was good hydration and had the added plus of helping warm me up from the inside.

In the morning I checked the clothes—**wet**, but not too bad. I put all the wet stuff in a mesh bag, and packed that on top of all the dry stuff still in baggies. When we stepped out of the motel to begin to pedal to Poughkeepsie, we immediately felt chilled. The temp was 38° but the good part was that it was not raining. I searched everywhere for my balaclava, as this was the perfect morning to wear it. Nowhere in sight! That really ticked me off. All biking stuff seems to come in black. I have black gloves, black shorts, black hydro socks, black arm and leg warmers, black rainpants, and the list goes on. All these blacknesses are in baggies, and I thought I had looked in every bag, but no balaclava. It makes me very irritable to be going out in the cold with no cover for my ears and neck. But hey, whose fault is it anyway? *MINE, so get over it.*

A good breakfast helped, especially since the eggs, ham, potatoes, and toast only cost $3.99. In Manhattan they would have probably cost $9.99. So that cheered me up a bit. I proceeded to drink enough hot coffee to crank me up for the entire day, and away we went. Bryon navigated us to a bike path that would save us the dreaded Bear Mountain climb. Everything we had heard about it— little or no shoulder, heavy traffic, exhausting climb, etc., said, *AVOID Bear Mountain.* (But, on the other hand, no one we talked to had ever taken the bike path that we were considering, down along the river, and they knew next to nothing about it. One person thought that it might not be in passable shape.)

We took the bike path anyway, and thankfully it turned out to be pretty good, though not paved (graveled), and it was beautiful. We wondered if we would see anyone else on it and sure enough it wasn't long before we met a cyclist riding in the opposite direction. He gave us some tips about the roads to Poughkeepsie. It seemed 9D was the road of choice, a small, not too well traveled road. The sun was out, the air warming, and we were thoroughly enjoying this little graveled trail along the Hudson River. Every now and again the trees we were riding through dropped away and gave us stellar views of the river, and valley. As we rode along this river, I felt one of those moments of profound well being. I still had a cough and a little sore throat, but that didn't detract from the moment. All cares drifted away and I was living in just that peaceful, joyful moment, feeling thankful for this life, and so lucky to be doing this ride.

Once we made it to 9D, the countryside was full of grand old homes with trees erupting in a palette of newly opened blossoms. There were miles and miles of some knock-your-socks off, drop-dead-gorgeous old estates that had mostly been turned into private schools, youth academies, churches, etc., even catering businesses. (I'll bet there were some pretty lavish parties in these whereabouts.) What a ride it was! But it was also a lot of up and down, up and down. We were earning every mile. The wind kept shifting, sometimes in our faces, other times at our backs with the wind nearly halting forward progress in one tunnel. I started having some brake troubles, so we paused for a bit and Bryon worked on them. (That bike repair class has been paying off.) We realized that with such a new bike, the brake cables would stretch and need to be adjusted, so this was not too alarming.

We made Poughkeepsie by 5pm, but the ride into town, through the suburbs, with no shoulder, was not heaps of fun until we discovered a sidewalk/bike path that helped ease the frazzled nerves. The motel we found even had a washer and dryer, so we were quite content. With a shower, newly washed and dried clothes and dinner under our belts—what more could we ask for? (Maybe less prune juice?)

I drank too much prune juice last night. Thought I would never feel secure enough to leave our Econo Lodge room in the morning. Ugh.

At last, things calmed down and the pedaling began again. Within a few miles we sighted a public library. Lucky for us, most libraries across the country seem to have computers for us to sign up to use. So the drill evolved: I would stay outside and watch the bikes while Bryon snagged a computer and typed up a group email. We were totally paranoid about someone stealing our gear and especially our bikes. So we always tried to have the bikes in sight of one of us. I took to writing in my journal, while Bryon sent the emails. So we settled down to this routine where he touched on the highlights of the ride, and I filled in some of the other details, in longhand. You can never put enough details down, though, and had I known that I would some day try to write this trip up in book form, I would have spent a lot more time trying to capture the trip in words.

As I sat in the sun, outside the library I wondered how many miles we would log in by the end of the day. Though the air was cold, the day was sunny, and the weather report for tomorrow was—DELUGE, all day. (What's new, eh?) The trip has been a bit, you could say, sloshy, making us both concerned about the speed of our progress. As of April 27th, we have been pedaling for more than three days and we have only made it about half the way to Albany. If we kept at this pace, I figured it would take us about 15 days, AFTER Albany, to get across the state of New York. (Of course we have to go faster than that. *Somethin's gotta give.* Either the weather has to improve, or we will just have to start riding more in the frigid rain.) We have 10 states to cross all totaled, and if New York takes us about 20 days to navigate and we have 10 states to cross, the math looks bad. It would take us, like 200 days, to cross the continent at this pace. That was a stunning realization and I sat there taken aback. As I ruminated, my innards pruninated, and I was glad to see Bryon emerging from the library, so I could make use of the library resources too.

Our ride through New York State has been beautiful, even with all the rain, and this morning proved no exception. By 10:15 we were rolling by the Culinary Institute of America Campus, and *Oh my, my, my*, what a gorgeous spot, on a bluff near the river. We wanted to tour the place and sample some of the food, because Bryon has a nephew who just graduated from there. But alas, the restaurants didn't open until 11am and we couldn't afford to wait around. (Turned out to be a good thing; you want to be able to linger at such a place, and not feel you have to quickly hit the road. We found this out several years later, when we traveled by car and did take the time to have lunch there. Gasp! Lunch, I say **LUNCH** ended up costing, hold your hat, $80.00! Caught us by surprise. For that price you want to linger most of the day. No, for that price you'd like a share of the business.)

On down the road we rode onto the grounds of FDR's Hyde Park, where the President had his "country" home. We would have loved to take the tour, but if we stand any chance of getting home to Oregon (we have friends coming from New Zealand) by the 1st week in July, we have to start picking up the pace. It's too bad, because there is so much to see and do.

April 29th

We spent 2 nights in Hudson, NY due to more, you guessed it, **rain**. The temperature topped out between 40° and 45°. The normal temp for this time of year was supposed to be 60°. When Bryon researched our trip on the internet, we were using the "normal" temps in our plans. Oh, well. But it's not so much the rain, or the cold that is a problem for us; it's the rain and cold *together* that is the problem.

We arrived in Albany, at long last, around 2pm, but it was the getting there that was really eventful. We were still riding along the Hudson River, and there weren't places to duck in and out of the rain. (Just imagine you're on your exercise bike, in your bathtub, with the air conditioner on to 39 degrees, and the shower head pelting you with frigid water, riding hour after hour…that is what our ride was like.) I had taken to wearing my colorful Household Heavy Jobs Rubber Gloves to keep my hands dry, which they did, but they did nothing much for warmth, or as a fashion statement. Then nature called and there was nothing to do but use the great outdoors, and the great outdoors was raining and freezing. Sigh. Damp and frozen, we continued on and on until we rode by a bar/tavern around 10:30am and stopped in search of something hot to drink. No coffee, but they could make us hot tea. As we sat there, our grumbling stomachs embarrassed us into ordering coffee break snacks that escalated into a food frenzy of greasy burgers, oil-sogged french fries, and just to complete the nutritional package—macaroni salad. Yumm. Why we didn't drop dead of heart arrest right then, I do not know. Haven't had that much grease and fat at one time since high school. (I'm appalled to say it tasted grrrrreat.) The friendly, helpful barkeep gave us directions to the nearest bike repair shop in Albany (I had noticed that Bryon's rear wheel was wobbling, and we suspected loose spokes.) and even though she let us sit right next to the heater, I just couldn't warm up.

Not long after that, we were making good progress even with the cold and rain, when I was startled wide alert. PLOP! My bike got instantly harder to pump. *What the heck is this? Geez-a-Luigi...I have a flat tire.* The first flat of the trip. It was not nice, standing in the cold rain, watching my husband pedal further and further away in the dark grey afternoon. I shouted, "Hey Bryon!" but he didn't hear me. I began to walk my bike and shouted some more (I won't say what I shouted). I sat down in a puddle, because I wasn't paying attention and at this point I really didn't care anymore, while passing trucks sprayed me. I examined my tire carefully, and woefully. At last, Bryon either heard me or saw in the mirror that I wasn't there, and came back to find me. *Bless him.* I am embarrassed to say, that I have no recollection of ever having changed a flat bicycle tire, personally, all by myself, and I was MOST grateful for his help.

Now, this was where our luck got very, very good. It was almost a miracle. Well, that might be stretching it a bit, but at least it was very good luck. It was rural, on this stretch of road, few homes and almost no businesses. But, alas, we could see that a little ways up the road, there was a car repair business. How amazing was that? I rolled the bike up to their garage, and we began to chat with the mechanics. They were quick, with the New York friendliness we have found in abundance, to make a space for us out of the rain, to work on the bikes. But Bryon's hands were so cold he could hardly *feel* the tire let alone work on it. Mumbling and fumbling around he did at last manage to get the spare tube in, but it looked like what I really needed was a new tire. There were some sinister slices where pieces of broken glass had slashed into the rubber. If we had had to deal with this problem out on the road, in the cold and rain, Bryon's stone cold hands might never have gotten warm enough to do the job. We were so thankful for the covered area to work in. Also, we had the repair shop's electric air pump to help us along. (*Is that cheating?*) Thank goodness, the air finally stayed in the tire.

We headed on, trying in the rain to find our way over the Hudson River toward Albany, with Bryon's wheel wobbling away, and my slashed tire on the verge of a repeat flat.

The first thing we learned about Albany, New York was that it is a HILLY place. Up and Up and Up and UP Madison Street we struggled toward the bike shop only to be greeted by a very unhappy looking chap who immediately pronounced, "I don't know if we can help you…" (It appeared that "walk-ins" were not appreciated.) After listening to our sad saga, and more importantly, realizing that we weren't going to go away, he relented. We ended up getting a whole new wheel for Bry's bike as 2 spokes were broken, a new tire and tube for mine, throw in a break adjustment and voilá, the visa card had a new $180.00 cha-ching! We gave these guys high marks for efficiency, though they could work some more in the friendliness category. But, we needed speed and competence from them, and they had it.

Well, we made it to a motel, and will wonders never cease—we actually turned west. This was a BIG milestone—**WEST! AT LONG LAST WE WERE HEADED WEST!**

We propped ourselves up on pillows and turned on a TV station that was showing the local weather news, and the weather guy said that, "…the weather today has Stunk!" Those where his words exactly. But I'll bet he hadn't been out riding his bicycle all day in that *stinking* weather. Ha! It had rained all day and the high had been a measly 43°.

The motel we stayed in (the only one we had the patience to find in the cold rain) had recently had the name Howard Johnson removed (more like it had peeled away). You could see what it used to be named, but it had no name now. Despite not being big on maintenance, it was, at least dry, and so we signed in. Motel No Name smelled of curry as we drug the bikes up the stairs and down the soiled carpet to our room. Stomachs growling, we just glanced at the room and headed off to find food. There were no restaurants within our desired walking radius, but there was a gas station. Umm, nothing like gas station food, eh? *For nutrition, and comfort after a hard day's work, try Gas Station Food.* Back in the motel the first thing we noticed about the place was that the bathroom sink wouldn't drain, it would not drain at all. So we washed our hands in the bath tub, which drained ever so slowly, like a swamp. While we brushed our teeth, camping style—with little plastic glasses full of water, spitting into the john, we heard the bed collapse. (No, really—we heard the bed collapse.) We stood there mesmerized by this turn of events. (You couldn't dream this place up.) So we dragged the mattress onto the floor for the night. Well, at least it was a warm and dry place, and our previously washed out clothes were actually drying. *Sweet dreams…*

The Last Day of April

Numerous folks had been telling us, "Whatever you do, do not get off the main roads through Schenectady. Its really bad, you don't want to get lost wondering around there." Taking this advice to heart, we stayed on our friend the #5 bike trail road and headed up along the Erie Canal. The morning was dry and sunny. We made good time on this stretch, over 30 miles before lunch. "See, we can cover some miles, when the weather cooperates," I told my bicycle, whom I thought could use some words of encouragement. After we stopped for lunch, we intended to find a nice place to stretch out in the sun and rest. Of course, as soon as lunch ended it began to rain. The next 25 miles we pedaled in the cold and wind and rain, a combination of elements increasingly familiar. Every time we ran across anyplace to get in out of the rain, we did. We stopped and purchased untold cups of coffee and hot chocolate, just to get under somebody's roof, and near a heater.

Finally, after 57.4 miles, we rolled into Palatine Bridge, a little rural New York community, and began the search for lodging. There wasn't too much to choose from and we settled into an old motel run by a wonderful Native American woman. She rated right up there with the nicest of all people in the universe. She volunteered to do a load of wash for us, no charge. We protested that we needed to pay her for doing that, but she would have none of it. And then, since it was raining, she offered to let us borrow her car to drive to dinner. Absolute strangers, we were, and she wanted to loan us her car. You talk about a giving, trusting soul; there she was, in Palatine Bridge New York, running an old motel. There have been a few times in my life when I have felt in the presence of such sweet goodness. Two of those times were on this bicycle trip, and she was the first of the trip. She wanted to make us French toast for breakfast, on the house of course, and we wouldn't let her, because she had been already so kind and generous. Since we wouldn't let her make the French toast, she brought us coffee, cinnamon rolls and donuts for breakfast and stuck around to see us off when we left. I am sorry that I didn't keep track of her name, because I would mention it here. She was a gem of a human being, just full of goodness. These moments are some of the best and the most humbling of the trip. We won't soon forget her kindness and generosity.

There were times during the ride to Palatine Bridge when the rain was coming down so hard that when I tried to breathe through my nose, it was like trying to breathe under water. So I breathed through a slim slit between my lips, and even then my front tire spewed enough of the road slurp up in the air and onto my face, that I was soon chewing road grime. Crunchy.

May 1ˢᵗ

Yesterday our struggle was with the cold and rain. At one point the rain drops were so big and cold when they dropped through our helmets and hit our scalps, that we stopped, took off the helmets, donned motel shower caps—pulling them taut over our ears, and stuck the helmets back on. We may have looked like bicycling cafeteria staff, but our ears were warm and scalps dry.

Today though, it was supposed to be NICE. With that information on hand last night, I decided to wash my *seal skin* rain socks which I had been wearing for days on end. Bad idea. I figured the room was heated and they would probably dry out, and if they didn't, well—it was supposed to be nice, so they could dry while we rode. Well, what happened was nothing dried and today was the coldest of our whole trip. I had some dry wool socks that I thought would do the job, but since my never-get-dry shoes were so wet, the socks didn't stay dry for long after they became acquainted with the shoes. Once we started out, and the cold air rushed over my feet, each foot felt like a block of ice. It was so miserable at one point that I stopped and checked my shoes because it felt like I had a big chunk of something in my socks, but it was just that the damp socks had lost all flexibility and had frozen stiff with an uncomfortable bulge. Bryon has been cold all morning too, because he dressed for NICE weather. And then to top it all off, we weren't mentally prepared for the HILLS that Bike Path #5 had in store.

Though the #5 was called a "path," it was not a bike path as such. It was basically a "route" that went along small, less traveled roads. Anyway, we had no idea of the never ending, grueling hills Bike Path #5 intended to inflict. We struggled up, up, ever upwards to the first high plateau, in biting cold winds, only to see that we would have to go all the way down and then repeat the process untold times. We were as high up as anything on the horizon, and looked down through the clear icy morning air, at the Erie Canal below. We had thought Bike Path #5 would be flat, like the canal. Bryon had worked so hard to plan a route that minimized climbs. He was completely blindsided by this curve ball that Bike Path #5 threw. It was the most sullen I had seen him in a long time. He wasn't speaking much, and the smile had left his eyes. When we expect difficulties, and get mentally prepared for them, we roll with the hills much more easily than when we're ambushed. We had 30 miles of these hills, before it flattened out a bit, relatively speaking. I became exhausted and started to lag behind, as we pressed on toward Utica, New York. The last 2 days had been a grind.

OH! And then there was always the additional problem of trying to figure out where we were, and how far we still had to go. I am now very appreciative of how Oregonians do the "sign thing." In rural Oregon, when you come to an intersection, there are usually signs that not only point you to the various destinations, but also tell you how far away the destination is. That was not the case in rural New York. They had very few mileage signs (at least on the roads we traveled). So we would ask people and they would say, "It's not far, just 10 minutes down the road." Ten minutes to someone who drives it in a car, can be 100 minutes to someone who rides it UP and down the road on a bike. But, on the other handlebar, we like the way New Yorkers do the "dog thing." They must have stiffer penalties, or else New Yorkers are just more considerate dog owners than Oregonians. Even out in the country, dogs are in kennels, behind fences, or tied up. We have not encountered one dog that was left to run loose and make a sport out of attacking bicyclists. I wish I could say the same for Klamath County, where we have an enormous population of growling, snapping and snarling bike chasers.

May 2nd

We were fast becoming among the most boring people in the universe. Not only had The Weather Channel become our favorite program, but the weather segments of local news broadcasts were our next favorite programs, and the morning of May 2nd was no exception. As we stared out the sliding glass doors of our Utica, New York motel at the cold, blowing rain, we listened to the weather lady. Last night the report was for "…less rain in the middle of the day today and then all hell will break loose." The morning lady said "…thunder showers likely, possible snow tonight as temperatures dip…" and then she smiled and cheerfully wished us all to have a great day. Arghhhh…

We put the news on *mute* for awhile, choosing to read about the weather in the newspaper instead. We just didn't have the heart to saddle up our gearshift ponies and ride. Actually, we read just about every line in the Observer Dispatch, and then around checkout time, the clouds parted, the rain stopped and we hightailed it to Wendy's, wolfed down breakfast and dashed back out to hop on the bikes so as to not miss any moment of rain-free riding time. Naturally, that was when the rain started up again.

Oh well, what the heck. We weren't too cold, **yet.** So away we went. As motorists passed us it occurred to me that they were probably feeling sorry for the two nutzoid bike riders, pedaling along in the cold, windy, rain. They must have thought we were feeling miserable. But alas and alack, nothing was farther from the truth. We were having a blast! You might wonder how such a cold, wet ride could be a blast? My enjoyment wasn't even unhinged when I had a little problem. Shortly after we left Wendy's, I had to stop to rearrange some gear, and was in a hurry to leap back on my bike. Too much of a hurry. As I threw my leg over the bar I snagged it with my foot and the bike and I tumbled into a mud puddle. Not only was I soggy from the rain, but now I was mired in a coating of mud as well. BUT, I DIDN'T CARE. I didn't care about any of that because I was having so much fun. We were chock full of fun. It was fun beyond belief. And it was all because of Mr. Wind. WIND. Wind! AT LONG LAST WE HAD THE WIND AT OUR BACKS! Hooray…Hooray…Hooray! For the first time, cycling was effortless. We couldn't believe it was the same sport we had been engaged in all these days. Bicycling was fun, fun, FUN! Bryon later extolled that it was the most fun he had ever had riding his bike. Euphoria! We were FLYING along, gobbling up the miles!

But, after awhile, we were also getting cold. No matter how much fun we were having with our friend Mr. Tail Wind, it was still raining, and it was still fricken cold, so we sought out a place to grab some coffee, and warmth. The bar tender was so surprised to see our soggy selves drip into his bar, that he paused as he processed us and our request for coffee, and then announced the coffee was on the house. He wouldn't let us pay a cent and chatted the whole time we sipped away, wanting to learn about our trip. One more really nice New Yorker to add to the growing list.

We wanted to keep riding with this wind all the evening long, but that wasn't practical, as the motels weren't where we needed them to be down the road. So we ended up staying at the Turning Stone Casino, and played blackjack long enough to quit ten bucks ahead. We washed our clothes in our room and then went for a swim in their indoor pool. This was starting to feel like a vacation. We basked in the memory of the wind at our backs! Ahhhhhhh, life was good in the extreme.

Mike Reynolds, the 400-miles-in-one-day guy, shared with us many things before we left on this trip and one of them was, "On a bike tour you will meet with more highs and lows than you will in any other activity I know of." True words. From the frustrations of flat tires, never ending cold and rain, the trials of Bike Path #5, and on and on, there came to pass the time when we had the wind at our backs. Fortunes change.

Meanwhile, back in our room at the Turning Stone Casino Hotel, I took stock of my deteriorating rain jacket. There were many things I loved about that jacket: light weight, easy color for motorists to see, breathable, packed up small, and it fit well. BUT, we hadn't even made it out of New York yet, and it was looking terminal. Chunks of the yellow outer layer, which looked a lot like finely corrugated thin vinyl tablecloth, had delaminated from what looked like a gauze backing, and had blown away in the wind. On the left sleeve there was a two inch hole straight through both layers, exposing my bare skin underneath, and the right sleeve was worse. With my jacket on I looked—well—tattered. At this rate, I thought, *pretty soon I'll just have a short sleeve rain jacket.* But even with all the imperfections, the thing had kept me dry, and that was what I had asked of it, and that oddly drew us together. I started searching for the duct tape, to mend my friend and was horrified to realize, WE HAD NO DUCT TAPE! What? How can this be? We needed duct tape. Duct tape was definitely on the list of needed items. Heaven forbid I should buy a new rain jacket when I could bloody well duct tape this one up.

May 3rd

Before leaving the Turning Stone Casino Hotel we, of course, watched the weather on TV. The forecast was for sun (partial), and some chance of rain. But the unsettling thing was that the whole region we were in the center of, was ominously colored blue on the map and had the word **WINDY** written across it in bold letters. That was the first time we had seen that particular graphic on TV. It was unnerving. We didn't quite know what to make of it.

Turned out there was reason to be unnerved.

It took us two hours to go just 9 miles. At one point we were actually stopped dead in our tracks by the wind. We couldn't advance the bikes at all. It was howling. We got off the bikes and turned our backs to the wind and leaned against it, pulling the bikes with us as best we could. It was insane. I was blown off the shoulder twice and once into the center line. When we could make some headway, we were in granny gears and achieving three miles per hour. Occasionally the wind subsided a titch and we cranked, red faced, as hard as we possibly could to get up to 10 mph. But those times were rare, just gusts of time. We were basically heading straight into this driving wind. The thought crossed my mind, that if we met anyone on this trail going east, they would just be a flying blurrrrrr…. We had acquired a new respect for the blue area on a TV weather map when it was emblazoned with **WINDY** in bold letters.

We were freezing. Every chance we had to get out of that wind, we took, but buildings were few and far between. We spent awhile in a small restaurant that gave new dimensions to the words "greasy spoon." The cook was not about to have ANYTHING stick on HIS grill. He must have used a cup of grease on my breakfast alone. But the food was hot, and the coffee was hot and we started to warm up a bit, but not fully. I started to shiver, and that surprised me. That wind had done a bonzer job of sucking out my body heat. I shivered away for about 1 ½ hours and gradually warmed up marginally enough to push off.

Once out in the elements again, it was still really cold and blowing like the devil. It didn't take long for our lips to start turning blue, and for enunciation to become a real struggle. The only way we could keep going was to stop whenever we could, and get in out of that cold wind. We stopped at just about every little restaurant we rode by. I cannot begin to say how much coffee we drank. When we rode, I stayed way back of Bryon so that we couldn't get blown into each other. We were pedaling so hard my right leg started hurting in that old herniated disc, down-the-leg nerve pain way. Ominous.

But the good news was that the *promotional signs* we rode by were TRUE. For many cranks of the wheel we had been straining past signs extolling the virtues of Flo's Diner. Among many other wonderful qualities, we learned that Flo's still had coffee for just ten cents a cup. Now this was hard to pass up, and we wanted to verify, for the record, that this astounding price was true. It was indeed, and as we sat there drinking yet one more cup(s) of hot coffee, we figured that, at this rate we will make possibly, 1,000 coffee stops before we get home.

We struggled through the community of Bridgeport, and its one hotel which turned out to be only a "drinking" hotel, no rooms for us. Cicero was next, 10 miles into the wind from us, which meant it could end up being 3 hours of non stop hard pumping. Bridgeport had had snow last night, and that was easy to believe; gees it was cold. The road was taking us along Lake Oneida and that was a sight to behold. The wind had kicked up the lake and the waves were violent.

Along that road, the INCIDENT occurred. Since Bryon has a different fantasy life on his bike than I do, I'll give you the story straight from his emails home:

The event of note is that we are surely the two slowest cyclists on this planet. The day we left New York City all the studs were out on their speed machines and just flew by us. It was depressing as could be, I mean they just zipped past us so fast we were left speechless, while we ground down the road at our paltry few miles per hour. We tried to mutter to ourselves that we have big loads to carry and such. But still it hurt. I spent the first week of the trip fantasizing about what it would be like to pass somebody, someday. How would it feel? Would I say anything to them? Oh, I covered miles and miles of New York countryside as this scenario played out in my head.

Then it happened.

We were headed west across New York, nearing Cicero into an arctic blast. We were both fighting hypothermia (we really were), our lips were so cold it was hard to pronounce big words. I was leading as usual, into this fierce headwind, going all out, doing maybe 4 miles an hour, when out of the corner of my eye I saw this bike come coasting down a driveway toward the street about thirty yards in front of me. I thought, "Who would be crazy enough to be riding in THIS?" Then I saw that the bike was a rusted up old Schwinn one speed, the type with a basket and bell rusted solid. On this old steed was perched a 90 year old geezer who appeared to have no teeth and really thick glasses. He was a living caricature out of some Patrick McManus story, riding right out into our path. He had pretty good speed, coming down the driveway when WHAM, he turned into the wind and just shuddered to a stop from the headwind. He had great balance for such an old codger as he kept her upright and moving a bit.

That's when it hit me.

I can take him!

Sure enough, I cranked for all I was worth and on the corner going into Cicero, I overtook my first cyclist. I felt like the crowds were cheering me on. Lance-Lance-Lance, they all cheered. I may never wear a yellow jersey, but I know now the feeling it must bring (sort of).

Pray for tailwinds and downhills.

-Bryon

Then suddenly, the sun finally came out. Ahhhhhh! Glorious. Then the wind lessened a bit. Ohhhhh! Supreme. Bryon stopped at a hardware store to buy some rope to use to string up the bikes, so he could work on them later. The sales guy took pity on me in my tattered rain jacket and gave me enough duct tape to shore it up. I keep sinking to ever lower fashion depths. I ask you, the reader—*have you ever gone out in public with your clothes duct taped together?* I doubt it. I think Garrison Kieller said it well and it applied to me, "…she had done the irreversible slide from fashion to comfort."

Every mile you have to ride, out of your way, on a day like we had just had, was a mile you didn't want to ride. But, after a few false starts, we finally found a motel, and they gave us some flyers for a "We Deliver" establishment. As we chomped down on the delivered chicken wings, salads, breadsticks and Diet Pepsi, we regained our good humor and started to think about the future. This pace we were making was not going to get us to Oregon. We needed to start adding significantly more miles per day. We needed some help from the cold and rain, and especially the WIND.

May 4th
Bryon finished the book he was reading, and he recently came across a copy of the Stephen Ambrose book, *Band of Brothers.* It was bigger than the book he had finished, and he could not fit this new one in his bags, try as he might. So he discarded a shirt, in order to be able to fit the book in. That just goes to show you how cramped he was for space, and how much he likes to read.

Yesterday was interesting on many levels. My knees held up, and I was worried they wouldn't, and that fierce wind could have driven us mad. Truthfully, if either one of us hadn't been so committed to this trip, yesterday could have been the end of it. It would have been easy to give up. But after a few chicken wings and a good nights sleep, we surprised ourselves and were ready to roll, again. My muscles were sore though, as we headed off in the morning, and I wondered about them. I was worried that another day of the kind of abuse my knees had just endured could do them in.

The morning sun was shining, the day was supposed to get up into the 60's, and there was a lot less wind in our faces as we rolled away from the Cicero motel. Bryon had been having some troubles with his gears and we stopped at a Wal-Mart while he strung the bikes up over a cart return area with his newly purchased rope, and went to work on both the bikes.

It was a really nice day, with just a light wind in our face, and we managed to go 67 miles. I have to admit though, that I was too tired to write in my journal, too tired to do almost anything, and this time—slept well.

May 5th

We rode most of the day within sight of the Erie Canal, or actually on the path that used to be used by the mules as they pulled the old barges along the canal. It felt like we were seeing the area as the folks of the early 1800's had.

Erie Canal and Tow Path, New York

The Erie Canal was quite the engineering wonder when first conceived and built. There were no schools of engineering in the country at the time, but the then New York Governor DeWitt Clinton had a dream he wrestled into reality, of linking the Hudson River and Albany, New York to Buffalo on the Eastern shore of Lake Erie. It was nearly 400 miles, an unheard of distance to dig a canal. But, they dug it and it transformed New York and the settlement of the country. The seven million dollar price tag was recouped in just 9 years. Settlers poured westward along the canal. New York was transformed into the busiest port in the country, and set the stage for it to become a giant of international commerce and finance. The legacy of the canal persists, as all but a couple of the biggest cities in the state of New York are along the Erie Canal. Other canals were added and some locks as well. The canal system is today a National Heritage Corridor, and rightly so.

The tow path we rode our bikes along, was beautifully peaceful with sunshine filtering through the trees. It was encouraging to see so many people out making good use of the canal tow path on a Sunday, by bicycling, walking, jogging and even skating. Some sections were paved while others just graveled. The paved sections got the most use, and became pretty congested, at times. A family passed us with a little six year old with stout pistons for legs. Look out Lance Armstrong. Piston Pete was in the lead and not about to give it away to his older brother, just behind him. He was pedaling for his life, turning his head often to look behind and make sure his brother wasn't about to overtake him. The rest of the family had bikes with several gears, but not Piston Pete the gearless wonder, he drove his pedals with maniacal determination.

Luckily, Bryon and I later happened onto a paved section away from the most populated areas, and had it to ourselves, gliding along in complete reverie, not speaking a word. The recent rains had made the countryside a luscious green and with the trees all blossomed out to the max, it was an exotic passage, alive with geese, swimming holes and peppered throughout with farms. It was an idyllic day; we had gone back in time to a place with no loud motor vehicles and their polluting ways, and no fast food trash to annoy and destroy the beauty of the setting.

Most of the canal had a graveled surface though and this made for hard work. At one point, tired of cranking along the gravel, I lobbied hard to leave the path for awhile and take our chances out on the roads. (The grass is always greener?) Though the roads were paved, as soon as we left the canal we were into the hills of New York. Up and down, up and down, up and down we went until the level gravel canal path began to look very good again.

Finally, after several days of sticking along the water, we left the peaceful canal behind and headed toward the belching city of Buffalo, New York, and the biking nightmare that awaited.

Perhaps if we had had some local knowledge of the roads, things wouldn't have been so dicey. The road we used to enter Buffalo, Route #78, had a nice shoulder when all of a sudden, with no warning at all, the shoulder simply disappeared. Without warning, we had nowhere to ride and there were huge trucks thundering past, just inches away. I was nearly hit by a bread truck, but was able to swerve onto a patch of dirt that existed in just the right spot. The driver appeared to have not seen me at all. With my heart pounding to beat the band, we spotted a gas station and swung into it. Bryon purchased a map of the city while I tried to steady my raw nerves. He then did a super job of navigating us down residential streets, going north to south, until we emerged at the enormous stadium of the Buffalo Bills. The place had the feel, on this day in May, of being a very COLD place. We could only just imagine how cold it could get there during the football season.

Finally we got on Route # 20, along the edge of Lake Erie, heading toward the border between New York and Pennsylvania. About 6 to 8 miles from Irvine, where we had hoped to spend the night, the heavens opened up on us like never before. I have never experienced such rain. My shoes instantly filled to the brim with water! Squish, squish, squish, I pedaled along noticing that my leg warmers and shorts were totally sopped as well. Luckily I had on my raincoat (for warmth) so my upper body stayed relatively dry and since the temperature was not as terribly cold as in the past, I was able to keep pedaling and generating enough heat that it kept me from freezing to death. The visibility factor became a worthy opponent, though. Have you ever been riding in a car when the rains hit so hard that your windshield wipers do no good? We had that happen in Georgia once. We couldn't see a thing, couldn't see the road and couldn't see the other cars. We crept slowly and blindly to what we thought was the shoulder of the road and stopped. Fortunately, all the other vehicles stopped too. Now, picture this same scene, but you are riding a bicycle, and the visibility is just a titch better, so that car drivers can just intermittently see the white line in the middle of the road, so they keep going, but they can't see bicyclists on the side of the road, so they don't try in any way to avoid them. Fortunately, after a while, the really hard rain subsided enough that we reached Irvine in one piece, soggy though it was.

Irvine was a crossroads little community and we went out on the town, such that it was. We never go to bars in our normal life, but decided to be daring in Irvine, as the tavern was on our path to the restaurant. We stopped in for a light beer, but they had none, and we were about to leave when the guy next to us insisted on buying us drinks. (Once again, doing well in the free beverage department.) We swapped stories for awhile and had a gin and tonic to toast what we hoped was our last night in the State of New York. Now, don't get me wrong—New York was a beautiful, friendly place, but we had been crossing it for too many days! It was time to move on.

Tailwinds

We started out the grey morning with the wind at our backs. Oh blessed wind! At 15, 17, 18, 19 miles per hour we **flew** along on the level road. I kept thinking, *someone is pushing me*, and I would actually look behind me to see who it was, but it was just Mr. East-to-West Wind and he had now become our best friend. We were zooming along the enormous, never ending edge of Lake Erie. It is no wonder they call the NY #5 road the SEAWAY TRAIL. There was certainly a lot of seaway. Well actually, it was a lake and not a sea, but it was so big that it behaved and looked like the ocean. The winds can whip up some pretty good waves here, and these huge Great Lakes produce their own weather, like lake-effect snows which have been among some of the heaviest snowfalls on record. There is a LOT of water in the Great Lakes. If someone snatched you out of your home, blindfolded, and plopped you down beside say, Lake Erie, you would swear you were at the ocean.

We were getting tantalizingly close to the state line, just a few minutes out of Ripley (believe it or not?), when there arose a terrible fierce noise from Bryon's bike. He slammed on his breaks and we could at once see that a bungee cord had partially liberated itself from his bags and wedged itself in his spokes which loosened one spoke at least, and maybe broke it. Anyway, freed from the rogue bungee cord, the bike continued to make distressing clicking noises. Not to be outdone, my bike had decided, a couple of days earlier, to make irritating tapping noises. So we were going down the road like some kind of little percussion band, *Click, click, tap, click, click, tap,* when we saw THE SIGN.

It had seemed at times like we would never get out of New York, but there it was. The lovely blue sign that boldly read, ***Welcome to Pennsylvania***. It was about time.

Chapter Four

Pennsylvania & Ohio

Ahhh, wondrous progress! We finally slipped the grip of New York and rolled across the line into State # 2. A tailwind ushered us into Pennsylvania and we annoyingly clickty-tapped our way toward Erie, Pennsylvania, looking for a bike repair shop. On the outskirts of Erie our eagle eyes spied such a facility. Unsuspectingly we crossed over the threshold and into the realm of the world's most gabby bicycle repairman/king of his domain, ever to set wrench to bike. We had been thinking for the past few days, that Great Lakes People were pretty talkative, but no one could hold a candle to this Erie Mechanic. We were there for 45 minutes while he alternately worked on the bike and expounded on a wide range of topics…I say alternately, because every time he spoke, he stopped working, and vice-versa. It seemed to us like he spoke a lot more than he worked, so after the 45 minute mark we decided to wander around his shop and try not to speak to him, lest he never find the time to get the bike fixed. He still managed to tell us one more time, about how we were *going the wrong way.* "You're nuts. You can't go East to West…" he expounded. *Yada, yada, yada.* He also decided that the last repair shop had mounted a wheel backwards, so he fixed that and tightened all the spokes correctly, "…which is an art in itself." (There was in his shop, an entire book just on the subject of the bicycle wheel.) Then he commenced to go over the bike with a fine tooth comb, tightening some stuff in the steering, and readjusting the brake. He cleaned a pad and who knows what else. Braced for a huge bill, we were shocked beyond belief when he announced we owed him $10.00. Well, I had seen a little $25.00 bag that would fit my bike frame, but had seemed too pricey, earlier. I raced over, nabbed it and added it to the bill. It seemed only fair. And then, as we left his shop he made us take a free water bottle, too. My word, this bicycle trip was reaffirming our faith in our fellow man. People have been overwhelmingly so kind and generous. This stop had also reaffirmed the notion that though the bicycle may look like a fairly simple machine, it is actually a pretty complex piece of engineering. Simply tightening up a spoke requires skill as there are at least 3 different dimensions you can screw up, and make the thing worse than when you started.

I was glad to have the new bag, because as the weather's been getting warmer, I have started packing some of the layers I've been, up until now, wearing. My bulging bags were beginning to stress out, and this new one helped relieve the strain.

In the last 5 days we had ridden 291 miles, not too bad for two grey haired gum drops...

May 9th

The weather report: Tornado Warnings.

It was pouring in the motel parking lot while we packed, but as we headed out the door, the picture suddenly turned brighter. Though humid, with the temperature in the 60's, it had stopped raining. The motel had provided us each with a cellophane wrapped Danish of undetermined age which had the look of being frozen and thawed a number of times before it found us. We gobbled the things down, nevertheless, and headed out into the wind.

It was a struggle to get going into the humid headwind. Bryon kept looking behind himself and asking me if he was pulling a trailer. I kept looking back to see if my back tire had gone flat. After a couple of hours of head/ crosswinds and fighting some pretty good gusts, we were looking for a restaurant to get some real nourishment. NO LUCK. We finally ate cellophane wrapped brownies from a bait shop. Another 6 miles down the road we scored cappuccinos from one of those little machines that make them too sweet, and some cookies. This was shaping up into the culinary morning from hell.

Then the barking snarling dogs got wind of us just as we headed into Ohio. I waited till they got within range of my pepper spray and gave 'em a good blast. Talk about "turn tail and run!" That pepper spray works! New York was great for cyclists when it came to the dog problem, Pennsylvania was not so good, and Ohio appears to be worse yet. The condition of the roads seemed to mirror that of the dogs. The roads we pedaled through New York seemed pretty good but when we crossed into Pennsylvania the road and shoulder deteriorated a fair bit. Then, when we crossed the state line into Ohio the roads took a big turn for the worse and looked like Ohio road crews had been trying to repair the numerous cracks and holes with left over roofing supplies, and the shoulders petered away…

But the people of Ohio seemed determined to win the award for the "Friendliest People in the World." For example, in Conneaut, Ohio we stopped at a local eatery for lunch and the waitress and all the customers debated which motel would be the best for us and then even phoned the motel and made reservations for us. The price seemed right and they said it was down by the lake, so that sounded good. With that chore out of the way, I was able to linger after lunch and drink coffee, while Bryon sought out the library to do the emails. This was going to be a half-day off for us, quitting at lunch, and we are looking forward to it. *I can't wait to get a shower* (I thought to myself) *as I look a fright after riding through rain showers, and having my little front tire do its job of spewing road brew into my face.* My yellow riding shirt was freckled with clumpy brown spray and so were my legs. *I'm a mess and everything I have on, and most of the stuff in my bags, needs washing.*

However, on our way through town and toward the motel, we asked some locals where to have dinner, and we got some good ideas, but when they asked us where we were staying and we said the name of the place, they looked oddly at us for a moment and said, "…oh."

Hmmm…what have we gotten ourselves into this time?

We pedaled toward the lake address and soon learned that this was no chain motel. This was an old house and the proprietor greeted us with his 6'7" height and 125 pound frame, complete with bell bottom jeans and a long ponytail. He appeared to be the original hippy and he perhaps got together with Moonbeam and put together the most eclectic inn in the hemisphere. The bathroom was a testimony to the Cleveland Browns with dog biscuits everywhere and NFL Browns paraphernalia abounding. The kitchenette was a temple to South Western Art/Frogs/Native American/Desert décor. The living room with couch and bed and TV had stuff EVERYWHERE! I can't imagine dusting it all. I counted 7 throw rugs, and on the TV alone, seven bits of pottery and odds and ends. (It was a very small TV.) Where the wall met the ceiling there was a plastic row of ivy all around the room. There were colored scarves and cloths draped over mirrors and chairs and it is just hard to describe it all. The bedroom was Star Wars crossed with Astrology. It was overwhelming at first. But the bell bottom fellow was so nice, and was so impressed and proud of the fact that each room had a different theme, that we began to relax and enjoy the place. It was all very clean.

After our "viewing" of the unit, we walked around the lake beach area, and ended up visiting a Biker's Bar where they were so astounded to have a couple of old bicycle people drop in that they wouldn't let us pay for our beer. We headed to the next bar with hopes of a repeat performance, but had to pay. Two beers being our limit, we headed to Biscotti's for dinner, as everyone had recommended it. It was a tasty recommendation, and it felt really fine to relax and give our muscles an afternoon/evening off.

The next morning we started out riding at 9:00am. The wind was in our face with force and stayed that way all day. Bryon had troubles with his saddlebag attachments, and needed a proper nut and bolt to fix his foot strap on one pedal. A stop at Home Depot corrected all that and we plowed back into the 25 to 30 mph headwinds. The road we were on slowly ran out of shoulder and became very busy. It was no fun and was getting dangerous. So Bryon pulled out the Adventure Cycle Maps he had brought along and figured out how to make it over to their route through Cleveland. For a few miles we actually got the wind at our backs, but as soon as we caught the Adventure Cycle Route and turned west, the wind was in our faces again. We found ourselves making about 4 or 5 mph, with forward-progress-stopping gusts. One gust threw me against a curb with such force that when I put my foot out for support and stability I was slammed bone crackingly hard. What a wind. We only managed 31 miles, but I was so tired at dinner that I fell asleep between the salad and the main dish.

May 11th

We arrived in Cleveland, Ohio. This was perhaps the most beautiful, scenic day of our trip, but it was also one of the hardest days to appreciate the beautiful sights we saw. We had been following the Adventure Cycle maps and not only was the route extremely hilly, but there was just about NO shoulder anywhere along it. We hadn't counted on such a hilly route and our morale took a big nose dive. Also we were fighting too much traffic, with too few shoulders. For safety's sake we took to pushing our bikes on many stretches, and pushing on some of the hills, just because we had grown too exhausted to try and pedal any more steep hills. We were really getting tired of it all. But we did, even in the face of all this, register some of the beauty. I can still see the green groundcover, the treed landscapes with picture book streams and waterfalls running through. Most of the homes could have been on the cover of Architectural Digest and many were adorned with their own private ponds. I would like to take that same ride with cars and trucks removed for a day. It would be wonderful to have "No Vehicle" days, ala *Bike New York*, all across the land, so that citizens could occasionally see the country without the noise, pollution and dangers of the motor vehicle.

We finally made our way to the fabulous greenway of trails that run through Cleveland. This gorgeous, majestic, peaceful, and safe parkway system captured our fancy. People were zipping around on racing bikes and all sorts of other bikes. One parkwayer pointed us in the direction of the nearest Holiday Inn which was within an hours ride. (This was a vast greenway project.) Fearing that a predicted storm was about to unleash, we picked up our pace and soon were checking into the friendliest Holiday Inn in America. Fresh baked cookies to munch, and they brewed a pot of decaf coffee, just for us. There was a pool, a hot tub, and a washer and dryer. (We always feel so relieved when we check in, especially a place that is sooooo comfortable.)

The storm we had heard about waited to let go until we were strolling back from dinner to our hotel. Because it is supposed to rain hard for several days, and tomorrow is Mother's Day, we decided to have a layover day tomorrow. Maybe we'll rent a car and see some of the sights.

May 12th
A very dark Mother's Day greeted us, with huge amounts of thunder and buckets-o-rain. And even though this is a nice motel, the weather can (and frequently will) get us down a bit.

Bryon's email on the 15th paints a pretty good picture of our stay in Cleveland:

> Hi All,
> Thanks for all the emails.
> Things are getting frustrating here. First it was, "We need the rain to help with the drought," but now as we head to Indiana we are getting, "Did you know there are floods up ahead?" NO friggen wonder!!!!! All it does is RAIN, then BLOW, then RAIN and BLOW! If you note a titch of frustration with the weather you are right. In fact it is causing thoughts of doubt to creep into our minds as we mold away in motel rooms. We got as far as Cleveland when this latest bout of storms blew in. We moteled Mother's Day and caught a showing of Spiderman (Grade B). The next day we rented a car and drove in a deluge down to Canton and took a look at the Pro Football Hall of Fame. Pretty good, and we even saw our friend and current

house sitter, Coach Merle Moore in one of the films. Then we drove back to Cleveland and the Rock and Roll Hall of Fame which was VERY well done. Could have spent days there. We really have enjoyed Cleveland. Drew Carry is right. Cleveland Rocks! Crappy weather though. Saw 'The Rookie" that night (Grade A).

So yesterday, in rain and wind, we pulled out and rode through the marvelous park system to get out of town and yet again got caught in a thunder storm and huddled in one of those million dollar federal outhouses (no kidding) to wait it out. Today we are riding to Sandusky, along Lake Erie. Yikes what fantastic homes! Tomorrow is suppose to be HEAVY RAIN. Crap! Oh well, it's fun when its sunny.

—Bryon

We rode out of Cleveland on the Rocky River Reserve Bike Path. It ranks right up there with the best bike paths in the country. *Holy Smokes*, did we ever have fun. No traffic, of course, and the trees, wetlands, river, and park made for a spectacular ride. The wind had been 20 mph, but inside the Reserve we were protected. It was so beautiful, and enjoyable that we felt like we were on a vacation again, instead of just slogging the days away.

A fellow bike rider in the Reserve gave us some new hope about the future of our ride, which cheered us up. He thought that from Cleveland on, through the rest of Ohio, our going would be much flatter, "This is where the mid west really begins and leaves the east coast behind." He felt, "…not only does the landscape and topography change after Cleveland, but also the architecture and everything else…" There is hope for us, Todo.

After having to say goodbye to the Rocky River Reserve we were once again thrown out onto more of Ohio's shoulder-less roads. We commenced to set aside our pride and ride on the sidewalks, as the road seemed just too *kamikaze* for our tastes. We were in a section of the metropolis, that was the home of something called the Tuesday Races, and two cyclists who were in town for the competition, started to give us directions to the Lake, when they abruptly decided they would just escort us there. We had to really work hard at convincing them to just give us the verbal directions (we were too embarrassed to have them see us ride down the sidewalks and we were not about to risk our lives on those roads, even with knowledgeable guides to lead us).

So, armed with directions, off we went heading down the sidewalks, again. After a while we spotted a homeowner on his riding lawnmower (good grief the lawns are big in NY, Pennsylvania and Ohio; maybe we should sell our store and become riding lawn mower salesman out here...). We stopped to make sure we were going the right way toward the lake, and this lawn mowing curmudgeon wanted to know how far we were going. When we told him, *Oregon,* he fired out, "Excuse my French, but you guys are Jack Asses!" He spoke these words in such a friendly, even congratulatory way, that we couldn't be offended. He couldn't wait to get in the house and tell his wife about the two old fogies on bikes, riding to Oregon. Seems he had bought his wife a $400.00 bike for a gift and it had been sitting in the house for ages and had NEVER been ridden. He couldn't wait to rub THAT in! What a funny character.

The lakeside homes were unbelievable. They were more like embassies than homes, with enormous, even monumental grounds overlooking Lake Erie. And there was amazingly, a shoulder to ride on. It was bliss. OK, now I want to blast Ohio and every other state in the union that undervalues cycling to their tourism industry. THINK ABOUT IT. It takes us 6 times as long to ride across your state, as it does to drive across it. We stay 6 nights more in motels, we eat huge amounts of food, way more than paltry car drivers do. We stop early, before dark, and get bored and go out and do the town up, way more than car drivers do. We are a great population to cater to. So for crying out loud—put some shoulders on your roads. Put shoulders on all your roads. We spend a fortune riding our bikes across your state. THINK ABOUT IT!

May 15th

Made it as far as Avery, which is pretty much the dead center of the top part of Northern Ohio. We have joined the Adventure Cycle route again, and it has been good so far. We especially loved passing through the little town of Vermilion (named after the red clay that the Indians painted with). They know how to do things in Vermilion. They have canals all over the place with homes and individual docks and there are sailboats galore, moored at this bay and that. We liked the place so much that we had an early lunch there, just so we could linger, and brought out the maps for some needed study time.

The big problem we're seeing with the Adventure Cycle maps is that the motels are farther apart than our sorry legs take us in a day. So our plan of attack evolved into this: get up really early and make a sustained dawn to dusk push.

We got only 48 miles before Bryon's tire started to go flat. We walked the bike into the nearest town, watching it slowly going flatter and flatter. By the time he got it fixed, and we did a test ride on it, it was 5:30 pm, riding to the next possible hotel was going to be a real haul, and we still weren't sure the tire was truly fixed. So we bagged it for the night, resolving to get an early start in the morning. After dinner the healthiest thing we could find to buy for breakfast was a bag of 15 miniature donuts (you should have seen the other choices) which said, "Fresh until May 29th." Since it was May 16th we bought them, but heaven only knows when they had actually been packaged. Each donut provided 180 calories, so if I ate half the bag or let's say—7 teeny weenie donuts, that's 1,260 calories. OH WOE…

In the morning we opened the bag and withdrew the first small donut, which had the topography of a tractor tire. If the donut had been a piece of wood I would say it was the "pressure treated" variety. It was very heavy with what I presumed was part grease and part preservative. Perhaps I could have stacked enough of them up into a fence post that would last 25 or 30 years in bad weather. But instead I started to eat the things. It reminded me of something our son Andrew had said as a tiny boy eating his way through a HUGE banana split, "I'm nearly full; I'm already sick." We couldn't handle the whole bag-o-donuts so left Motel 6 with five of the little gems, and headed out into the WIND.

It's hard enough to carry on a conversation between two cyclists who are cycling one behind the other, on narrow country roads, in the best of conditions. But when you throw in a howling wind, it's even worse. As soon as we got started I shouted out, "Look at that billboard (it was anchored down by 12 big telephone polls) it's built to withstand a hurricane!" That was what I said, but what Bryon heard was, "whewlkitatbwhrilbfhewd…" So he shouted back, "What…?" And then I either said, "Never mind," or I just gave up talking. Anyway, after that "communication" I started to look seriously at the weather, the look of the land and clouds and horizon and I started to feel very uneasy. I pressed hard, caught up to Bryon's rear tire, and yelled, "This area looks just like all the film clips and photos of tornado country."

Bryon looked around and hollered back, "Thanks a lot; that's all I needed to know!" I could see him looking around some more, before he added, "The clouds look like all those clouds you see in tornado movies too."

We were pushing hard, heads down/eyes squinting, into strong headwinds. We were both very quiet for awhile, inside our own thoughts. We both knew that it was tornado season and we had been hearing tornado warnings, but so far—not in the areas we were heading. We'll just keep our fingers crossed I guess, and our eyes open, as best we can.

The Adventure Cycle designated motels, all seemed to be 5 to 10 miles off the route. Drat! We began to talk about freelancing it once again. We commenced stopping at every local library to research the route ahead. Bryon threw himself into the internet, obtaining bicycle shop phone numbers all along the route and contacting them for more details and recommendations. Also, we had been noticing the Adventure Cycle routes, around these parts, seemed to be really rural, with no place to stop for *morning or afternoon tea*—as the British would say. This also translated into *nowhere to use the loo,* which put us out into mother nature and a LOT of poison oak type looking stuff. Shudder.

May 16th

We made it to Freemont, Ohio which, unbeknownst to us, is where the Rutherford B. Hays Memorial Presidential Library and Museum is quartered. But before we got near the Presidential quarters, Bryon had an errand to run.

He had begun to suffer dearly from the ailment of the long distance, upright bicycle rider. His bum was killing him! Here is his report:

> My Highlight of Freemont came this afternoon when I got directions to "Chicks Awnings," where I was told I could buy some foam rubber to tape on my bike seat to ease my butt ache. I thought it was on Hayes Road but as we advanced, it looked too residential, and as it turned out, too Presidential, as well. I spied a mailman whom I figured would know where "Chicks" was. So I stopped and asked, hoping to get an answer like, "Yep, it's about a mile up there on the left…" But NO!
>
> I had met the real life version of Cliff Claven, the mailman from "Cheers" TV show. He got real serious and announced it was, "…on Hayes Road!" So I asked if this wasn't Hayes Road we were on. "…why yes it is!"
>
> "So where is Chicks?"
>
> "Well, if you go up to the business past the railroad tracks, that's 2008, and it's the next one, so it's 2011," he surmised.
>
> That was an interesting wrestling out of directions from a postman, but Chicks was at 2011 Hayes Road and my mission was soon accomplished. Ahhhhh…

After achieving this seat of cushiony foam, we advanced on the Rutherford B. Hayes Presidential Library. Never having been in a Presidential Library, we really wanted to see it. But, there was nowhere safe to leave our bikes, and that had us worried. Plus, heavy rains were due anytime after 3:00 pm. We hadn't found a motel yet, and the guided tour was going to put us out on the road at 4:30 pm, just in time to wander around in a rainstorm looking for a motel. Buggers.

The kind lady at the desk, though, volunteered to give us a "Rutherford B. Hayes in a Nutshell" tour: Apparently having grown tired of the "spoils" system of politics Rutherford started the Civil Service, so that all the government jobs didn't get handed out as political favors. You see, he had this wacko idea that experience and competence matter. How refreshing. If the current administration had kept up with that idea in their appointments to the likes of FEMA, we might have had a competent aftermath of the hurricane Katrina in 2005, instead of the botched and incompetent mess we got. I have great appreciation now for Rutherford B. Hayes and his hopes for competence over cronyism. Go Rutherford!

May 17th

The storm that was coming, pummeled us during the night. In the morning it was a grey 40 degrees, but dry. Crosswinds were only a little annoying, and we made good progress to Bowling Green, Ohio. We stopped a couple of times to get some coffee and warm up along the way and each time the proprietor wouldn't let us pay. "It's on the house," is becoming the theme song for Ohio. What is it about these people? One bartender who served us coffee was a single mom who held down three jobs and yet when it was time for us to pay up, we heard again, "It's on the house."

Bowling Green seemed like a great place to live and raise a family, a nice college town.

We needed some info from the Library and found that it had been moved into an old grocery store. They hadn't taken down all the grocery signs from the walls, though, and when I asked where I would find the restroom, they said it was in the FRESH MEAT DEPARTMENT (I kid you not). We would hire any of the ladies who run the Bowling Green Library, to work in our store, in a flash. The friendliest, most helpful people you could find; they went way out of their way to assist. One lady ran out of the library and caught us in the parking lot, to make sure that we didn't end up on a road with heavy construction that could prove dangerous for us.

We wanted to work our way to a more northern route that held out hopes for more frequent motels. We had gotten up early and wanted to go as far as our little legs would push us when, once again, events conspired and at 50 + miles we hit Grand Rapids, Ohio (No, not Grand Rapids, Michigan) and another glitch.

Coming into greater Grand Rapids, we rode by two ladies working in their yard, one quite elderly. Mr.Cold Wind had taken his toll upon us and we were looking for directions to the nearest establishment where we could warm up. The ladies gave us directions, but would not let us go until we had been given the tour of Francis' "Proper English Country Garden." Now, we are not gardeners. We have not planted one flowering plant around our yard, not one. There are some wild roses in one spot, and we pretty much leave them to do their own thing. But Francis and her gardening friend didn't know that about us, and they were so darned proud of their garden, that we just couldn't refuse the tour, even though we were already many degrees colder than cold. Well, it was still like winter in Grand Rapids, and as far as we could see, not the time to view a Proper English Country Garden. But Francis' garden had made some of the "Magazines," and was therefore not to be missed. To us it looked pretty much a mess at the moment, but no doubt when winter loosens its icy grip, the true beauty of the place will blossom ten fold. We were fondly told the name of every sad looking, winter ravaged plant, before we made our getaway. You had to love their commitment and enthusiasm. It is so wonderful to meet people with such a passion for something in life. We would need a lot fewer shrinks if we all had more things that interested us, and especially interests that get us out and doing something. Good on ya ladies.

Grand Rapids proved to be a little gem of a village. The villagers had worked hard to retain the historical flavor of the place and you kind of walked back in time there, picturesquely, along the river. We had intended to push on for another 25 miles, but we were so cold by then that we stopped at the first place open, which was ironically an Ice Cream Parlor. Forgoing any treat with *ice* in its name, we opted instead for the hot chocolate, with the emphasis on HOT. I don't know how the two high school girls running the place managed to bring me a steaming hot cup of chocolate and Bryon a cool one, but they did, and rather than interrupt their conversation, we poured the two cups back and forth until we each had one with some warmth to it.

With renewed body warmth, we headed back into the cold and up the hill. Immediately I could see that Bryon's tire was low and shouted the news to him. We looked at our watches and calculated that the time to fix (maybe?) a flat, and still go 25 miles, was pushing our luck in this weather. Luckily, right across the street there was an old mill that had been converted into a Bed and Breakfast. It might have been the only place to stay in a 25 mile radius. They had room for us so we checked in. We took the bike up the road to the gas station and commenced to try and fix the flat. Turns out the very same kind of odd abrasion that had done-in the last inner tube had done in this one as well. We went through the tire and rim carefully, over and over, but could find no culprit. We were confounded. To top it off, the tubes they told us would fit, when we bought them, amazingly wouldn't. The 50 cent air machine wouldn't work (after gobbling up numerous 25 cent pieces) and neither would our hand pump. We do admit though that the problem is probably more with our hands (arthritis?) than with the pump. As our mood grew gloomier, a customer overheard our problems, and volunteered to drive Bryon to his personal compressor and back to the gas station. With newly pumped tire in place, Bryon finally took the bike for a spin and the tire was at least holding air for the time being.

By the time we got back to the Mill, and cleaned up, it was raining again, still fricken cold, and we were glad NOT to be out riding in it. We watched the news and it had been near-record lows for the day. The prediction for tomorrow was for RECORD LOWS.

Breakfast was a gourmet delight, especially compared to some of our recent mornings. For starters there were deliciously fresh baked apples, followed by a platter of tasty French toast and sausages, juice and coffee. We felt comfortable, warm and well fed as we opened the door to be blasted by the arctic Ohio morning. It was hunker down cold, the coldest yet of the trip. We headed out but had to stop several times for Bryon to get some feeling back in his fingers. I had to stop twice to get rid of all the coffee, and this proved to be an extremely chilling, fumbling affair, out in the forest. Approaching Napoleon we pulled into the first possible coffee stop and were once again the center of attention. The curious customers, all of whom knew each other, discussed Bryon's (once again) broken side mirror and one lady pulled out a phone and called the only store, this side of the brand new Wal-Mart, that might carry a mirror. Bryon went there, while I waited companionably with the coffee crowd, until "Miracle Jack" arrived and wanted to know, "Who rides the *incumbent* bike?" Miracle Jack, you see, had elections on his mind. He loudly told me, and all of us, that he was running for congress, but no place in Napoleon, "…including this coffee shop, will let me ask for signatures to get me on the ballot!" For the next 25 minutes I heard about how Jack came to be called "Miracle." It was a rambling story, but I guess Jack was in a coma once (from a brain tumor?) and then he woke up. He also lectured us all on the constitution and the salaries congressmen get paid, and shared many of his ultra right wing political philosophies. Jack was exhausting. After he pronounced the name of every business in town that wouldn't let him solicit (which I think WAS EVERY BUSINESS IN TOWN) he finally wound down and left. Phew!

Bryon returned from the "bicycle" shop he had been directed to, which was really more of a fur buying establishment. No mirrors, so we decided to head out of town toward the new Wal-Mart Store. As we rode, Bryon's tire started looking softer and softer. We found a gas station pump that helped us get to Wal-Mart. Here is Bryon's (whose patience was all ready running thin with this never ending tire saga) account:

> We rode out to the new Wal-Mart hoping for a few bike supplies, and surprise, it was a brand new Super Wal-Mart Store that was having their Grand Opening. (We know something about Wal-Mart Grand openings now, but we didn't then. Just this past year in Klamath Falls we had a Super Store Opening and it was complete with a preacher telling us, with great conviction, how, "Jesus Loves Wal-Mart." It was quite something.) We found a secluded spot to hunker down on the concrete, out of the wind and rain and remove the tire. This time we were very careful (in the light of day) to mark the tire precisely where the damage was occurring and finally we could see that the tire was ruined and it was causing the tubes to go flat. Now all of this wouldn't have been too bad, except that the Grand Opening Celebration was now going on in full swing and we seemed to be the center for all the action. A helicopter landed next to us, and then to top it off the baton and drum corps of 5-8 year olds came marching around us and the cute little tykes on the marching xylophones were mercilessly banging out, "Whistle While You Work," over and over again as they stopped to do their prime performance right next to us (at full volume). As I sat there listening to their crummy rendition of that lousy song, I was just about to grab the 5 year old xylophonist and shove her through the bass drum when it occurred to me that that would be the height of bad manners in Ohio. Sheryl calmed me down and we got the tire fixed, and rode out of the parking lot. Almost. Before we got to the street she said, "I think your tire is going flat."
>
> OHHHHHHHHHHHHHHHHHHH! What a mess! We needed a new tire and there was not one to be had, that would fit (28"), in all of Napoleon or anywhere near it. We spied the Grand Gala Hot Dog Sales Stand and asked if there were any rental cars in Napoleon. Well siree, this was Ohio so naturally a lady said, "Come with me," and pushed me into her SUV full of kids and off we went, but alas, there

were no rental cars to be had until Monday. So, she decided to loan me (whom she didn't know from Adam) her husband's truck so I could drive to Toledo! He said it wouldn't make it, and I would not only have a dead bike to deal with but a dead truck too, so she took me back to Wal-Mart. We once again inquired of the Grand Gala Hot Dog Sales Stand and a lady said, "My husband will be happy to take you to Toledo," (about 40 miles away). He showed up shortly, after she phoned him, in the church's van and hauled us to Toledo. Two bike shops later we had two new tires, four new tubes (two for spares) and we were back on the road. Ain't life wonderful!
—Bryon

Bryon ended up with over $100.00 in new tires and tubes, and with much thinner tires than what he had had. But it was the best we could do at the time, and we just kept hope alive that these tires would work for him. The really bright spots in this saga were the people of Ohio, once again. It turned out that the man driving the church van was the Pastor of his church, and was a true *Good Samaritan*. We were amazed at all the time he gave us and the expense he went to. He did all of this without once asking what our religious beliefs were, or trying to push his beliefs onto us. He was just helping. Once again we were humbled. He insisted on driving us back to Napoleon and dropped us off at a motel. We tried to arrange to take him and his family out to dinner, but he insisted that his wife was committed to the Wal-Mart Cart, as it was a fund raiser for the Church, so they couldn't join us. (We were able to find out the name of his church and sent them a donation, which made us feel a bit better.) We will never forget how kind these "strangers" were to us.

A milestone (from Bryon's emails):

Hi All,
Not much to report here other than record cold today to go with our record droughts and rains and winds. But the big news is we hit the 1000 mile mark, in Bryan, Ohio. Hard to believe, but it's true. You probably think that means the pounds have melted away and I look like that guy on the Bowflex commercial and Sheryl looks like the babe on "Buns of Steel!' HA! We have sat around in so many motels that we decided, when looking in the full length mirrors, that we look more like "Archie and Edith Bunker Go for a Bike Ride."

Sheryl actually feels her legs getting stronger but is not using her arms at all, and feels she is beginning to look like a kangaroo. Not what we had hoped for...
—Bryon

I guess I had been hoping that the days would get warmer and warmer as we rode on toward summer, but the opposite keeps happening. We keep getting record lows, and colder and colder weather. I know it will change at some point and I will be sorry I ever groused about the cold. It will no doubt get really hot at some point in this trip, if we last that long, but right now it is hard to imagine it.

There is one other thing that has occurred to us as we've ridden through Ohio. We had only been cycling Ohio for a day or two, and the countryside had just seemed so lovely, and blessed with trees, water, wildlife, rich soil and all, that we wondered about the American settlers who had passed through here and what it was that kept driving them on. Ohio was so beautiful and so potentially productive, once you got there, why would you ever leave? I think I would have voted to stay.

Chapter Five

Indiana & Illinois

May 19, 2002

The 60 miles today—from Napoleon, Ohio to Angola, Indiana, was not an easy ride. We started the day out at a chilly 37 degrees. I wore every layer I had, including my Household Big Job Rubber Gloves again (which reached most of the way up to my elbow and served as another layer of clothing on my arms) and my balaclava, which I finally found. The combination made me look like a house-cleaning terrorist. What was worrisome was the 80% chance of rain. With the wind-chill, it was to be in the 30's all day.

As we rode, we managed to stay ahead of the encircling rains, until we could tell a thunderstorm was about to overtake us on our then remote, underpopulated little road. Fearing an absolutely chill-drenching downpour, Bryon knocked on a door of one of the few houses within sight and the teenage girl who answered said we could follow the path through their property, into the woods, to the cabin by the pond. We hurried down the tree lined path to discover a clearing with one of those man-made ponds we had been seeing all over Ohio, and a little cabin that looked like "kid's paradise." We rested at the table and chairs inside, listened to the little portable radio and imagined all the local kids playing at the foosball table and enjoying the pond. The rains came, but not as hard as we feared. Nevertheless, we found it hard to drag ourselves away from the scene, even after the rain stopped, and felt we had gotten a little glimpse into the lives of folks in these parts.

After the storm passed we soon found our roads had gotten more and more narrow, with fewer and fewer sign posts. We were not sure where we were. OK, we were lost. Finally we knocked on another farmhouse door and this time a young fella answered, who seemed a pretty bright lad. When we asked him how to get to Angola, he just lit up. "My friend and I once rode our bikes all the way to Angola and back, from here!" He added enthusiastically, "As soon as the paved road ends, and the dirt and gravel begins, that's where Indiana starts. Wish I could go with you guys."

The young guy seemed quite confident, so off we went to enter Indiana by mud, it seemed, as the rain was starting up again and the dirt road was approaching. We were certainly off the beaten path now, and had our fingers crossed that this kid knew what the heck he was talking about. He turned out to be a good lad; we soon pedaled into greater Angola and were so tired that we snagged the first motel we found, which was one VERY BIG FAT MISTAKE.

The first big problem we noticed with *The Worst Motel in the World*, was that our room was about 100 to 110 degrees. I naively thought that we could turn the thermostat down, but it soon became apparent that the thermostat was just for decoration. We found the manager and he explained, "We can't do anything about the temperature because some people are from warm climates and some are from cold climates, so we just leave the heat on all the time." When we pointed out that it was too hot to sleep, he said, "Open the windows or turn on the air conditioner." Talk about contributing to global warming— we were aghast. On careful perusal of our air conditioner I decided I didn't want to touch it, let alone breathe any air that might come through it, should it even work. We opened a window instead, and a metal gizmo fell off and landed outside on the ground. We had to prop the window open with our Instant Coffee jar. This was not looking good and why we didn't pack up and leave right then, I will never know.

We opened another window and got the temperature down to maybe 80 degrees and noticed that most of the occupied rooms had their doors wide open. It was supposed to get to 30 degrees tonight and we could have snow, according to the Weather Channel. Things were not looking sane.

There were, amazingly, two sinks in our room and while I was washing my clothes in one sink, Bryon was washing his clothes in the other. But, his sink wasn't draining, so he was moving the little plunger up and down when I noticed that he was getting some drainage all right, but it was all going straight onto the carpet below, where he had placed his clean socks. (Incredibly, defying common sense, the pipe under the sink just drained the water onto the floor.) So we moved his socks and put the wastebasket under the drain. Bryon thought about telling the manager about the carpet and the plumbing problems, but he thought the manager would just reply, "Some people are from wet climates and some are from dry climates so there is nothing we can do about a moisture problem."

I then took a shower and guess what? It had a **VERY** slow drain. (Who knows where that went, but at least it wasn't onto our floor.) The only saving grace about this place was that it was already 9:30 pm by the time I finished my shower (the drain took half the night to finish) and we would hopefully soon be asleep. Of course the remote on the TV didn't work, but who cared at this point? When we woke up in the morning, we would get dressed and leave this place behind.

May 10th

Last night was by far the worst night's sleep of my entire life. I thought I was so tired that any reasonably flat, soft surface would do. But the bed had troughs in it, that just defied comfort, and the neighbors were so noisy and there were so many comings and goings that I wondered if the inhabitants of the place had "evening work" going on. At 2:30 am I was still wide awake.

By 6:00 am we were haggard but dressed, packed and ready to roll. The "manager" or "outlandishly negligent person in charge," had assured us upon check-in, that the coffee shop next door to the "motel," or whatever it was that we had spent the night in, opened at 6:00 am. Since our "motel" served no coffee (no surprise), we took solace in the idea that we had a coffee shop to go to in the morning. Our walk into the freezing cold morning, was rewarded with a "closed" sign on the coffee shop door. It seemed it was Monday, and this coffee shop was always closed on Mondays. Fancy that. Duh, you would think our "manager" might have picked up on that little tidbit of information.

Now, I know I have said this over and over again, but truly—this was our coldest day yet. It was really cold for us old folks! Brrrrrrrrrrrrgeezies!

Riding blurry eyed and coffeeless, we soon found our route deteriorating into a shoulderless, truck intensive road, which we abandoned in short order, for rural and often unpaved roads. Most of the rural roads we had ridden in Ohio were paved, but not so in this stretch of Indiana. And whoever told us that Indiana was flat, hadn't ridden this area. Up and down the unpaved roads we cranked. At noon, in La Grange, the temperature had risen to a nippy 41 degrees.

Negotiating the gravel/dirt back roads, trying to find some paved ones, we labored around a bend in the road to be greeted by an entire family of the most beautiful, golden horses I had ever seen up close. Spotting us immediately, they came prancing across their field to say hello. It was a fairy-tale scene. The horses were so inquisitive and powerful and the day was so lovely that I was mesmerized. They followed us along the fence as far as they could, and as much as I would have loved to linger with them, we said our goodbyes. Later we learned that these horses are the breed of choice for pulling the Amish plows.

Unbeknownst to us, we had made it to the Amish Country of Indiana. Of the 34, 000 people in La Grange County, about 37% are Amish. The town of Shipshewana reportedly swells from 525 people to 30,000 on Tuesdays and Wednesdays each May through October when they hold their "world renowned" flea market. A talkative fellow at the local library insisted, "…this is the second largest settlement of Amish people in the country."

Pedaled by some pretty lakes this morning with attractive communities nestled up to them. Rode amongst lots of dogs, too, and I used my pepper spray again, with good results.

The neatest sound though, was the *clip-clop, clip-clop* of horse hooves pounding pavement, pulling Amish carriages hither and yon, which reminds me of the following email from Bryon:

> "Hello Mudda,
> Hello Fadda,
> Here I am at,
> Camp Grenada…"

Remember those lyrics, about the "unhappy camper" moaning about everything until the weather got good, then winding up saying, "…kindly disregard this ledda." Well, kindly disregard all of our past whining, bitching and lamenting of the bad weather. Your prayers (and incantations from Ashland) seem to be working. We whizzzzed across Indiana in three days with TAIL WINDS! Yep. And it's been record cold (coldest since the 1700's) but we'll take it with tail winds. Yesterday we did over 70 miles and are about 1/3 across Illinois as of today. Whew, moving at last.

You all seemed pleased to hear that we had managed to pass that old guy in New York. Well…

Anyone who has ever ridden a bike is a big fat liar if he/she won't admit that when they see someone up ahead, whom they think they might be able to pass, that they don't give it just a little extra and find a sinful thrill in THE PASS. We all go for it. I'm sure that the legions of cyclists that have swooshed past us feel some of that thrill, though passing us must rank low on their list of thrills in life. Anyway…

It seems a couple of days ago, we were riding through northern Indiana, on our way to South Bend (where we rode around Notre

Dame, saw "Touchdown Jesus" and all things Irish) and were buzzing down this country lane when up front, about a mile away, I spotted a slow moving object. I soon realized that again we might execute "The Pass."

I got real excited.

Soon I was sweating like a pig as we closed the gap. In cycling terms, I think I should say, "...we reeled him in," and soon I had my victim right in the cross hairs of success. It was an Amish Buggy!

Man did that get me fired up, but as I maneuvered into position and worked out my timing (we had to pass on a downhill, that horse was too damned fast on the uphills) I realized that this sort of competitor could play defense! How rude. Yesserie, as I lined up for an attempt, the horse, shall we say, began to download. Piles and Piles of hot greenish horse goo began to get lobbed my way like hand grenades. As you read this, you may think it funny, but as these mines were laid, there was no humor for us. We have no fenders!!!!!!

Smacking into one of these steamy piles would have been our final undoing.

Oh, it was close, but we bobbed, weaved, and executed THE PASS in style.

Pass the Yellow Jersey.

I was full of testosterone.

Sheryl was full of testosterone (I think).

So, it was another great day in Amish Country, nearly bought a rocking chair, and it was another great day on the road.

—Bryon

Amish country hitching post + recumbent

(Road Trivia—If the pretzel place called "Jakes" is publicly traded, we should all buy stock in it. We had the best soft pretzels ever made by man, in a shopping mall in Illinois. It was hard to tear ourselves away from Jakes, but Oregon wasn't getting any closer as we sat there eating pretzels.)

Amish furniture is just gorgeous, with clean, classic lines, comfortable and so beautifully crafted. We pulled into one home studio, where I would have said, "Back the van up," if we had had a van, and then would have proceeded to buy (if we had the money) the dinning room table and 6 chairs (two of which were chairs for two), two rockers, two dressers and *while you are at it throw in that bed.* I loved their furniture. But we were on bikes so we just drooled and left.

May 24th

We spent the morning along the old I & M canal in Illinois, and was that ever gorgeous. It was also flat, which was mainly why we were on it. What a stroke of genius Bryon had in plotting out his "canal route" across the country. It is the flattest and straightest route possible.

We finally surfaced from the I & M, after pushing hard along it all morning. My stomach was growling madly as we waited for our PIZZA-4-U to be baked, and I scratched away at my first mosquito bite of the trip.

Two days ago we had made it to South Bend, Indiana. I knew Bryon had been wanting to go there to see Notre Dame, but I didn't know the full story. He gave me the camera and said he had a particular picture in mind. I was game to see the university campus and he kept talking about the "Fighting Irish" as we pedaled toward the place. It was a beautiful campus, and I kept seeing great photo ops, "You want me to take a photo here?"

The answer was always something like, "…pretty soon, pretty soon."

We rode by the gorgeous Gold Domed Duomo but even that didn't rate a photo. When we got to the stadium and there was a large statue of someone no doubt significant, I thought, *AHA, this is it!* But, no it wasn't the coveted spot, either. Finally, after circumnavigating the stadium we came to a large quad, which had as its central feature, a HUGE mural of Jesus. The enormous mural portrayed Jesus with his hands high in the air and apparently is affectionately referred to as "Touchdown Jesus," by football fans. Bryon said, "Get out the camera," as he headed out onto the lawn. He held his hands up, just like Jesus and asked, "Am I lined up?"

So this is it? This has been the quest? You want to line up with Jesus and make the touch down signal?

I hastily glanced around thinking, *If this isn't the height of tacky, what is?* But no one seemed to be concerned; luckily graduation had been the previous weekend, so I snapped the photo of Touchdown Bryon in line with Touchdown Jesus, which seemed to tickle Bryon's funny bone to no end.

Touchdown Bryon with "Touchdown Jesus" Notre Dame

Finally, we started to get some warmer weather and decided to try and tally up some heftier mileages, so we left the canal paths for bigger roads, with decent shoulders. Though these roads were busy, noisy and less scenic, they did have *TRUCK SUCK*. It is amazing, when big heavy trucks roar by at great speeds how they create an air blast that propels your bicycle forward with a great surge. This is particularly gratifying when you are laboring into headwinds. All the noise, commotion and *TRUCK SUCK*, also is energizing, and you really get to hauling. We went a touch over 70 miles today—our new personal best, but last night was a struggle.

Late in the evening we entered the south Chicago area, which is not a great place to bicycle, if you don't know where you are going. Getting a bit lost and concerned, we happened across a couple of cops who had pulled a car over. Asking for assistance, we explained that we were trying to find our hotel, but every road we took, got increasingly less and less "friendly," and we didn't know which roads were safe. It was starting to get dark and we were hoping for directions to a bike path that would go toward our hotel. One of the cops gave us directions all right, but they got us even deeper into neighborhoods where we stood out like clowns at church. I was feeling very uneasy; the book titled "The Gift of Fear" came to mind.

Luckily, we stumbled across a guy at a car wash who tried uncomfortably and unsuccessfully to help us, when abruptly he gave up on all things verbal, reached into his car's mezzanine and grabbed a $17.00 map book of Chicago which he thrust at us, "…here!" We thought he was loaning the map to us to look at and we began to leaf through it, trying to include him in figuring the thing out. He obviously had NO map skills at all and became quite agitated at this, "Take it, just take, I don't want it, take it away," his voice kept rising with each word. Not wanting to irritate him further, thanking him profusely, we took the thing and pedaled out of his sight to look at it in a more relaxed atmosphere. Bryon then navigated us to a hotel just as darkness fell.

The next morning we easily found the I & M Canal Trail, right near our hotel and happily followed it all day. It was paved part of the way, and we just sailed along. The rest of the trail was gravel, but well packed and relatively easy to ride. Even though the wind was blowing pretty solidly in the region, the path's tree lined canopy afforded us much appreciated protection. It was a very easy 50 miles, and we were rewarded with the company of birds of every color, as well as bullfrogs, geese, ducks, ducklings and goslings, squirrels, chipmunks, and you name it. Then, when we were surprised and mesmerized close-up by egrets taking flight, a reverie descended upon me, such that it brought tears to my eyes. How lucky we were to be doing this trip. We were lost in time—back in the 1800's in a world of canals and wildlife, mules and quietness…it was bliss…until a techno-cyclist passed us, promptly pulled over, and started talking loudly into his cell phone. Sigh.

May 24th

It rained a lot last night and the personality of the I&M changed noticeably. It wasn't muddy, or very puddled-up, but the rain had demonstrably softened the canal trail and we found it much harder to cycle. The good news was that the wind that was now making it through to the trail was a tail wind! Hot Dog! The bad news was that the rain induced softness of the trail kept us going about 7 or 8 mph, even though we were making our hardest sustainable effort.

Illinois had a planned, Grand Circle Trail that, who knows, might be finished by the time I finish this story. When completed, it will make a loop around the top northern part of the state. Along the section of the trail that we rode, there were little clearings, here and there, where trail *pilgrims* could pitch their tents and use fire pits. If we had been set up for it, it would have been neat to camp on the I&M. But even without camping, the trail was a gem. We didn't see Illinois precisely like the settlers did, but our experience was close enough to get a whiff of what it had been like for them. It must have been grand.

The trail began to be less and less a canal trail, and more and more a rural/ wilderness trail. The canal was being reclaimed by nature, and as we approached the end of the I&M, it appeared there was no ongoing attempt to preserve the rest of the old canal system.

There have been some interesting bits of history, along the canal. Some authority, had erected at various mileposts, a bit of "history on a post." When we went through Ottawa, Illinois we learned of the Abraham Lincoln— Stephen A. Douglas debate on the issue of slavery. As I read the brief history of the debates, I was struck by how incredible it was that there was ever a "debate" about the issue. How could any person ever, come to the conclusion, the belief, that slavery was right, and just and moral? It is so disgusting. And yet today we have similarly disgusting "beliefs," expressed daily across our own country and in other countries. There are always those who don't want "freedom" to apply to anyone except themselves. In later years I read the full text of the Ottawa Lincoln-Douglas Debate and what really hit me was that they were lengthy debates of over an hour for each person (maybe 90 minutes?) and then rebuttal time too. Can you imagine that? You might actually learn what kind of mind and temperament a candidate had if you listened to them that long, on one issue. Our current political debates, especially those for the Presidency of the United Sates, are so lame and pathetic in contrast. An ignoramus can manage to sound OK for a minute or three, but in an hour, ON ONE SUBJECT, we would have a better grasp of the person on which to base our vote. And intelligence does matter, no matter what anyone says.

The night of May 23rd was memorable. We were jolted awake by the loudest thunder either of us had ever heard. The thunder and lightning display was so spectacular that we opened up the curtains and watched the show throughout the night.

On May 24th we added to our canal wildlife count, the following: a deer, a turtle, a snake, a black and red bird I hadn't seen before, and a raccoon. For bird lovers this canal has been a dream. On more than one occasion I have found myself so riveted on a beautiful bird flying across my handlebars, that I nearly crashed.

We were going to miss this *corridor from the past* called the I &M, at the trail's end in La Salle, which was quickly approaching.

Memorial Day Weekend

You could see The Deck Motel from a long way away because of its ENORMOUS sign reaching into the sky and proudly advertising in nine foot letters: MOTEL FOOD. *Oh brother, what kind of establishment have we gotten ourselves into this time, Motel Food?*

For the first time since N.Y. City, we reserved a motel three days in advance, due to the holiday weekend. We wanted to take a day off, and we could see that motels were starting to fill up as we got closer to the weekend. We wanted to be sure to have a room, and were quite proud of ourselves for planning ahead, because as we rode through The Deck Motel's parking lot, it looked full to the brim. However, the sunny smiles we arrived with quickly evaporated, as The Deck was *full* for the weekend, and they had no record of our reservation, "No vacancies, sorry."

I whipped out the sheet of paper I had saved from the phone reservation process, and I guess I had recorded enough specifics and to whom I had talked, that they believed me and worked the computer for 45 minutes until, somehow they found us a tiny room with a small bed. There really was no option as it looked like this was the only room in town, so we took it.

Well, it came to pass that the mattress was way too soft, resulting in us rolling into each other, wedging into a Valley of Insomnia. Fortunately for me though, at one point I drifted off. Then, in the middle of the night I awoke to discover Bryon rolled up in the bedspread on the floor. So much for taking a "layover day" to *rest*! But here is the amazing part, in the morning Bryon announced that it had been his, "…best night's sleep of the trip!"

So, we took the day off, in this odd little room, and watched the Indy 500, and the Jack Nicklaus Golf Tournament. Bryon did some bicycle maintenance, and we both relaxed. Then, we rode our bikes into the delightful down town of Geneseo, Illinois. Neat old homes lined the road, with people sitting in swings on their front porches, enjoying the evening. We were beginning to feel the seasons were changing; temperatures had reached into the 70's! In preparation for a holiday concert, a swarm of Geneseos were setting up benches and decorations in the town park. Had we stepped into a Garrison Keillor novel? Maybe...

Geneseo, was a town of contrasts, as most towns are, I suppose. We saw, once again, the peculiar sight of Cadillac Farmers. We have seen Cadillac Farmers quite often lately. In one community along one of the canals, we stopped for breakfast and overheard two Cadillac Farmers discussing the "farming business."

"I hear Washington is really going to do right by the farmer, a dad-gum subsidy windfall," said one farmer to the other.

"Yep," the other farmer said, "We're going to do all right. Guess it's time to buy another Cadillac."

"Hell!" says the first farmer, I only got 10,000 miles on the old one, don't know what I'll do!" They both chuckled away, oblivious to our presence.

Now, I know the whole issue of farm subsidies is complex. It seems like "welfare" to many folks, to be paying farmers NOT TO GROW things. And I guess I don't mind the idea of farm subsidies so much as I am offended when I hear farmers voicing opposition to taxes that go to anything other than themselves. I also get dismayed when these subsidies (our tax dollars) don't even go to small family farms, but mostly go to enormous corporation farms. It seems to me that one of the political philosophies in our country appeals to its followers to be against any tax that doesn't benefit them personally, at the moment. The truth is, in my book, taxes are a good thing. We don't like to pay them, and that is human nature, but they are, in large part, what separates us from the third world, where everything runs on baksheesh (bribes) and the great masses go with no education and no hope. Here is my two cents—we need to work hard, as citizens, for INTELLIGENT use of taxes, but this day after day full-court press for less and less taxes will eventually turn us into a third world country. Once again though, that's my two cents. (Also, I know lots of farmers do support schools and libraries and all. I don't mean to paint all farmers with the same brush. Forgive me if it seemed that way.)

We were riding around Geneseo without any of our bags on our bikes and it was like going from driving tractors to sports cars. We just zipped around town, effortlessly. The late afternoon sun warmly caressed the town as we pedaled off to find the highly acclaimed "Cellar" for dinner.

What a surprise The Cellar turned out to be. We had no idea. You don't see Roast Duck on the menu very often, in the restaurants we go to, in Klamath Falls, and when we saw it on The Cellar's menu for $14.95, it was a done deal. Turned out we got a multi-course dinner, including half a duck each, tender as could be, swimming in a mouth watering orange sauce. (That meal ranks right up there with the best ever.)

The communities all along the canal tow paths and bike paths have been another of the pleasant surprises of this trip for me. They have added a lot of texture and flavor to our days.

Chapter Six

The Mississippi River & Iowa

Memorial Day lived up to its reputation as the *Unofficial Start of Summer*. As we headed off the next morning, I rode with no vest, no raincoat, no long johns, no arm or leg warmers, no extra T-shirts, and no gloves. Summer had come to us overnight. Bryon talked all morning about mailing his cold weather clothes home, instead of hauling them around. I kept thinking that we might need all these clothes when we hit the Rocky Mountains, so I wasn't as keen on the idea.

Out of Geneseo we navigated to the Hennepin Canal Towpath Trail which pretty much took us all the way to the quad cities of Moline, Rock Island, Davenport and Bettendorf which straddle the border between Illinois and Iowa. What is geographically significant about this destination is that it is also where the Mississippi River flows. The Mississippi River has been another of the long awaited milestones for our trip, so we were eager to reach the thing.

While riding along the canal, we met two couples who were **walking** the trail together. The foursome had walked the canal path from Molene all the way to Chicago (which is all the way across the state of Illinois). They only had weekends to accomplish this task, so they had been doing the walk in segments, each weekend. They knew the area well, and pointed out all the different places where we could catch the bike path along the river. The bike path seemed to come and go, and sometimes we had trouble finding it again once it spewed us onto the roads. We had a lot in common with these people and could have happily chatted the day away with them. When they invited us to spend the night at their homes, it was absolutely tempting to take them up on the offer. However, we had taken the day off for Memorial Day, and just couldn't justify more time off.

The canal path now, though it was gravel over tar, was very thickly graveled and hard to pedal through. When it deposited us onto the roads, they had no shoulders and lots of loose gravel. With all the traffic, gravel, and worrying about Memorial Weekend drunks on the road, we were nervous, jumpy, and exhausted as we came within sight of the Mississippi River. But the sight of the Mighty Mississippi revitalized us. We had never been sure that we would make it all the way to this great river, but we had at long last arrived and it was energizing.

It was also fun to hit the paved section of the bike path along the river, and it wasn't long before we came across a group of about 10 cyclists who were all riding recumbents. They were a lively group and if I had lived in the area I would have joined their club in a flash. One fellow gave us some recumbent specific literature and encouraged us to write our story up and submit it to one of the recumbent magazines. (I lost the info on the magazines, but who knows, maybe I can research it on the internet, and submit something after all, one day.)

The Mississippi River used to be home to, among other things, pirates and steamboats which Mark Twain brought to life in his book *Life on the Mississippi.* The steamboat races must have been grand. Though there were no steamboat races for us to see, there was a Criterion Bike Race in the Quad Cities and it was in full swing as we approached. We caught the start of the race and it was unnerving to watch as there were so many bicycles jumbled together, rocketing round and round the city streets, that I was on pins and needles, just sure the whole pelaton was going to smash up in one jumbled mass. We also took in a sideshow of *Trickster Bike Boys,* or some such thing, doing wild maneuvers off a jettison ramp—flying mindlessly high in the air, daring their arms and legs and heads to stay on their bodies through crazy acrobatics and landings. It was nerve-rackin' to watch and the Mississippi River area appeared to be living up to its historical reputation as a place of action and excitement.

And though we encountered no pirates we did have to battle a drunk who told us he had screwed up his life and that he had a neutron bomb in his stomach and to prove it he lifted his shirt to expose his stomach, slurring, "I'm going to kill everyone." With that we got on the bikes and pedaled into Iowa. No steamboat races or pirates, on the Mississippi, but we did have bicycle races, and a bizarre drunken man threatening to kill us all. I guess that's poetically similar enough.

Iowa

"It is by riding a bicycle that you learn the contours of a country best, since you have to sweat up the hills and coast down them. Thus you remember them as they actually are, while in a motor car only a high hill impresses you, and you have no such accurate remembrance of a country you have driven through as you gain by riding a bicycle."

—Ernest Hemmingway, *By-Line*

*(*As found in *The Quotable Cyclist* by Bill Strickland)

Oh boy, we were in Iowa now. But we had been warned about Iowa. We were prepared for Iowa. I think most of America might, if asked about the topography of Iowa say, "I guess it's kinda flat." Boy, oh boy America, would you ever be wrong. We had heard that Iowa was hilly, and that we would really notice the hills of Iowa on a bike. We had heard right.

But before the hills began to catch our attention a little *Muskrat Love* distracted us. Captain and Tennille must have written their popular tune, *Muskrat Love,* back in the 60's or 70's, after an experience similar to the one we had as we pedaled toward Walcott, Iowa. It was a warm, sunny day and we had stopped near a little ditch to have a sip of water and a stretch. Some movement caught our attention and we gazed in fascination at an idyllic little grassy ditch, with softly flowing water, and two very energetically amorous little muskrats enjoying the sun and each other. We felt like a couple of voyeurs, but that didn't deter us. Ahh, to have been able to play the Captain and Tennille's song, as we pedaled away...

Bryon is getting increasingly annoyed at trying to carry all his cold weather clothes, now that we don't need them. When we stuffed so many of the garments that we had previously been wearing, into our bags, the bags began to bloat, with the zippers strained menacingly. When Bryon threatened to purchase and fill a heavy plastic bag with his unwanted stuff and drag it behind his bike, I could tell he was getting irritated. But we did manage to secure his stuff, without dragging it, at least for awhile longer. We are both in the market to add a small bag to our accumulation.

Iowa roads are living up to their reputation. *Crank, crank, crank, up and down, up and down.* Bryon bought a big Gazette Book of Iowa so he could get a better fix on the topography. But what Mike Reynold's told us seems to be holding true, so far. The paved roads do not have paved shoulders and the roads are not wide. So we rode ever mindful of the abrupt gravel shoulder that we might need to bail onto and kept a watchful eye on the rearview mirror. We were pleased though to be moving along at 14mph. Pretty good for us. At that speed it didn't take too long to work off the golf ball sized cini-minis the motel had provided. It seems that the chintzier the breakfast the more signs/warnings/prohibitions there are, DO NOT TAKE FOOD BACK TO YOUR ROOM, or LIMIT OF ONE ROLL PER PERSON, etc. To top it off there were usually only a couple of chairs in the eating area, so if you didn't take the food back to your room you had to stand up with the entire rest of the guests in a tiny room while you ate. Lovely. I furtively glanced around, avoiding reading any signs, balanced the little cini-minis atop the coffees, and high-tailed it to our room.

May 28th

By the time we pedaled into Iowa City we were ready to switch routes **again**. The little towns we passed through didn't get enough traffic to have motels, so every evening we had to head back to the freeway to find a motel, hating every extra mile that added to our ride. So as we wheeled into the very nice, University Town of Iowa City we were looking for a bike shop and some information. The most patient bike mechanic in the world spent a very long while with us and with his maps and suggested a route that Bryon hadn't researched, so off we went to the library again, to ferret out motels along that stretch of Iowa. Then it was off through the town's beautiful college campus and up what seemed to be the highest hill in town, where the hospital was, and down the hill to the first motel we found. It lured us in with free warm cookies and ham and cheese sandwiches. We're such guppies.

Earlier though, as we spun along toward Iowa City, Bryon filled me in on The Episode he had had a few days back as we rode toward Davenport Iowa. It later was the subject of the following email:

Hi All,
We fought our way through the "Quad Cities," crossed the Mississippi and were trying to escape all the urbaness. We had a big descent down to Highway 6 on some crappy old broken up road that had pot holes, chuck holes, hell holes, gopher holes and rat holes here and there. What a bad piece of road and it was just littered with broken bottles and such things that we fear so highly. Just seeing a

broken bottle in the road is a near death experience for us both. So I was zooming downhill, concentrating on weaving in and out and around the debris/obstacle course and must have been doing about 25 mph into a 20mph headwind when WHAP! My head snapped back as something had struck me. IT WAS A BEE!

Normally, of course, a bee wouldn't hit too hard, but this one smacked me at a combined air speed of about 45 mph and so he packed a wallop. You might also wonder how I knew it was a bee, at those speeds. It turns out that I am cheap.

Most cyclists go to the bike store and buy $75.00 riding glasses. Not me, I went to the hardware store and for riding in low light conditions I bought some clear safety glasses for $1.99. They wrap up both high and low and wide and fit so darn close to my eyeballs that I cannot see the edge of the lenses when they are on. They are fine safety glasses and as I went zooming down this hill the right lens had this bee splatted right onto it and because the glasses fit so close to my eyeball the bee appeared to be about 6 feet long, as it blocked half my field of vision. It was VERY disconcerting as I could tell the bee was holding on for dear life as he was not up on his 6 legs but spread eagled (spread beed?) right on my eyeball and using his little wings to balance. I am still flying down the hill, dodging cars, those various holes, glass shards, spent shell casings, etc., while shaking my head like a bad dog with your bedroom slipper, trying to fling off the bee. It was bedlam. I calmed down when I was sure he was finally gone and began to regain control of my bike, but no, there walking across the top of my field of vision were his bottom 3 legs going right to left. He was headed up under my helmet as I screamed past a bus and into the parking lot of a driving range in a wild rage trying to get my helmet and glasses off before he went on a stinging rampage. Oh, it was an exciting moment. Just another one of those many little daily events on The Trip.

Thanks for the emails, we love um. We are both worried about our knees now, but so far we are holding our own. Soon we will make the 2000 mile mark. I think we have both lost about 4 pounds. How's that for a diet. Want to lose 2 pounds? Just ride your bike 1000 miles.

—Bryon

Meanwhile, as we pedaled toward Montezuma, Iowa we kept looking for a place to have morning coffee. 10, 15, 20, 25 miles we went. No luck, nothing. We did come across a gas station, though, bought sodas and candy bars from the machine and took a break in the shade, standing next to the building. After that we finally made it to Millersberg for lunch. It was quite the place. Out in the middle of those rolling hills of Iowa farm country, we found the little community of Millersberg, which was feverishly preparing for their Sesquicentennial celebrations. They were putting in new sidewalks around the only restaurant in a 50 mile radius. The restaurant was nothing fancy, but it was everything to the people who lived in the area. They told us they were, "...really lucky to have this restaurant," recounting some of the great meals the restaurant had put on. "People come from miles around and everyone knows everybody else."

It was hot, as we sat there with this group of proud citizens, and there was no air conditioning. There were lots of fans though and lots of friendly folks. The room was set up with one long table extending down the middle, a bar along one side and booths along the other. The table was where everyone headed first. It was the focus. All the patrons were lined up along that table, chatting away, eating plates heaped with roast beef and mashed potatoes and gravy. This was their nerve center. Two TV's were on and they were both tuned to the Weather Channel. The weather takes on new meaning here. It is life and death. Thunderstorm, tornado and flood warnings are things you take very seriously. Farming becomes a dramatic endeavor.

We ordered hot roast beef sandwiches and the waitress disappeared into the kitchen. The moisture from our still dripping wet cycling shirts was evaporating and the fans were attempting to do their job of cooling us as well, as we waited for our order. Soon the waitress made her way to us with steaming plates of food that didn't look a lot like our order. She informed us that she and the cook decided there was not enough roast beef left for two sandwiches, so they made us each a half sandwich and added a couple heaps of mashed potatoes and gravy. If that was alright with us, she would reduce the price, since we didn't really get what we ordered. That was fine with us, a novel and personal solution.

Granted, we had been riding hard all morning with the temperature in the 80's outside so we were pretty hot, but I just couldn't cool down in that room, even with all the fans. I wondered what it would be like in that restaurant when the temperature climbed into the 90's and beyond. But no one in the room seemed concerned at all about the temperature. We downed glass after glass of ice water as we ate our lunch and then headed out into the sun where the sidewalk crew toiled. This email from Bryon describes the scene:

Today we found ourselves in Millersberg, one of those little hamlets that only has one café/bar/general store/post office that essentially is the town of Millersberg. It was lunchtime and we were hot. Actually we were hot, sweaty, stinky, maybe even putrid, as we opened the door and stepped inside the town of Millersberg. Ouch, this was uncomfortable as instantly all conversations stopped and all eyes turned to view the two hideous Martians that had just stepped through the front door. Obviously Millersberg had never seen cyclists before. If they had, they were sleek young Lance Armstrong types, not a stinking fat guy and a sweat drenched gray haired old lady wearing gaudy colored clown outfits. The murmuring began. We said our "Hellos" and sat at one end of this long table that seemed to house the entire population of Millersberg.

This was Mid-America and these are nice folks. Soon one guy muttered "ridin' bikes?" to which we quickly agreed and commented on how nice it was to share their air-cooled café. Soon we had a "Wheredja come from?" When we answered "New York City," mouths dropped open. That was all it took, the conversations exploded. They were our new best friends and wanted to know all the amazing details. Soon they were calling us "athletes" (a term we had not heard in about 30 years), and "cyclists." Our heads were beginning to swell. I was getting a bit chuffed by all their admiration now that we were the town's newest celebrities. Yes, we were Rock Stars and we felt it! Oh how proud can you be to have an entire town quaking with admiration?

But it was time to leave.

We gathered our stinking gear and headed outside with the entire admiring town following us to see us off on our grand athletic adventure (did I tell you they called us "athletes"). They oooed and awweed at Sheryl's red recumbent and gathered around as I began to mount my old upright. I really don't know how it happened, but there was the tightness of the crowd, it was a bit of an uphill, and as I pushed off and swung my leg over my bike, it caught on something for just a moment and I lost all my momentum.

Oh my God! The next moment turned to slow motion as, there in front of our "fans," I simply crashed in one big heap, laying on my side in front of the astonished Millerbergeans.

If anyone from Millersberg should ever read this account, and remember us, they may be surprised to know that we actually ended up riding our bikes over 3000 miles. I'll bet they were wondering how far we would get.

Before we left them, the Millersbergians warned us about Deep River. The name alone gave us pause. It sounded like a place that might take a lot of effort to climb out of. As we pedaled, sweating profusely in the heat, toward Deep River I concurred that it really was time to jettison some of the cold weather gear we were still hauling. It was almost June and I had to agree with Bryon that at least the long johns could go. So when we spotted the Deep River Post Office, we were ready. We rifled through our bags, retrieved the long johns, stuffed them into a Priority Mail envelope and mailed them home. That was kind of a big statement about our trip. The cold weather was over (knock on wood). We had crossed into the warmer part of the trip (famous last words). We had started riding on April 22nd, but now we were knocking with sweaty hands on summer's door.

As soon as we set foot out of the Post Office, a man across the street started pointing at us and gesturing, trying to catch our attention, which he did. He insisted that we should come into his house and have some cookies and orange juice and use his toilet. It turned out he had once ridden the legendary RAGBRAI (Register Annual Great Bike Ride Across Iowa). We were impressed. The RAGBRAI is talked about everywhere you go in Iowa. Even non-cyclists know all about it. The cycling legions dip their tires in the Missouri and Mississippi Rivers, at the respective start and end of the ride. In the middle of the ride they toil the ups and downs of the Iowa landscape, and they do it with an agonizingly fast pace. The RAGBRAI is a RIDE! Anyway, our host knew from riding the RAGBRAI that cyclists could always use a cold drink, a cookie and a toilet. It was very sweet. We learned about his family and his son's impending wedding as we chomped away on cookie after cookie...Lastly he told us about some people who had recently cycled by the house and visited with him, a German couple. After leaving, she was hit by a truck further down the road and killed. This was not a story that we enjoyed hearing, but it is sometimes useful to be told these things, it helps to elevate our awareness of the dangers out there on the road, lest we get too complacent. The chilling story gripped us as we also pedaled away from this unexpected cookie benefactor.

Finally we were getting close to Montezuma, but before the motel was supposed to be open. What to do? A beer and peanuts sure sounded good, so we stopped at the first bar we encountered, on the outskirts of town. When we crossed the threshold all conversation abruptly stopped and everyone just looked at us like, "...what in the world is this?" Everyone was seated at the bar, as usual; no one was in any of the booths. But there was no room at the bar, so we headed to a booth right near the bar. Silence. Silence everywhere. Then, after far too much silence, one curious fellow began to chat us up about our trip, and volunteered some local knowledge in answer to our numerous questions. Soon the bar recovered from its muteness and amiable chatter resumed. I guess it was decided that we were OK—nothing to worry about after all.

Bryon's knee has bothered him a lot today, so he is taking MSM and some antihistamines. We are both worried about the knee as it is swollen. We do knee condition inventory often.

As we headed on toward Montezuma, still a few miles ahead of us, we watched with unease as the grey sky to the south got darker and darker. Thunder and lightning began. But we were moving west, and to the north the sky looked good—blue sky and scattered clouds. There was a sharp divide, half the sky seemed fine and the other half looked demonically possessed. Slowly more and more of the sky took on that ominous look and we could see that it was raining really hard out there. It would not be fun to be caught in that kind of downpour, you wouldn't be able to see a thing in rain like that. We had been zeroing our sights in on the big blue Montezuma water tower, watching it grow ever bigger as we approached. But the tumultuous greyness was becoming blackness and was also zooming in on our landmark tower. When the storm reached the water tower along with a bolt of lightning that flashed right over it, we started looking for cover. Finding an old abandoned barn, in pretty bad shape, but good enough to huddle in (we hoped) we hunkered down to watch the show. The wind whipped up the storm and rattled our refuge to its floorboards, but then the path of the storm veered off to the south and missed us. It would not be fun to be caught out in the open in one of those fast moving fronts of lighting, thunder and heavy rain.

May 30th

Iowa is living up to its reputation. Hills, hills, hills, hills, hills, hills, hills. We are on county roads that parallel Hwy 80 and we are working our butts off. 12 miles of hills so far today. No flat, just hills. We struggled to the top of one hill and there was actually what appeared to be a little plateau on top, about the width of a football field. I rejoiced and yelled to Bryon, "Look a flat spot!" It was a memorable point in the day as we stood there and admired the one flat section we had seen the whole morning.

This is Iowa—green hills. Farm Country. Farm smells rolled over us each time the wind chose to anoint us. They say smells bring forth images from the past quicker than any other sensory input? These brought back memories of Greeley, Colorado where our youngest son, Tyler, went to college his first two years (basically to snow board). The school was downwind of some pungent feedlot smells. You might not notice them at first if you arrived and there was a wind blowing the other way. But before too long, the wind would shift, and then you would notice for sure.

We stopped for coffee some miles back at a restaurant with the now customary big long community table. It doesn't seem to matter what time of day we hit a restaurant in one of these small towns. No matter when we arrive, the table is animatedly occupied. It is a really hospitable thing, and something that we have come to look forward to.

But the winds, the hills, the heat and the humidity were conspiring against us. *Oops*, my sunglasses blew off the park bench I was sitting on whilst recording events. We were reassessing our goal of reaching Des Moines by the end of the day. It was supposed to get up to 97% humidity. We had gone only 18 miles and we were already pooped, and the headwinds were strong and getting stronger.

On our map, the community of Reasoner looked like a good spot for lunch, about the right distance for us, but locals told us that there was no place to eat there. They also told us that the Coffee Cup Café was legendary in these parts. A Des Moines Newspaper wrote it up once and ever since, people have been flying in and renting cars just to get to this little, unassuming looking café. It wasn't actually lunch time, but when you hear these kinds of things you are loathe to miss out, so off we went to the Coffee Cup Café, as their highly acclaimed pies were calling. I could hear them.

Well, the sandwiches were good at the Coffee Cup Café, but the pies were wonderful. I can vouch for the homemade rhubarb pie—it was delicious. And it was a darn good thing that we hadn't planned to eat in Reasoner. When we finally made it there, the temperature was in the 90's and we were sucking the last drops of water out of our bottles. There were no businesses anywhere to be seen. There was no drinking fountain or even a faucet, in the one park that we found. In desperation, I flagged down a lady in a car at the intersection, asking where a couple of thirsty cyclists might get some water. She suggested that maybe the post office would have water, but then thought better of that and said, "If you don't mind well water, you can follow me to my house and I'll fill your water bottles." What a sweetheart. We followed her the 2 blocks to her wonderfully cool well water and drank and refilled our water bottles and drank and refilled until we couldn't drink any more. When you are that thirsty, there is nothing in life that tastes as good as clean, cool water.

We revisited the little park we had come across earlier, and laid down in the shaded picnic area. With the humidity and the 90+ degree heat and the exertion of riding the bikes, I was as hot as I can ever remember being. You could have cooked a pizza on my face. As I laid there it really hit me how different our lives are lived in different parts of this vast country. The people who live in Reasoner have no gas station or grocery store, or you name it. Reasoner makes Klamath Falls seem like a metropolis of services and conveniences. If kids in Klamath think there is nothing to do, they should just go to Reasoner. But then again, with so few commercial diversions, the kids here are probably better at inventing their own fun, and entertaining themselves, than their city counterparts.

We were happy to make it to Prairie City, and hoped that tomorrow might be the start of a flatter terrain. At lunch, everyone told us that it would be, "…a good climb" out of Reasoner, and they were too right. But it just seemed like constant climbing all that afternoon, without let-up. Seemed that we were destined to just climb our way out of the Great State of Iowa.

May 31st

This morning the weatherman said, "Normally it's 77 degrees, but today it will be 91 with high humidity. Have a nice day." I considered throwing an object at him, and actually looked around for one. They are starting to break heat records across this whole country and our journey has become one of extremes. At the start it was so cold as to break the records in the East that were set back in the 1800's. Now we are riding our bikes through record heat in the mid-west. It got too hot yesterday for projected thunderstorms to develop. I didn't know that could happen.

The young folks who ride their bikes across the country are often doing it on a wish and a prayer, with little change in their pockets for extras, like eating out. And often we find at the end of the day we will just stop at a grocery store on the way into a town and buy stuff for dinner, or sometimes succumb to a Big Mac Attack, or just out of fatigue we'll walk to the closest pathetic place and order whatever. But every now and then we splurge and sometimes it's even worth it. Our motel last night was an example. "Steak Night," seemed just too good to pass up, and it was. The lady running the place found out that we were leaving early in the morning and since the restaurant didn't open till 11:00am, she went out of her way to round us up a coffee pot and rolls for the next morning. Those little acts of thoughtfulness sure are appreciated. In fact, when you're at the whims of nature, and vagaries of car, bus and truck drivers, as well as the terrain, and you're out there alone all day—all kindness, from all quarters, is keenly appreciated.

We ran into a snag in Prairie City. We could find no internet, which made finding motels and researching routes more difficult. Our route had turned bad with terrible traffic, and we wanted to seek out a new route. We looked at the map for smaller, rural, paved roads but couldn't get info on motels. It occurred to Bryon that we are only a phone-call-away from the internet and he called our friends the Reeders back in Klamath. We got their very tech-savvy son, Mark, on the phone and he did the research for us.

Sitting on a bench along the Raccoon River Trail which hooks up with the Greenbelt Trail, I appreciated what a great ride these trails made for folks from Des Moines, Iowa. A little community of Jefferson looked to be about 60 miles away and about the right spot for us to spend the night, but all the motels were booked. We figured it was just the right distance for people to ride and was probably a major weekend trip for Des Moines cyclists. So we wouldn't be going to Jefferson. But the trail had been blessedly flat and the shade from the trees had been a salvation. It felt, once again, like we are on vacation riding along this trail. I told Bryon how much I was going to miss the tree canopy when we leave it and he replied, "Well you better get used to it, cuz that's the last shade you'll see till we ride into our driveway." I didn't think that was a very positive thought. It kind of hung a cloud on my helmet. But it may have been somewhat prophetic as the rest of the day was hot-sun-in-a-cloudless-sky. My skin objected.

It was 95 degrees when we rolled into Audubon, Iowa and I was suffering. We had managed to make 74 miles in 90+ degree temps and with lots of hills (What else? It's still Iowa!) I was exhausted and sported heat rash and sunburn. My legs were roasted after 2 days in the hot sun, even though I used 40 proof sunscreen. I probably sweated it off too fast and didn't reapply it often enough. I tried to buy sunscreen with higher protection but couldn't find any. The good news though was that Road 44 had been great, with almost no traffic and the ups and downs were more easily cranked. But as we walked around Audubon (named after John James Audubon the naturalist and wildlife artist) my skin was screaming at me to, "Get out of the sun!"

Yesterday we passed over the summit of the divide where all the drainage on one side goes to the Missouri River and all the water on the other side travels to the Mississippi. We had made another milestone.

Something else was starting to happen to us, too. We were both almost afraid to voice this thought, but as Bryon put it in one of his emails. *"...we are beginning to think we just might be able to pull this off. Prey for those east winds, clearly the wind is THE issue from here on."*

Of course that jinxed us and the weather changed. The TV weatherman on June 2nd announced. "It may be the first days of June but it feels like the Dog Days of Summer." He added, "...there is a chance of hail, thunderstorms and tornados in Iowa North of Hwy 30," which was just where we were headed. Between our motel and Hwy 30, "...there is a possibility of severe weather."

Oh, boy. Just what does "severe weather" mean? They make these pronouncements, but what, REALLY, do they mean? Is severe weather worse than tornados? Are we facing imminent death by riding bikes in severe weather? Will we end up blown into the Land of OZ?

We had to head north for 10-12 miles to catch our road west, and the cross winds ripped straight through us. The powerful erratic gusts caused us to pitch all over the road. Good thing we pretty much had the road to ourselves. I guess most drivers were smart enough not to be driving in "severe weather." There certainly weren't any cyclists out (except us). Anyway, it was very hard on this Sunday morning to ride a straight line. When we finally reached the juncture and turned west we just hollered, "Yee Haw!" and started roaring down the road effortlessly with the wind at our backs. I think, but it's just a guess, that the wind was over 15 mph but probably under 22 mph. At 15 mph with the wind at your back you feel the wind at your back but not in your face. At 22 mph you start to feel wind in your face (at least that's what I wrote in my journal from my unscientific wind observations). Whatever our speed was, it was absolutely exhilarating.

Riding with the wind is one of the most genuinely fun experiences in all of cycling. Granted, its fun coasting down hills, however, you paid for that coasting by pedaling up the other side; so you have earned that downhill fun. But a tail wind all day is like a gift from heaven. I can't articulate how much fun it is. But it is the best. What a blast! Bryon took to standing straight up and letting the wind hit his shirt like a sail, turning him into a great orange bicycle schooner. My recumbent didn't allow me to catch as much of a tail wind, but I was having so much fun—who cared? (Anyway, he has to work harder in a headwind than I do, so fair is fair.)

146

(Recumbent Note: It just occurred to me that another advantage of riding a recumbent bike is that in the heat, I don't need to wear gloves, as there is no pressure on my hands requiring cushioning. Bryon though, needs to wear padded gloves all the time on his upright, due to all the pressure of leaning forward onto the handles.)

We are such novices at cycling that we learn something new related to it every day. Living in Klamath Falls we are on the dry side of the Cascade Mountains. Our climate is very different from the Willamette side of the mountains which is green and lush and gets a lot of rain (That is the greenness that most people picture when they think of Oregon.) But we live on the dry side and it is, well—DRY. Skin cracking dry. So it took me awhile to figure out what was causing the "smeary mirror syndrome." At first I just thought that once the weather had gotten warmer and I started sweating, that I was rubbing my sweaty arm on my bicycle's mirror, inadvertently, and gooing it up. I couldn't keep my mirror clean, making it very hard to see clearly. It was annoying. When Bryon asked if I was having trouble with my mirror fogging up, I realized that it was just so darned humid, that the mirror was fogging up almost as soon as I cleaned it. The air didn't look foggy, but it was laden with moisture.

And then of course there are the burp strips of the Iowa Roads. It took me awhile to figure those out. I would hear these growling loud burping sounds and at first I thought they were some kind of horns. It was curious. Unnerving. I came to realize that many Iowa roads have had deep, wide, parallel gouges cut in the asphalt all the way across the lane, at intersections with stop signs. These slow-down grooves loudly reverberate when a car is driven over them and do a startling job of catching your attention and everyone else's. On my bike I had always found a way to go around them as they looked like they would be hard on my bike. Every car and truck made its own unique sound or tone as it went over the grooves, a sort of cacophony of car farts.

The next TV news that we saw corroborated my earlier estimate of how fast the wind had been blowing. I had guessed between 15 and 22 mph, and the weatherman informed us that we had been riding in 18 mph winds.

And speaking of the wind, it was gusting something huge when we were nearing Dennison, Iowa today. My bike and I actually started feeling pretty light in the wind, now and again, like I was being lifted up off the road, ever so slightly. It felt weird. The crosswind was pushing so hard and I was trying so hard not to get blown over that it was a real struggle. Suddenly, while I was cranking hard, moving along at a good clip, a force violently hammered hard across the bottoms of my tires, where they meet the road. I thought I was going to crash for sure and go skidding along the pavement into the traffic. Someone had apparently shoved my tires out from under me. *"What the HECK?"* I recovered my balance, and managed to lurch to the side of the road. It really scared me. (It was not that hot of a day but I noticed my palms were ringing wet.) I had read about cyclists being blown over in the wind and I guess I thought if the wind pushed you over it would be more like being shoved over at shoulder height. But this was more like a football player being clipped. Anyway, I decided that it was not safe for me to ride if the crosswinds grew too powerful especially if there was any traffic.

But as we pedaled away from Dennison the next morning we couldn't have asked for better weather. The cool morning and cloud cover were just what the doctor ordered for my sunscreen slathered sunburn. We made 42 miles before lunch, thanks to some tail winds that had developed, and dearly wanted to go on, but soon decided to call it a day, as the wind changed in the afternoon to a strong headwind and the chances of thunderstorms and tornadoes were too threatening to ignore. We thought it might be nice to use some good judgment and sit the storms out. Plus, it would be good to let Bryon's knee and his ever more aching bum have a rest. My back had been talking to me (bad mattress the night before), so some R &R sounded pretty good. And besides, headwinds are just such a bummer. Yep, it was a good time to stop early.

Speaking of winds changing, here is another thing I have learned. When the "call of nature" hits you, and there is no bathroom anywhere to be seen, I have been known to disappear in high grass alongside the road, awaiting Bryon's "All clear!" shout before I stick my head up. I once even dropped my skivvies before I noticed I was perched over a pile of swarming ants. You have to be alert out there. Well today was a new low. I actually don't mind using the great outdoor loo, especially when there are no cars and you're way out in the woo woos and the scenery is nice. It beats a smelly ole box. But I learned today that trying to achieve the desired results in an extremely strong, swirling unpredictable wind, was not an experience I cared to repeat.

June 3

Last night we had a choice between two places to stay. We could either stay at the Park Motel or (can you believe this?) the Ho-Hum Motel. The Park turned out to be a good choice, but we will never know for sure how good the Ho-Hum might have been, as we didn't check it out. I guess we just took them at face (or name) value. Isn't it interesting how people name and advertise things? What are they thinking? We have a friend, Grant Pine, who once advertised this: *Reasonably good tent trailer for sale.* He paid to put that attention grabber in the newspaper. Basically, I think he is just too ethical to be allowed to advertise.

I do have a complaint about the Park Motel's recommendations for local restaurants, though. The motel lady must have rated food on the basis of grease content. When we sat down to place our order, the waitress announced that this establishment was, "...out of baked potatoes." *Seriously*—nobody is ever out of baked potatoes anymore. You stick a potato in the microwave for a few minutes and, "Voila!" you have a baked potato. But since we had no choice, we ordered the French Fries. Then we ordered chicken, but the only kind they weren't out of was broasted chicken, so we took it. There were posters up in all the windows proudly proclaiming the fact that they had this item in their restaurant. I was looking forward to trying it. I had possibly heard of this dish before, it sounded good, and I just assumed that *broasted* was probably some kind of *baked/roasted* chicken. But, not so, I soon learned, as my congealing plate of totally deep fried everything was plopped down in front of me. I eyed it for a moment (debating...) and then just resigned myself to eating 10,000 calories worth of fat in one sitting. At least the chicken was crunchy, if nothing else. I guess that was a good thing? Later I looked the word *broasted* up in several dictionaries and a couple of cookbooks, and could never find it. I even looked it up in a big two volume dictionary.

Tonight I found the franchise that will make us rich, if we just keep an eye out for it when it comes up for sale. That is, it will make us rich if it has business every night like the night we were there! It was the Dairy Queen. We went there after that lovely regional chicken/grease dinner I mentioned, and were amazed to see the place totally hopping and choc-a-block with ice cream devotees. On closer examination we realized it was packed with nothing but teenage girls, not a guy in the place, except Bryon, and no older folks, except us. We both noticed that fact at the same time, and wondered where the guys were. This place was a buzz of activity and the cash registers were cha-chinging non-stop. It was like music to our ears. After we waited in line, marveling at the brisk business going on, and all the bright-eyed, athletic looking young ladies, the missing contingent of guys began to show up in force and by the time we finished our blizzards they had begun to swarm around the ladies like flies in the outback. The cash register continued to cha-ching, cha-ching with gay abandon, the whole time we were there and I am sure long after we left. What a business! Of course it didn't hurt that it was a nice warm evening, and that kids need a place to congregate, and having a business with food, helps.

With all of the ups and downs of the Iowa terrain I had plenty of opportunity to observe how differently our bikes responded to different situations. Whenever we coasted down hills it was easy to see the differences. As we crested a hill and began to coast down it, we would both move at about the same speed (though I would be gaining slightly), if we both continued to sit upright. But if Bryon went into a tuck on his upright bike, he would pull ahead of me, and then if I went into my odd little recumbent style tuck, I would go faster and have to brake or pass him. Usually, he would have to start pedaling again on the uphill long before I needed to. I always enjoyed that part of the hill, where he had to pedal and I was still coasting up behind him. It always made me smile.

As we pedaled this morning toward Charter Oaks, Iowa, and on toward Nebraska, it was so humid that it was difficult to strenuously exercise. It was really hard for me to breathe on the hills.

But Charter Oaks was a delight. Here are some of Bryon's email observations:

> We have crossed that special part of hell known as Iowa. Hills, hills, hills, but the winds and weather have been good. Unfortunately the Podunk libraries have no internet.
>
> We stopped in Charter Oaks for breakfast at the town café/bar & grill/ social center, and four guys seated at the one long table eating breakfast waved to us to sit down with them. Then they announced that we should go get our own coffee from the pot and if we wanted to eat something we should go see Alice back in the kitchen and tell her what to cook. "Great, is there a menu?"
>
> "Nope, just tell her what you want, then when you're done, leave as much money as you think its worth on the table."
> —Bryon

Their breakfast looked good, so we asked for that, and soon had plates heaped high with French Toast. We were both a little uncomfortable about this unusual approach to pricing our meal though, what with no menu and no prices. We guessed $6.00 all total, cuz we noticed the other guys had left two bucks each, but they hadn't had coffee. We hoped that was fair.

About the time we were done eating one of the guys asked if we would like to check our emails, "Yes, thank you, we would!" He took us to his insurance office across the street to use his computer. Then as we were leaving his office, one of the other guys brought us a list of all the people he knew who lived along the route we were taking, as we might need help. (We were overwhelmed with how much trouble people were willing to go through for us. It was very touching) And then amazingly, as we were getting on our bikes a lady showed up to take our picture for the newspaper and then another guy brought us flag pins with September 11 written on them, so that we wouldn't forget Charter Oaks. Mind you, this entire town is pretty much the sum of a restaurant, a gas station, and a feed and seed store. This is some country, and we have sure come to enjoy these little towns. As soon as we walk into one of these café/tavern places the world comes to a hush, all stare at us as if we are pink gorillas but soon we are telling our story and getting to hear theirs. Its been fun. Couldn't ask for kinder people.
—Bryon

Its noon and we've made it to Onawa, Iowa, which is close to the Missouri River and to Nebraska. We realized a few miles back that we had just come down off of our last Iowa hill. There was a real feeling of accomplishment, having ridden the hills of Iowa. Someday we may have to come back so that we can see all the sights we've had to pass up. We were right near Madison County at one point, and it would have been fun to go see some of those bridges of Madison County.

Today's ride was through some of the loess hills, and they were gorgeous. We would have loved to have explored the area more as it is so very unique. Shanxi, China is the only other place in the world that has the extreme thickness of loess layers that exist in Iowa. Loess is, according to the USGS web site, "...a gritty, lightweight, porous material composed of tightly packed grains of quartz, feldspar, mica and other materials...the source of most of our Nation's rich agricultural soils." The German word for crumbly is "loess," and loess is just that. It presents many problems for farmers, as it wants to crumble away and return to the Missouri River Valley from whence it was originally blown, (glacial dust deposits being the source) starting some 150,000 years ago and laying down in three major layers up until about 25,000 years ago.

The loess hills have been described as pie-crust shapes, and erode easily leaving gullies that wash out bridges and roads, sediment in streams that harm fish, and drainage ditches in need of dredging. Many farmers practice terracing and contour farming to help control erosion. But the loess hills provide wonderful grasslands and forests, and Iowans are trying to reintroduce native species there, that have nearly been lost. It was a beautifully green, exotic landscape and one well worth trying to protect. In China the hills no longer look anything like these in Iowa, having been changed by both natural and human activity.

When we first started this westward journey of ours and spied our first cornfields, the crop was barely visible, just beginning to poke out of the soil. Today I walked out into a cornfield and it hit me about mid-calf. We are not a fast moving tour.

This morning didn't start out so good though. We had gotten up at the crack of dawn to get an early start but my tires were looking pretty soft. I decided to make a "quick" stop before leaving town and top them off at the gas station right across the street from our motel. They had a free air machine but it wasn't plugged in. I plugged it in and pressed the button to be sure it was working. It made appropriate machine noises so I attached it to the nozzle of my tire and it made one *pufft* and that was it. I could tell air was escaping the tire and yanked the hose off but the damage was already done. The tire was flatter. I asked the attendant if I was doing something wrong and she said matter of factly, "Oh no, it's broke." I thought, *Great! It sure would be nice if you would put a sign up to that effect.* She suggested that we could try the next station, but didn't know if they had a pump.

I hand pumped the tires, but hand pumping by me doesn't get these tires pumped up enough that I trust them, so we rode carefully to the next station. No luck. I walked the bike to a third station and finally got some air. But our "early start" had deteriorated.

That night in Onawa, we went to another restaurant on the recommendation of the motel lady. Oh my, we are going to have to stop taking these recommendations.

The restaurant had very big posters on the windows, though that proclaimed with great pride, "We serve ESKIMO BARS." Bryon and I were curious as to why the place was so happy to have Eskimo Bars on the menu. Well—Onawa, it just so happens, is the home of the original Eskimo Bar. It all started here, the birth place of the Eskimo Bar, and we didn't have a clue. Well it wasn't quite as amazing as unknowingly stumbling across the Amish Country, but it was something that might come up some day in a trivia game, you just never know.

The next morning we lingered at Motel 8 contemplating the 20 mph winds outside and the next series of thunderstorms that were coming through. We knew we couldn't get too far in such winds and were trying to time our move from one little community to the next between storms. We really didn't want to get soaking wet with the temps in the 50's. So much for our warm weather.

As we prepared to cross the Missouri River and head into Nebraska, it felt like we were heading into another country. We asked untold numbers of people around the area if they knew if Decatur, Nebraska (just across the river from them) had a motel or restaurant. They all pretty much replied, "Don't know, never been there." Amazing. Curiosity was not big in the genes hereabouts. They didn't seem to know what was on the other side of the bridge from where they lived. I guess they all headed south to Omaha for shopping or something, but even so...

We had very little information about this new country called Nebraska. I guessed we would be like Lewis and Clark and just discover it on our own.

Chapter Seven

Nebraska

"It is when you come back to bicycling after long dispractice, that you realize how exquisite a physical art it is."

—**Christopher Morley,** *The Romany Stain*
(As Found in *The Quotable Cyclist* by Bill Strickland)

"Everyday I am grateful for this recumbent bike that has allowed me to come back from dispractice *(or in my case* no-practice*) to experience the joys of riding a bicycle."*

—**Sheryl Van Fleet**, *The Recumbent and The Upright*

June 4th

We crossed the Missouri this morning. Unfortunately we were going so fast, because of all the traffic on the bridge that we couldn't stand around and appreciate the moment. But Lewis and Clark went up this Missouri River with their Corps of Discovery in 1803. As I write these words, that would have been round about two hundred years ago. They passed right under this bridge we rode across, except of course, there was no bridge then. No bridge, but a lot of Sioux Indians who thought seriously of killing them all. It's hard to believe that was just a little over 200 years ago. How the world has changed in that short time. If we could have told Lewis and Clark about all the changes, I can't imagine that they would have been able to believe what we said. It would just have been too far fetched. But then again, they were men of science and vision, not like our current anti-science administration in Washington. They were men of wisdom and competence. Perhaps they could have appreciated the various possibilities. Oh my goodness—to have leaders once again that are men and women of science and competence, vision and wisdom…

Nebraska is hilly. At least the Eastern part is. Matter of fact it seemed hillier than Iowa, but we managed to ride it, which kind of surprised us. There were hills pretty much all the way to Wisner and they slowed us down considerably. We were on the road from 10:30 am to 6:30 pm with the most minimal of stops and only made about 48 miles. The country side was green with farming all along the way, but we saw very few farm houses. Maybe a lot more corporate farming going on than small family farms? On the way to Wisner we passed through the little town of Bancroft where the Poet Laureate of Nebraska and the Prairies, John G. Neihardt, lived and worked from about 1911 to 1921. From the internet sight *pacbell.net* I learned that Neihardt had worked among the Omaha Indians while in Bancroft, and that he, "...befriended many great cavalry and American Indians who fought in the Great Indian wars and who participated in the fur trade. Thus, it can be argued, that Neihardt's portrayal of American Westward Settlement is the most authentic version available." He wrote *Black Elk Speaks* (after he left Bancroft) and about 25 volumes of poetry, philosophy and fiction. Nebraska has a right to be proud of this Native Son. *Black Elk Speaks* is a perennial best seller and lauded by scholars. The internet sight notes this exchange:

Bill Moyer: How can you experience this ultimate ground that the shamans speak of?

Joseph Campbell: The best example I can think of in our literature is that beautiful book by John Neihardt, *Black Elk Speaks.*

Neihardt wrote the book from the interviews and a close relationship with the Ogallala Sioux Holy Man—Nicholas Black Elk that arose out of research he was doing on another project, *A Cycle of The West.*

Once again, we have another interesting area of the country to return to one day, when we have more time.

June 6th

We stayed last night at what could have been named the *Cement Figure Works and Motel.* There was a nice looking little motel of only a few rooms that the guy from the *Cement Figure Works* owned. The fellow told us his main business was the cement figures (apparently he had just completed the mold for a small horse—as the sign out front alerted everyone to the fact that: *The horse mold is now finished.* He had quite a display of animals, and what-have-you. Arranged on the lawn between his house and his motel were cement bears, elephants, dogs, deer and so forth. He was a nice guy, an inspiration really, in doing the right thing for your community. He came to buy the motel unexpectedly. The older couple who then owned it, were talking to him one day about the prospect of eventually retiring. On the spot he mentioned to them, kind of off hand, that if they ever decided to retire to let him know because he might be interested in buying the motel. Well, that got the couple thinking more seriously than ever about retirement. Before Mr. Cement Figures knew it, the couple said they were ready to retire and would put the motel on the market, but first wanted to know if he wanted it.

The *Cement Figures* owner was taken by surprise. It was much sooner than he had thought this might happen, but it was kind of a "put up or shut up" moment. He gulped hard and bought it, and it is now making the payments, so he's relieved. But the main reason he bought the place was that he wanted to be sure that the town had a motel. He thought a town should have a motel for weddings and graduations and what not, so people who came from out of town would have a place to stay. If he didn't buy it, it might not survive. I think he was sincere about this. The motel was not going to make him much money, but since he already lived next door to it, it was easy to have his house be the "Office." It was a good fit for him, so the town was able to keep its only motel. We had a very pleasant stay there. The room was actually two rooms so we had plenty of space for our bikes, and it was very modestly priced. Citizenship shows itself in many ways.

Engaged in the long haul across Nebraska now, we managed to make it to Norfolk today and more "celebrity" excitement. We went through the home base town of *Eskimo Bars* as we crossed the Missouri into Nebraska and then John G. Neihardt's stomping grounds and now, as if all that weren't enough, we pedaled by the huge road side sign announcing that Norfolk, Nebraska is, "Johnny Carson's Home Town," complete with a giant smiling face of Johnny Carson. What could possibly be next? Like Lewis and Clark, we will just have to discover it.

The topography from Wisner to Norfolk just about did us in. More hills. We had been hoping for some flattening out of the landscape. The head winds had been a battle and Bryon felt them more on his upright than I did on my recumbent, and bonked-out in the morning so we even stopped for a GU break, which we don't do that often. But finally we came to the top of the last hill and could see that Norfolk looked like it would be the start of at least some semblance of flatter riding. We were not kidding ourselves though; we knew that we were going to be doing the gradual, but continual rise to the Rockies. That was a given. But all these steep ups and downs of Eastern Nebraska were wearing us old farts out.

We'd been hearing about a Nebraska "Cowboy Trail" that would take us west, but we didn't know if its surface would be easy enough to pedal to be worth it, and since we had finally found a road with a good, wide, paved shoulder on it, we reckoned we could make some comfortable miles—so if the "Cowboy Trail" was too hard to push on, we would give it a pass. The other side of the coin, though, was that if we took the trail, it would be more pleasantly removed from the traffic, and the scenery was supposed to be wonderful.

The day was lovely in the friendly town of Norfolk. The 70 degree weather was just right for sitting on a bench in front of the extremely active Senior Center next to the Library. Bryon was researching the next part of the trip and checking emails. I had just got invited to use the internet at the Center too. And before I could do that, someone came to invite me to have lunch with them at the Center. See what I mean, Norfolk was a friendly place, and had been growing in leaps and bounds recently, according to the locals we met. They had a thriving steel business that converts or recycles steel. Sounded like the way of the future to me. But then we don't hear enough about innovative technologies and green technologies that actually make the country better and the world better. I've been writing this story from pre 9-11 to 2007 and what we hear about is how many people we need to bomb next.

We opted not to take the cowboy trail at this point and headed off to ride the Eastern Nebraska Alps, or so it seemed to us, then we cranked the rest of the day into a headwind, riding from 6:30 am to 6:30 pm. 66 miles of climbs and winds.

On this day, 56 years ago, it was D-Day. I have been reading *The Band of Brothers* by Steven Ambrose, and so this day has a special poignancy. I am mindful and thankful of the sacrifices made by our military throughout our history and our current ongoing wars as well, but this year I am even more keenly aware than ever of the sacrifices made by all those who fought in WWII, and so very grateful to them and their families.

We've been following the Elkhorn River and noticing every time we cross it that it looks like a moving duck pond. (Perhaps that always happens in June?) It's that fecal green color and it's just a guess but could it be that farming and ranching practices contribute to excessive runoff and/or maybe lack of fences encourages the cattle to use the streams and rivers as their personal johns? As we rolled toward the little community of Clearwater, we both wondered what their stream would look like. Actually, it was clearer than the Elkhorn, but as we might have guessed, there was a whole little family of cows, looked like moms, kids, & cousins, standing in the creek, doing what cows do while standing in a stream. But this obviously is the range land of Nebraska, The Cattle Country. I don't recall seeing any crops but grass growing along the route today. Beef is king here I would think, and so I guess they just aren't overly concerned about the water quality in the Elkhorn.

It was 88 degrees when we finally made Atkinson at 5:00pm. I am sure it was well in the 90's earlier in the day, as we cranked ever westward. We were not use to this heat, though we were getting more resigned to it. But what really did me in was the combination of heat AND wind. That combination dries out a body fast. I filled up all my water bottles at lunch and so did Bryon, but within 18 miles (which took 2 hours) we were running low again. We would drink water and 5 minutes later we would be really thirsty again. The wind (we later learned) was gusting over 30 mph. When it's hot and does that—LOOK OUT. Better carry lots of water.

We took a break to restart our circulation, and drank some more water. We talked again about how, for both of us, this trip surpasses anything we have ever done, or may ever do again (in our entire lives) in terms of sustained, hard, challenging, physical activity. We also realized that the longer we take to finish this trip, the hotter the weather will keep getting. So we stopped talking and started pushing on again.

We had lunch in the Irish town of O'Neill, at the Blarney Stone. Bryon had a prime rib sandwich that he said was the best of the whole trip. Then, that night, farther along the road, for dinner we both had steaks and I have to say that mine was among the most flavorful of steaks I have ever eaten. This Nebraska beef is really good.

But times are changing, and we seem to have lost the long community table in the combination bar/café/meeting place. We are back to little booths where you have to sit in smaller groups.

June 7th

At 11:45 am we reached the 2000 mile mark, between Newport and Basset, Nebraska, with hot winds in our faces. Nothing like hot headwinds, and to top it off, Bryon's bum was the most painful that it had been the whole trip. He had taken to dropping his shorts when there was no traffic, and trying to get the area aired out, and some of sun's rays targeted there. I kept scanning the surrounding areas, in fear of a Department of Transportation Weather Camera beaming his bare bottom around the internet. I felt so bad for him, though. And I feel so lucky to be riding the recumbent, as my biggest complaint is the occasional numb toe. I use to think that the biggest threat to the completion of this trip would be when one of us injures a knee. Although that is something still to be concerned about, it is being replaced by the worry that the trip could end because of Bryon's ever more painful bum, guess you could say the trip could get *bummed-out*. That would be a *bummer*, for sure.

We are currently in Bassett, at Jules Drive-In, and Bryon is resting his head on his hand and he is asleep.

Coming into Bassett I was once again aware of the size of the storm drain openings along the curbs in this part of the country. Every Nebraska town seems to have these things and as I looked at the ones I was pedaling by, I figured that if I slipped and skidded toward one, I think my whole recumbent and I could have slid through the opening, never to be seen again. These people are prepared for mega-storms.

We got lucky this afternoon with some cloud cover, and although we battled the winds, near the end of the day they died down, which was good as we were racing against an approaching thunderstorm. We could see the lightning in the grey clouds in front of us and the curtain of rain out there. But it was hard to figure out the direction or speed of the coming mass. We sighted some buildings on top of a nearby hill, near Long Pine and rode up there to check for some possible shelter. But on the gravel road, we met the land owner who encouraged us to carry on toward Ainsworth. He was not interested to offer us shelter from the storm, and said the weather report was for evening storms. It was 3:30 pm and we figured we would make it if we raced the rest of the way. The lightning and thunder kept getting closer. It was closing in on us as we sped into town as fast as our legs would haul us. There was a really good lightning display right over the Motel 8 sign. I counted 3 seconds between the lightning and thunder. That was close enough for us! We called it a day with 48 miles ridden.

Ainsworth advertised itself as the town, "…in the middle of nowhere," which seemed pretty accurate. And a billboard coming into town proudly touted another of Ainsworth's claims to fame: *Mike Baxter—the 1995 Champion Cattle Auctioneer*. I did not know that there was such a competition. But you can go to the website for the Livestock Marketing Association and on the page titled World Livestock Auctioneer

Championship (imaweb.com) you can scroll through the past champions and click on any one that you would like to hear. I clicked on Mike Baxter and it was an exhausting listen. My untrained ear couldn't follow it all, but I did have the sense that Mr. Baxter was among those who turned auctioneering into a melodic art form. He was very good. What other "favorite sons" were we going to learn about as we rode across this country?

I have had an odd, undiagnosed tapping noise in my left pedal for most of the trip. We tried to figure out what was causing it and even strung it up in a tree to work on it. But we couldn't figure it out and eventually I just decided to accept it. Well, a couple of days ago Bryon started getting the same sort of tapping noise in his right pedal, and we once again tried to figure it out, but it just remained one of those mysteries of this trip. Even more mysterious than the tapping though, was the fact that on the day his started—mine stopped.

We left Ainsworth in the morning with a tailwind of over 15mph and we just sailed out of there. Thunder was clapping off to the north as we sped west. We would keep an eye on the sky and see how the day progressed. Since we were moving along at such a (for us) good clip, we decided we could spare some precious time to read the historical markers for a change. We went by a World War II Training Camp, and a Sod-House School Site, and we learned that Johnstown was the home of the TV show, *O' Pioneers*.

Hwy 20 had a wonderful paved shoulder and this morning was a gift to us of cool weather and good tail winds. Even a slight drizzle was no concern at all, as we were in seventh heaven riding along on this reasonably flat land. The road went up slightly, inclining toward the Rockies, with very ride-able little hills now and then. We really enjoyed finally cranking up some speed.

I hadn't seen any signs but I figured we were approaching the Sand Hills of NW Nebraska. It looked like buffalo country of the old-west movies. Native looking grasses covered a profusion of hills. And that is pretty much what the Sand Hills are. They were formed by Pleistocene sand (glacial erosion from the Rockies) and are mostly stabilized by vegetation (grasses). They cover a big chunk of Nebraska, and abruptly end (to be replaced by flat Nebraska). Where portions of the hills had collapsed, it looked like ill-kept sand traps on a golf course. It is very pretty country, wild and windswept. Looks like a giant coastal golf links. There isn't enough population out here though, for a golf course. We stopped in Wood Lake (population 72) for coffee as we headed toward Valentine. The billboards proudly proclaimed the area to be a "Vacation Paradise for Hunting, Fishing, and Canoeing." The Sand Hills would also be worth returning to, when we have more time to explore.

This morning the weather channel said it was snowing in Wyoming at 5,000 feet. That caught our attention as we plan to cross the Rockies in Wyoming at 9,000 feet. Of course we have a while to go before we get there, but we sure hope it warms up enough by then so it doesn't snow on us.

It hit us as we first crossed the state line, that Nebraska seemed "Midwest." But today, as we breezed into Valentine, Nebraska we have definitely crossed over into "The West." It is mostly ranching now, not so much farming anymore. There is a totally different feel now, and Valentine's aura is one of an "outpost," reminiscent of of parts of Alaska. Heaps of road construction was going on through the town, and lots of dust and disorder. Any which way you go out of Valentine, you have to go a fair piece before you will hit any kind of a large population.

We headed off for a fast food/ Subway type dinner and then on to the movies to see the new Star Wars film, *Attack of the Clones*. As we walked through the streets of Valentine, it was 90 degrees and the wind was blowing. That kind of heat was too much for me to enjoy. We heard about some great waterfalls and a lake and about some fine canoeing, hereabouts, and Valentine was certainly experiencing growth.

I wondered about how much Nebraska pays its teachers though. We ran into two Valentine Public School Teachers who hold down two jobs each. One was a PE teacher who works as a waitress in the summertime, and the other was a Special Education Teacher who works at the desk of our hotel in the summer. The Special Ed. teacher drives 800 miles **a week**, during the school year. I looked up State by State Salaries, and my State of Oregon was 14th in public school teacher salaries, while Nebraska was 42nd. No wonder these gals were working two jobs. Nebraska teachers averaged $11,000 a year less than Oregon teachers. It would seem that education is not a very high priority in Nebraska. I imagine that the cost of living might be a little less in Nebraska, but not that much.

Oh yes, on the way to town we were told about the river canyon we would have to ride down into and then, of course, have to crank back out of, just a few miles out of Valentine. But if we took the Cowboy Trail and the old bridge across the canyon, we could avoid the climb out. We debated this, because the road and shoulder were soooooo good. Finally we decided that we hadn't ridden any of the Cowboy Trail yet, and thought it would be interesting to ride some of it. The problem was that our bikes weren't mountain bikes and they didn't do well in gravel and soft stuff. But we did opt to take that section and were very glad that we experienced even just that bit of the Cowboy Trail.

In those instances where the trail moved away from the road we imagined ourselves as cowboys of old, thoroughly enjoying the ride. On the bridge over the beautiful tree lined river canyon, we met a family with a mom who loved to cycle. She was trying to impart her love of the activity to her kids. The kids though were all ready to go back; the whiny little buggers felt they had had, "…too much exercise already." Actually that is a bit harsh, they were very nice kids, and not just "whiny little buggers," but clearly I felt sorry for that mom. I tried to keep hope alive that kids do change, as they grow, and I just hoped they all might learn an enjoyment for some kind of outdoor activity as they go through life. Being inactive is to me a curse, and staying inside too much, a killer of the spirit.

When the Cowboy Recreation and Nature Trail is completed it will have a horn or two to toot:

It will cross 321 miles of Nebraska.
It will be the nation's longest rail to trail conversion.
It will be Nebraska's first state recreation trail.
It will pass over 221 bridges and through 29 communities spaced 10 to 15 miles apart, which will provide camping, restroom and showers for the "cowboys."
This trail was already turning into a gem.

The Valentine Gap:

Dear All,

Hoorah! We survived the "Valentine Gap!" This entire trip I have been haunted by the name "Valentine." (It is from Valentine that we have a 92 mile gap facing us, with no motels at all.) I've been WORRIED.

The most we have done in a day is 74 miles. We think we could do 92 miles if it was reasonably flat, and we had a tail wind or maybe a cross wind, but we've had head winds so often, that if that happens during that 92 miles there is NO WAY we would make it. Every time I asked someone (about motels or ideas) they just murmured, "Tsk, tsk," and looked worried for us. So as we approached the dreaded Valentine, I was praying the winds would shift.

They didn't shift…but…

When I called the Valentine Super 8 from Ainsworth, for a reservation, and I again asked about motels in The Valentine Gap—BINGO! The receptionist said she thought there was a lady in Cody (midway) that rented a house out to hunters. So she gave me the number of Cody Oil and I called. Cody Oil said I needed to call the Husker Hub (a bar). So I did. BINGO!

Pat, the nice lady who owned the bar, also owned the house and yes, it was available. Yippppieeeeeee!

So last Sunday we headed from Valentine to Cody. By the time we reached the near ghost town of Nenzel, we had run out of water. We saw a guy coming out of a church and we asked him if there was anywhere we could refill our water bottles. He said sure, and took us inside the church where we were generously presented with biscuits, coffee and all the water we could use. It turned out this fellow, Mr. Johnson, lived in Cody and he invited us over to chat that night.

So we made it to Cody, right out of the movie set of a dying town of 177 people. Cody was, according to the dilapidated greeting board on the way into town, "The Town Too Tough to Die." We called our contact lady and she told us where to find the house. When we opened the door we couldn't believe our good luck in finding not only a place to stay, but a whole house. We cleaned up, went down to The Hub, drank beer with the locals, including local Native Americans, and a lady from Oregon. After our cheeseburger deluxe dinners we headed over to visit the Johnsons who were teachers. We sat on their porch, ate hot cookies and continued one of the best evenings of the entire trip. Ain't life amazing?

—Bryon

The actual ride that got us to Cody, though was another story. Yesterday, getting to Valentine, we just flew with the wind, but today was a struggle. The Weather Channel said South Winds 30mph gusting to 50. My legs became leaden in no time. It took a lot out of me trying to keep my bag-laden bike steady, in crosswinds like that. We weren't out on the road long, when I had a headache, backache, and soon a leg ache. I got blown onto the shoulder twice, and then while going downhill, trying to shift into the big gear, I threw the chain. Again. That was starting to happen more often. Could the chain have stretched enough to cause this? Anyway, while trying to put it back in place in the howling wind, I managed to get a kink in it and that got wedged in the derailleur and by the time we got it all straightened out, the derailleur was a bit catty-wampus so that the chain rubbed almost all the time, no matter what gear I put it in. STRESS. That was wearing me out and adding to my sense of fatigue. I decided that the recumbent's long lanky chain had problems when I tried to change to the big gear on bumpy roads, and during strong winds. I wasn't going to try to shift in those conditions anymore, if I could help it.

I couldn't keep up with Bryon today, and had to have a Gu **and** a Power Bar before arriving in Cody at 1pm. I'm not even sure that helped. It was my biggest bonk-out day so far.

People in Valentine told us there was not much out there in the direction of Cody and they were right. We browsed each little "community" or collection of buildings, for somewhere to get coffee or lunch—NO LUCK. We would have just been happy to get in out of the blazing sun for awhile, to find some shade somewhere. Finally, with our water running out and still one or more hours of hot riding to go, we passed by Nenzel and the church that Bryon described in his email, and where we met Mr. Johnson. What an oasis that church was to us.

When we finally got on the outskirts of Cody we were famished and stopped at the first cafe we saw. While Bryon phoned the lady about getting into our house, and we waited for our meal, I read "Food for Thought from Cody, Nebraska" (…wisdom from the West and other places). I especially liked these:

"Remember, we all stumble, every one of us. That's why it's a comfort to go hand in hand." Emily Kimbrough

"Lord, help my words to be gracious and tender today, for tomorrow I may have to eat them." Unknown

I thought those were good thoughts to keep with me the rest of the trip .

It was wonderful to have that nice roomy house in Cody. We drank gallons of water, took showers and then got all of our clothes out of our bags, hand washed everything but what we had on, and hung it all outside from the tree branches to dry (which took about a minute in that hot wind!) and made the yard look like a hurricane had hit it. Bryon cleaned and oiled the bikes and I washed out the water bottles and relaxed by the air conditioner. It was bliss.

June 10th

One of the locals we met last night grew up in Alaska, her dad was a fisherman. She retired to Cody partially because she just loves the terrain. The Sand Hills reminded her of the ocean. I sure do agree with her. It is an *ocean-scape*. The hills look much like waves out on the open ocean. There are even lots of birds that look like shore birds. We were scolded as we pedaled these sand hills, by one and then two shore bird looking creatures. The needle nosed complainers were not very happy to be making our acquaintance.

There is a lot of water in these sand hills. The depressions between the hills form untold numbers of ponds/lakes, and there are heaps of marshes and birds of all sorts. There are even turtles, which we sadly saw the unlucky remnants of here and there; those being the ones who had navigated the roads unsuccessfully. The whole feel through these Sand Hills is one of remote quietness. It is very attractive. The ranch houses appeared to be set a long ways back off the road and out of sight, down long earthen driveways. So, as we rode along, we rode with pretty much just windmills pumping water for the cattle, the cattle, the sand hills, the birds (some cranky, some not so cranky), and today—THE WIND.

We needed to go 58 miles in strong winds today. It was hard work and we were trying to pace ourselves. The wind was from the north with some headwinds. It was a struggle because it was just blowing so hard, and gusting even harder. I looked up from my journal at lunch and Bryon was asleep with both his hands propping up his head. It is amazing the postures that people can sleep in.

We weren't at all sure that we were getting any fitter with each mile. We may just have been getting more worn out. Whenever we got to talking with people and they realized that we were riding all the way to Oregon from New York City, they often exclaimed, "You must be so fit." We usually answered, "Wish we were, but just look at us, we've got a long way to go before anyone could call us fit." But at least at this point we could do 50+ miles a day, and get up and do it again the next day, and the day after that, and we'd be tired, but not too tired to keep repeating the process (unless the winds were BAD).

I found the following weather report with my observations, in my journal, but it was out of place and I couldn't give it a date really, so I am throwing it in here because I think it sums up a portion of the ride:

> The weather report was for highs in the 90's and plenty of winds up into the 25 to 35 mph range, with occasional gusts to 50mph. Lovely, eh? Nothing like more really hot, strong winds to make our day. By lunch I was turning into a crust of my former self. The combination of heat, wind, and exertion really is an assault. But we have no choice. We can't sit-out the heat, we have to keep moving if we are to make our July 4th deadline…

We had another sad hamburger today, compared to the ones we are used to on the west coast. I don't mean to be disrespectful, but a hamburger with no tomato and no lettuce, and no onion, is really just a meat patty in a bun with a slice of dill pickle. It is always a shock, and we should know better by now what to expect, when these "hamburgers" arrive. Today they also got the award for the "World's Worst Coffee." I think it was the, "second pressing" of the used coffee grounds that put them over the top. The visibility to the bottom of my coffee cup was extremely good, you could see for miles. But the mom and son team who ran the place were quite the duo. The son couldn't have been much older than 12 and he did everything but cook—she did that. But he brought the water, took the orders, brought the coffee (and I suspect he made the coffee) brought the meal, and we paid him at the cash register when we left. He was a nice kid, and did his jobs carefully and with pride. I had the feeling that these two were on their own in the world and this restaurant was their life's blood. They must just love it when new people, "tourists," blow in.

After lunch it warmed up quite a bit and we decided to change to our sandals. We pulled over to a wide spot in the road, and sat down to remove our shoes. Bryon said, "I could just lay down here in the dirt and take a nap."

I replied, "You can do whatever you want, it's your vacation."

That made us both start guffawing and he balked, "So now we're calling this MY vacation, are we?"

I then launched into what MY vacation would be like,

"…pool, beach, margaritas, dancing, music…"

Well it was a nice thought, but the reality was we were sitting in the dirt in Nebraska, and we still had about 4 hours or more to ride if we were going to get to our motel in Gordon.

A few miles before we hit Gordon, we came down out of the Sand Hills. I was sorry to leave them behind; they were so unique. Since Bryon had planned the trip, he may have known more about them than I did. But to me they were a wonderful discovery.

We kept climbing westward. The road was one long, continual incline. We were basically back to farming country again, in this area around Gordon.

As we zeroed in on our motel, we went into our tried and true routine: Bryon went in to see about the room. I stayed out with the bikes. After that we had dinner in a "Mexican" Restaurant that had not one single taco or enchilada or anything like them on the menu. How can they call themselves a Mexican Restaurant? Bryon had steak and a salad and I had pork chops, but once again I didn't ask enough questions and they appeared to be breaded and fried in Valvoline. Sigh. Yuk. Bryon's steak was grilled, and I thought it sure looked good as I wiped the pork grease off my chin.

In the morning we woke up at 5:00am and headed down to the "continental breakfast" which turned out to be (once again) one store-bought cinnamon roll in cellophane, and coffee. But we got to chatting with some of the other guests and one fellow said the sand hills to the south would be even harder to ride as they get, "...pretty choppy out there." Once again, another use of nautical terms to describe these hills here in the center of a continent. This guy had been a rancher out in the sand hills but had had to give it up when he had a brain tumor and a heart attack to deal with. So he moved into town. What a difficult time that must have been, losing a way of life and your health as well.

As we pushed off into the wind, we were already on the prowl for some food to supplement our "breakfast." All the little "towns" on the map, though, didn't translate into eating establishments. We finally came across a gas station/food mart and all they had were more of the same rolls, so we each had another. One of the little communities we rolled through had a sign that read, *Population—33.* You would be lucky to find a candy bar for sale there, and we didn't.

The landscape was changing. A few miles outside of the Chadron area we spotted a ridge with pine trees. There was something almost breathtaking about it. It really charged us up. We had pedaled through the Mid-Atlantic, we had cranked across the Midwest and some of the Plains and now we were starting to cycle across the West. As we drew nearer and nearer to those Pines up on the ridge, with a lovely river running along beside us, we thought once again of the pioneers. What more could they have been looking for? Everything was here, and it was such a pretty area. It would have been quite the decision to pass up such country, hoping for something better. You can just imagine the pioneer family discussions:

"Henry, this place has everything we need, let's just stop and live here."

"Now Marguerite, I know you and the kids are weary of all this, but I've heard about this country further west..."

"You said that same thing in Ohio. Henry I'm not sure we'll ever settle anywhere..."

Or maybe he says:

"This place is just what I have always been looking for, this is it!"

And she says, "Are you kidding, we can't live here, it's so far out in the wilds, what are you thinking. There are no schools, no shops..."

But the great thrust of our young country was to go ever westward, like Henry, and likewise for us. On we went.

We happened across the Museum of the Fur Trade, in Chadron and paid our bucks to go see an old trading post that was dug into the ground. The Trading Post's history taught us that the Sioux would camp up on the ridge, in the pines, when they came to trade at the post. You could just picture the scene. But the Army closed the place down, probably because the Sioux were mostly interested in trading for guns and ammo, which was not really to the army's advantage in the long run.

June 11th

Tonight we are only 50 miles from Wyoming. You may think by now that we have become Superman and Superwoman. NOT. What we are becoming is worn out. My rear end is one big sore. Rather than making ever more miles each day, we are usually happy at 50, so Wyoming has some challenges for us. First of all we have more 80-90 mile gaps ahead, and then there is this little issue of the Rockies. We are talking about buying a little tent to help cross the motel-less gaps. Who knows? But it is exciting to be back in the trees and to know the prairies are mostly behind us. We now need to cross only two more states and we'll be in Oregon.

There is hope.

Thanks for the emails.

—Bryon

June 12th

Well, yesterday was our first sighting of a pine covered ridge, and today was our first sighting of antelope. We spooked a mother and offspring in a field, on the left-hand side of the road, as we rode by, and they took off racing and alerting a few more antelope who emerged from their hiding places and joined in on the dash to be rid of us. On the right side of the road, deer were hopping about in the waving wheat, headed themselves for thicker, taller vegetation. It was lovely, and we couldn't have enjoyed the moment more. It wasn't long before we sighted our first real Old West Movie-type looking ridges. One ridge was where the Crow and Sioux once had a huge battle, and another, Scott's Bluff, was a major landmark for the pioneers along the Oregon, California and Mormon trails.

But there was more than the past and the interesting countryside that had our attention. As we rode through all this historic country we were both grinning from ear to ear, as we discussed the news we had gotten the night before from our oldest son, Andrew.

Yesterday, Bryon printed off the email from Andy that said for us to call him because he had "life altering" news and that it was "good" news. As soon as we got to our motel we commenced to try to phone him. But this was one of those motel phones whose printed instructions say, "To make a credit card call press 9." So I did that but it didn't work. I reread all the instructions and nothing worked so I tried a few other numbers and was getting nowhere fast. I kept getting recordings telling me this is not a valid number, or yada, yada, yada.I was getting more and more frustrated, until finally I came up with a combination of numbers that worked and the phone started ringing, halleluiah! Soon a voice answered saying, "911, what is your emergency?" I got so freaked out that I started trying to explain and apologize all at once, interrupting myself and sounding brain impaired. Finally I just apologized and hung up. Crap! I called the motel office and got the new, "revised" set of directions which worked but only got us to Andy's answering machine. We left the motel's phone number and waited for him to call back.

When we were just about ready to call him again, our phone rang and we got his news. Andy and Madri had gotten engaged. We were just thrilled, and he was obviously so pleased with his news that we had a wonderful evening hearing, among other things, all about *The Proposal*!

His proposal was unique. He took Madri fishing, and he tied, unbeknownst to her, the diamond engagement ring on the end of her line. After that ring went into the water and sunk below the surface, he nearly had a panic attack, worrying about it getting snagged up and the line breaking. He had brought his goggles, just in case, but he could hardly contain himself. Finally he asked her to check her line and she reeled it in. She got the biggest surprise of her life when she saw that ring, and as soon as he saw it come out of the water, he was able to breathe again. I also was able to breathe again at that point in the story, as this diamond was a family heirloom that had come down through several generations on Bryon's side of the family. My heart can't take too many of these stories.

So today we smiled as we rode west, we were going to have a wonderful daughter-in-law, the diamond hadn't sunk to a watery grave, and our family was growing.

It was a nice spring day, with some light winds but the temperature was good for riding. We enjoyed the morning and made it to Crawford by lunchtime, after which we headed to the Crawford City Park for a siesta on the picnic tables. After a pleasant little nap, we realized that we didn't really want to take the same steep road out of Crawford that we had come in on, in order to get back to the Highway. So we took off through town looking for alternative directions out of Crawford. We hailed a 6th grade boy on a bike who was a very nice young man but just happened to be severely directionally impaired. Nevertheless he tried mightily to be helpful.

"You want to get onto the highway? Let me see…" He paused. "OK, wait a minute!" He paused again and this time rubbed his eyebrows really hard. "You go down this street till you hit a dirt road, 2 blocks…NO wait a minute! 3 blocks." He put his hands to his ears and pulled on them, trying to extract some better information, but it didn't work. "No, wait a minute! Do you know where the school is?" (We didn't and that nearly deflated him, but he sprung back to life with, "Well, it's up that street there and…Oh, wait a minute!") "You could go back through town and up two streets…NO, NO—wait a minute…" He was looking in so much stress that we were sorry we had asked him the question, but he was trying so hard to help us out that we felt committed to sticking out his directions, no matter how long it took. Finally he started indicating which way we were to turn at each intersection, by turning the handle bars on his bike in the direction we were to go, "You turn this way here, and go that way there, then you go this way again…" and so on. We listened respectfully, but were having trouble following the map he had in his head. At last he stopped talking for a second so we seized the moment and told him we thought we understood and thanked him profusely for all his help. As we mounted our bikes for our getaway he looked at my recumbent and volunteered, "I haven't never seen no bike like that."

We eventually maneuvered our way back to the highway, but the wind got stronger and stronger and the hills got hillier. The 2000 ft. (or whatever) climb out of Crawford was exhausting.

We took our time reading the historical markers whenever they presented themselves. One today, was particularly sad and moving. It was the story of the Cheyenne, who were forced out of the area and sent to a remote, awful reservation. They couldn't bear the terrible place and quite a large contingent of them headed back to their homelands and proceeded to fight a bloody war, where many on both sides died. It was one of the Big Indian Wars, and such a profound tragedy.

June 13th

It was windy again and in our faces in the morning. The motel owner in Harrison ("Where the West Begins") told us that it was pretty flat to Lusk, Wyoming. We crossed our fingers and headed out to find pretty much nothing but hills. Nebraska has not been particularly easy to cross, but we began to miss the wonderfully generous shoulders they had, as soon as we hit Wyoming.

Chapter Eight

Wyoming

"A Cyclist can ride three-and-a-half miles on the calories found in an ear of corn. Bicycles consume less energy per passenger mile than any other form of transport, including walking. A ten-mile commute by bicycle requires 350 calories of energy, the amount in one bowl of rice. The same trip in the average American car uses 18,600 calories or more than half a gallon of gasoline."

—**Marcia D. Lowe,** *The Bicycle: Vehicle for a Small Planet (As found in The Quotable Cyclist by Bill Strickland)*

I was struck by two things when I read the above quotation. It is absolutely amazing, isn't it, how little energy is required for a human to ride a bike 10 miles? Just one bowl of rice? Isn't that something? But on the other hand, it alarms me that I am not burning more calories. I had hoped to lose some weight on this trip. But if I ride my bike for 50 miles I will only burn off about four bowls of rice and a couple of ears of corn? I am eating way more than that in a day, and I am suspicious that I haven't lost a single pound on this trip and we only have Wyoming and Idaho to cross before we reach Oregon and the end of the trip. Oh well, whatever happens, it will be interesting to get on the scales when we get home and see what the result, weight-wise, will have been in crossing the continent by bike.

As soon as we crossed the state line the generous Nebraska shoulder turned into a 3 inch wide Wyoming afterthought, and the traffic didn't lessen a bit.

As we rode we watched coal train after coal train race by. We stopped on a bridge to see what we were crossing over and looked down in amazement at all the coal. We have had about 6 coal trains go by us in the last hour alone. Bryon counted the cars in the last one, and on that train alone there were 117 cars. That is a lot of coal. There must be a big coal deposit near here somewhere. The curious thing is that during all the time we had been riding; only full trains had gone by. There was a double track, so you would think empty trains would be headed back to pick up more coal but we hadn't seen a one. The mystery was solved though, as later in the day all the empty ones started the return trip.

I think today was Bryon's hardest day—it was brutally windy. Ironically, as we crossed the state line I was singing to myself, "Oh give me a home, where the buffalo roam, and the skies are not cloudy all day…" (It had been clear blue skies for a day and a half!). But just as soon as I finished the song the clouds rolled in with a passion, the temperature dropped, we felt a few drizzles, and the wind began to blow seriously in our faces. Teach me to sing happily along. Bryon, sitting so tall on his upright bike, really had to struggle for all he was worth, into the ever strengthening headwinds. He got very down and out over this as the day progressed. At one point he growled, "I'm on the verge of throwing this bike off the cliff and hitch-hiking!" I could tell by his face and body language, that he was on the verge. It was a bad day. We rode from 8:30 am to 2:00 pm, and we only went 32 miles. But, luckily, we found a nice motel in Lusk, Wyoming and quickly turned on the golf in time to see Tiger Woods take the lead at the US Open. We love to watch him play the Majors, so we relaxed in front of the TV the rest of the afternoon. That was like an elixir for us both and we were much more chipper by lights-out.

June 14th

Up at 5:15 am and on the road in short order, with calm winds, and not too many hills, we were rewarded with a beautiful day. We have really learned to appreciate these days, and coming off of such a hard one yesterday, this day was extra sweet. When we pedaled by some antelope and deer, it occurred to me that they had become such a regular sight to us that we no longer even pointed them out to each other. We disturbed one antelope that was nestled in the grass, right next to the side of the road. It is always so lovely to see them curled in the grass like that, and so close to us. But the bicycles always spook them no matter how quiet we try to ride. Ohhhhhh, they are just so pretty lying in the grass and so full of vim and vigor when they bolt up and race off. I have never seen more than one antelope curled up like that at any one time, never two or more. I felt so blessed though, to be seeing these sights in the early morning hours of such a gorgeous summer day.

As we rode, we could see the Hensel fire, or rather the smoke from it. It had thus far consumed 1,400 acres and was "…the largest wild land fire in

Wyoming (so far this year) and still growing," according to the Casper Star Tribune. The fire was thankfully south of us by a fair piece (about 5 miles northeast of Laramie Peak). So it didn't appear that we would have to ride through any of the smoke from it. We kept as careful track as we could of all the fires because riding a bike through one could be big trouble. Today we hit the highest point of the trip so far. A sign announced we had crested 5,377 feet.

The word "town" out here, takes on new meaning. It apparently doesn't take much of a population to get your "town" on the map. One community had a sign that read *Population 3*. (I think it might have been Keeline, Wyoming but forgive me if I'm wrong.) Anyway, I don't know about you, but I don't think— *population 3*—is a town, it's a family. One cannot assume out west that a place has any services, just because it is on the map.

I spent a long time last night going through all the info we had—to see if there was any place to stay between Casper and Shoshoni, but no luck. It was too long a gap for us to ride unless we got really lucky with the tailwinds. We were giving serious thought to buying some camping gear in Casper. But between Shoshoni and Dubois I did find a bed and breakfast, 12 miles west of Crowheart. That was good news. We mapped out how long it would take us to get there so we could call for reservations. We signed on for a room, 6 days hence, but the place was booked solid after that. This area was in the heart of tourist country and at a busy time of the year. Booking ahead was becoming even more important than ever.

At Orin, Wyoming we got on the Interstate 20/26 to Douglas, which turned out to be a very good move as the that section of the freeway was brand new and had a hugely generous shoulder. ALSO, we got the wind at our backs! We just cruised into Douglas effortlessly, and were able to get a motel earlier than we had thought we could, and once again watched the US Open. Tiger was ahead after 2 days by 3 strokes. He doesn't lose many when he gets to playing like that.

June 15th

We woke up at 5:00 am and quickly departed Douglas, but once again, what a difference a day makes. An unfriendly wind was picking up, Bryon's posterior was complaining loudly, and my knees were talking to me. But we plugged along OK until the construction on the highway turned the route into a very dicey situation. We kept our eyes tuned into our rearview mirrors as the four lanes had eroded into two lanes causing the traffic to become really heavy. Too many trucks! We had to share what was our bike lane with trucks and that meant whenever they came roaring through we had to bail off into the gravel next to the road. The trucks couldn't swerve out and around us because of the temporary posts down the road to separate the two directions of traffic. So it was up to us to get out of their way in time. We struggled on this way for 5 or 6 crusty miles and it was way too exhausting.

Bryon noticed some dust from a vehicle going down a dirt road, and he checked it out on the map. If that dirt road connected with the River Road, we would have an alternative road into Casper. We took the chance and headed off down the roughly graded "road," rattling every tooth in our collective heads. It wasn't long before Bryon hit some deep, soft dirt that pitched him over and banged up his legs—but he was otherwise OK. I swerved around to miss him, in my own little version of a wild ride, but managed to stay upright somehow. When the dust settled we carried on and did eventually hit the River Road, and were so happy we had taken the gamble. There was almost no traffic and a good shoulder to take us to Casper. What a relief!

All morning long we had been looking to find a place to get some coffee and take a break, but had found nothing until a few miles down the River Road we spied a tavern. It was the first business that we had come across all day. The establishment was another of those "biker bars" that have been (mostly) so friendly to us along the way. This was no exception, and the proprietor we chatted with was a really helpful guy. He called around for us and found out that the construction workers had booked up all the accommodations around the area. Oh woe was us. Then he proceeded to call his friends for ideas and someone suggested that Hell's Half Acre had recently reopened and since it wasn't in the phone book yet, it might be worth contacting. We were dubious about the place, with a name like Hells Half Acre, but we had no choice, and when the lady running it said they had a vacancy, we booked it up fast! So we don't have to buy camping gear yet. Local knowledge is great, isn't it?!

We made it to Casper and collapsed in our motel, in front of the TV to follow the developing saga of the third round of the US Open. Tiger was still ahead.

We had been emailing Mike and Pam Reynolds, and they were headed our way (by car). We hoped to catch up with them in Casper and were delighted to learn that they had made reservations at our motel. We had a great dinner with them and thoroughly enjoyed trading the "war stories" of bicycle tales from the road. They were on their way to the Black Hills of South Dakota and it was just great to have some time with friends again. It was the first time in 2 months that we had come in contact with people we knew. And it was especially nice to see them, as they had been our inspiration to do this trip.

June 16th
Father's Day!

We decided to take a layover day. Bryon's hamburger bum was really becoming a major problem. The worry about it, as a possible trip-ender, is replacing all other concerns. Besides, Dads should be able to relax on Father's Day shouldn't they?

Over the motel's continental breakfast Mike and Pam encouraged Bryon to try using Bag Balm for his ground-round rear-end. They are the best cycle advisors anyone could ever want and so when they speak, we listen. What is Bag Balm you might ask? Well, it is nearly pure lanolin that was initially used in the dairy industry to combat chafed cow udders. In the process of using the stuff the farmers noticed it soothed their rough hands and made them softer and smoother. Chafing of tender areas is a given when riding day after day on an upright bike and it didn't take long for cyclists to find their own use for this smeary glop in the bright green cans. While Mike took Bryon off in the car to find the potion, Pam and I took their dog for a nice long walk. It was wonderful to walk for a change, and stretch my legs. It felt really good.

With the new anti-friction, lanolinizing balm in place we waved goodbye to Mike and Pam and then settled in for the 4th Round of the US Open. As we alternately watched the golf and napped the afternoon away, we also took note of the howling wind outside which was blowing the wrong way all day which made us feel quite smug having decided to take the day off. We also tried to reach both the boys, but we couldn't get through to Tyler. He has one more year at Oregon State to finish his degree in Spanish, and is working his butt of this summer at Jeld-Wen Windows and Doors in Klamath, pulling heavy boards off a conveyer belt at breakneck speeds. He also plays rugby for OSU and tends to be a hard man to get a hold of sometimes. Tyler has travel in his blood and while we were in Alaska he headed off for a term to study in Spain, which turned into a year of study and work. When 911 hit he was trying to get home from Spain and got stuck in Madrid until our country sorted things out and flights resumed.

But, happily we did manage to get hold of Andy and he had yet more good news for us as was reflected in this email from Bryon:

> To top everything off, Andy announced that he had just been hired to teach next year in the same slot that he was a student teacher this year. There has been a teacher freeze in most Oregon districts this year so he was VERY lucky to land this job, and it is

a nice compliment that he must have done a fine job as a student teacher, so we are VERRY proud of him and just overjoyed with all his good news. It sort of makes my sore butt insignificant!
—Bryon

June 17

Slept in today, as we didn't want to leave before the continental breakfast opened at 6:00 am. The weather report was for wind in our faces, but it was calm in the morning and we felt like we were getting away with something, at least for the first 5 or 6 miles. Better enjoy it while you can! Then we hit more road construction, which consisted of 12 miles that we were mostly able to ride through, but it wasn't fun. Finally, we made it up to where the pilot pickup was waiting to guide the next group through the construction mess for the next 2 miles. It would have been a nightmare to have had to ride through this section. So we asked the flaggers what cyclists were supposed to do and they took us right to the pilot truck. We put the bicycles in the back of the pickup and hopped up front with the young Wyoming lady pilot for the next two miles and were just happy as clams to be in that truck, and not eating her dust and fighting the bad road and riding like a bat out of hell trying to not slow up the traffic behind us. But once deposited, we had to keep focused so as to get off the road in time whenever trucks and RV's came barreling along. It was not a relaxing ride.

Wyoming had been looking pretty dry to us, but there was some green to the hills now, which we heard was unusual for this time of the year. There were antelope everywhere! There must be a lot more antelope in Wyoming than people. Our biggest problem though, was that just before noon the headwinds came with such a vengeance that we almost could not ride into them. It was a Herculean struggle to gain any ground at all.

It has seemed to us that often the mornings have been relatively calm and then the winds pick up around lunch time. We may start getting up earlier and earlier, not just to avoid the heat, but to beat these cantankerous winds. No place to find food or drink presented itself between Casper and Powder River, so we dug into our stores and found some energy bars to tide us over. As we kept pushing on into the wind it kept hitting me how far out in the woo-woos we were. There were so many vast stretches where there were no buildings, and no people whatsoever. There was just range land and fences, antelope, cows and us. Whenever we stopped on a rise, I would look back east, over the mountains and canyons we had ridden and think back to all the land we could no longer see, all the way back to JFK Airport in NYC. Then I would stand there agog. It was a marvel to me that we two people, at our age and our physical condition, had been able to accomplish this. Here we were in Wyoming, and it just seemed awesome looking east, that we had actually gotten here by this personal physical effort called bicycling. What an amazing adventure.

Powder River, out here in the way back of Wyoming had a Café/Restaurant/Lounge in a log cabin with attractive, comfortable chairs and tables crafted from tree limbs. But Powder River itself was a pretty unsightly conglomeration of old trailers, some newer manufactured homes, buildings falling down and caving in, a few metal and wood buildings, one Quonset hut, and lots of discarded and broken down vehicles. There were officially only 50 people in Powder River, according to the sign, but there were a heck of a lot more derelict vehicles than there were people, if that sign was correct. What brought those 50 people to come and live here, what did they do here to earn a living and how did they feel about the place? The guy running the café was certainly nice, and the people eating lunch next to us were friendly, too. But this little community looked, for all the world, to have been randomly dumped in the weeds and the dirt. My mom use to say often that, "It takes all kinds to make the world." She never meant that in a derogatory way, and I never took it as anything other than a true observation. People seek and require different things out of life.

We gathered up our tired bodies and headed back out into the hot Wyoming day, and once again, into the wind. It was only 6 miles or so to our motel at Hell's Half Acre, and we were leaving around 2:00 pm. But with this wind, I was thinking we would make between 2.5 and 4 mph. We would have to stop more often to keep our circulation going, and we would be drinking so much water, by the bucketfuls, that we would have more loo stops and so on. I estimated what would normally have taken about a half hour would take more like an hour and a half to ride.

Well—I wasn't too far off. We arrived at 3:40 but the manager of Hell's Half Acre was a talkative bloke and it took a while to actually make it to our room. Ohhhhhh….blessed windless room. We turned on the air conditioner and sat in front of it drinking glass after glass of cold liquids.

Hell's Half Acre Restaurant/Shop/Motel was located next to a chasm with magnificent formations.

According to roadsideamerica.com, Hell's Half Acre, "…is a geological oddity—a craggy horseshoe-shaped gorge that drops away from an otherwise flat plain...the 150+ ft. gorge—actually 320 acres total...is filled in one section with jagged rock spires, naturally sculpted into nightmarish chaos by an ancient offshoot of the Powder River." That pretty well describes the place in words, but as with most things, you really have to see it to appreciate it. The attraction's big claim to fame occurred in 1997 when the alien bug scenes for the movie Starship Troopers were filmed there. They used some locals in the movie but mostly as dead bodies.

The motel and restaurant were in operation when we came through, lucky for us, and they served us huge hamburgers for dinner (Regular sized were ½ pounders and doubles were 1 full pound.) They were hard to eat, they were so big. Dark Wyoming beer helped them go down and we also bought a couple pieces of homemade apple pie to take back to our room for breakfast in the morning. We planned to get up between 4:30 and 5:30 am and be gone as soon as possible.

June 18th

It was 54 miles to Shoshoni from Hell's Half Acre, and we intended to beat some of the wind and heat by leaving early. The apple pie hit the spot, oh did it ever. We were on the road by 5:45 am, and after pedaling away those apple pies, we started looking for some place to get our next calorie intake. We had learned to get food and water from wherever we could in these far-outs of Wyoming, cuz the next possible chance could be a heck of a ways away. In Hiland we found ourselves buying "food type products" from the archetypal "Red Neck Store." The folks at Hell's Half Acre warned us that we would be going into the middle of nowhere, when we left them, and they were right. They said there was a, "...store of sorts in Hiland," and that about summed the place up. The proprietor of the "store" (or perhaps more accurately referred to as the "sore" in Hiland) would have made Rush Limbaugh proud. "You've come from New York City? Why, you been out there where all them liberals is." Liberals were to blame for everything, "...Yup, no doubt about it." He heated us up some sad looking egg mcmuffin knock-offs that he pulled out of his freezer. We ate in silence as he told us about how the *guvmunt* makes it hell for the small businessman, and about *wacko vironmentalists, and yada, yada, yada.* We could tell the mcmuffins weren't going to get us far, so we bought some frozen chicken sandwiches (bad idea) and some other junk to take with us. As we rode away from the fellow I wondered if he had just been trying to rile us up? Or was he just so unaware that he thought people riding bikes across the country would actually think the way he did. There may be some bike riding folks who don't care about the environment, but not very many.

Further down the road, when we finally cracked out the "ready to eat" chicken burgers—they were inedible, so we ate them anyway. When I tapped on the bun it sounded just like tapping on a piece of wood.

We made 50 miles before noon, which was a new personal best. By leaving so early we got cooler temps, almost no wind at the start, less traffic and a chance to beat the storm that was supposed to materialize some time in the afternoon. We made it to Shoshoni a little after noon and spotted their extremely nice Senior Citizen Center. There seemed to be no one using their internet computer and they kindly allowed us to spend some time on it. It was an old snail paced relic and while Bryon struggled to figure out its idiosyncrasies, I had a chance to talk with a delightful, older Shoshoni woman, a real charmer of a lady, who clued me in on where the good fishing was to be found. Not that we would do any fishing—no rods with us this trip. Finally, when we headed back out onto the streets of Shoshoni, we were glad to have beat most of the wind and heat and to be headed to our motel early.

It was well past time for us to have a session at a laundromat, so I loaded up the bike with a giant sack of dirty clothes and struck out to find one. The motel lady said it was across from the Post Office, and that the Post Office was on Main Street. I rode up and down Main Street and found no Post Office, at which point I cornered a couple of people on the street and inquired where I might find the laundromat. They, of course had no clue, and questioned whether Shoshoni even had a laundromat. Finally they concluded that it used to have a laundromat, but not anymore. They did direct me to the Post Office, though.

The Post Mistress volunteered that she understood that, "...the laundromat had shut down because the kids in town had trashed it so badly." But, not certain, she referred me to one of the gas station/convenience stores that had some years ago had a laundromat on their premises. She was pretty sure they didn't still have one though.

As I approached the gas station, I noticed a beat up building, off to the side, in advanced stages of disrepair and neglect that had a faded laundromat sign on it. I hesitated but the door opened as I pushed on it and through the filth and mess I could make out some coin-op washers and dryers. The guy at the gas station said he thought it was open, so I bought some soap from him and headed back over to the unlit rubbish dump of a place. I paused for awhile in the doorway, wondering if it made sense to be doing this on my own. But finally I slowly made my way into the room. It looked dreadful as it must have been a decade since anyone had cleaned the place. There was grime covering everything. Most of the washers and half of the dryers had scribbled "out of order" notes taped on them. Before I put the clothes and soap in the washer, I put my coins in and turned it on. Happily the thing started pushing water into the tub, so I pronounced it to be in working order. Then I surveyed the dryers that didn't have "out of order signs." All but one of them had inordinate amounts of black globs on their drums, which looked suspiciously gross. I found one dryer that looked a bit better than the others and I chipped off a couple of the biggest globs and hoped for the best. I found a discarded shirt and dusted off the folding table as best I could. The floor was strewn with debris, and I was so appalled at the sink, that I don't even want to try to describe it. It was a very weird feeling, being alone in that place. No one else was there, and I almost felt like I was breaking in, and could get arrested at any moment; that the place actually wasn't open for business…But the machines kept taking my money, and they even seemed to work OK, much to my relief. I was very happy when I packed up all the freshly cleaned clothes and got the heck out of there.

Dear All,

Greetings from Shoshoni, Wyoming (it's about halfway across the state). Things are changing fast in our lives. After weeks and weeks of west pedal on the plains, our world now has contour. Our adversaries have announced their presence. We now can see the towering white capped WALL of the West. Talk about intimidating! Today we crossed the dreaded Shoshoni gap by starting our ride at 5:45 am before the howling winds struck. We are off to Dubois tomorrow, and then over the Continental Divide. That will be a day to remember! Then into Jackson and the Tetons and on to Idaho.

Yesterday we got out our Idaho map and began to plan that state. Talk about exciting! We can see OREGON on its western edge!

Thanks again for all of the emails and keep praying for east winds. It can REALLY Blow out here in Wyoming and we need all the help we can get. Bring on those Rockies!!
—Bryon

The grasslands have given way more and more to sagebrush. It is dry and inhospitable looking land, and we are seeing a lot fewer antelope now. It would be a hard scrabble existence trying to eke out subsistence here.

Since we have decided to get going at 5:00 am every morning, we are starting to hit the sack around 8:00 or 8:30 each night.

June 19th

In the morning the air was wonderfully calm. We started out climbing and just kept climbing and climbing, and the scenery kept changing and changing. A ways out of Shoshoni we started to see the snowy caps of the Wind River Range in the distance. They were wondrous as we crept ever closer and they got ever bigger. The sagebrush gave way to irrigated land, some crops and some grassland.

The highlight of the day though, was that we finally, after all this time, spotted a young couple laboring along the highway with their bikes loaded to the hilt with camping gear, and who knows what all. We were so excited to have found some other touring cyclists that we raced each other over to their side of the road. They were going from Austin, Texas to Calgary, Canada. He said they were even carrying a laptop computer so they could post the trip on their website as they went. They spoke English well, in a non-native speaker way, and asked us what kind of distances we did each day. They were from Switzerland and there was something about the rhythm and cadence of their English that made everything they said charming as heck. We couldn't stop smiling as they spoke. When we told them our average daily miles she was astonished, "That's the same as we do!"

"Yes," I countered, "but look at all you carry and then look at our light load."

At this he rolled his eyes, as he gestured at all their baggage and said, "It is very heavy," with a heartfelt groan.

They were both having a great time though, and just like us, they were ecstatic to have made it all the way to Wyoming. She said that every night they got the map out and traced their progress, and that they were always surprised and, "...quite impressed with ourselves, to see how far we have come." We wished we could have invited them for a drink and a chat somewhere, but there was nowhere to go, so we stepped aside and wished them well. We warned them about the rattlesnakes, though, before they headed off, which reminds me of this email:

Dear All,

Whew! Wyoming is exciting. Like two days ago on a 30 mph descent from Hell's Half Acre, I was zooming down the road when there in my fast approaching path was a rattlesnake. Missed him by 2 inches, but for the next 10 miles I had these horrid visual images of the possibilities, had I hit him.

—Bryon

The rattlesnakes definitely have our attention. I have never seen so many of them in my life and they are always unnerving. They seem to like to sun on the shoulders, in the gravel. They also seem to usually get squashed there. But every now and then I have seen one that appeared to be just fine, and simply having a snooze beside the highway. Sends shivers through me, as I am usually going up hill pretty slowly when I notice them and I would make an easy target. I also have to keep telling myself to be very careful when I go off the road for my "nature call" walks, and my heart skips a beat just seeing a snake-like stick. It makes the procedure fraught with unease.

Oh, and then of course there are the bears. Now it is one thing entirely to be in a car and see road signs that warn you about bears. It is entirely a different thing to be on a bicycle and see those same signs!

What do you think, pepper spray or a rock?

There are plenty of bear stories in Wyoming. Apparently it's not surprising to see bears in the area we are headed into. I just hope that none of them fancy a bicycle chase. We would be tempting, juicy, moving prey. We would be quite the sport.

By the time we got to Riverton, a determined wind had started to come at us again, making it a good time to stop for some shopping. We had been unable to locate anywhere to stay after Riverton, and so it was time to "comparison" shop at Wal-Mart and K Mart for camping gear. We ended up with two short, thin sleeping mats, 2 lightweight fleece fabric things with zippers that they called "sleeping bags," and a small tent. The total bill came to about the same price that a reasonably OK motel would cost for the night. We looked pretty odd when we strapped all this stuff onto our bikes. But once again the recumbent helped out, as I was able to tie a plastic Wal-Mart bag on each side of the seat back, for the stuff that wouldn't fit anywhere else. Bryon took the tent, which was the heaviest thing. It extended off the back of his bike like a tail. We looked unlike any other touring cyclists you will ever see. But it seemed to work. Tonight we don't know where we will camp, but there is no other choice, so camp we will, one way or another.

Newly purchased camping gear is strapped on in Riverton, Wyoming.

We had lunch in Riverton, before heading out into the no-motel-gap-zone ahead of us. A fellow recumbent rider noticed our bikes outside the restaurant, and rode over to talk to us. Wayne (or Wade?) had a flashy recumbent decked out with a clear plastic wind slick, or ferring, that really was an eye catcher. His bike was packed like a mule, for his journey from Washington State to Georgia. Riverton seems to be attracting some cyclists, who are all anxious to chat, compare notes, information, battle plans, and just tell stories.

After we left Riverton, the "ups" went up a couple notches in steepness. We climbed and climbed and climbed out of the town, only to be dismayed to descend and descend and descend back down again. The wind came up hard in our faces and the pedaling was tiring. We stopped at a little general store in Kinnear, exhausted, and learned that Morton, "…up the road a ways," had a good Mexican Restaurant. As we were taking time to recover from the climbing, we sat outside the store and talked with an old fellow who had worked on the ranch Ian Tyson sings about, the *Old Double Diamond*. He worked on that ranch, was in rodeos in his youth, and raced dogs in Florida. Wished we had time to hear more of his stories, but we had rested long enough so saddled up again, in search of the Mexican Restaurant.

The Mexican Restaurant was just what we needed. The folks were friendly, and the food was good. It was a good time to stop for dinner so we asked them about possible camping spots in the area. We had become concerned because all the land along the road was fenced off, we couldn't see any farm houses to ask permission, and we were loath to trespass. The people who ran the restaurant offered us the use of their backyard for our tent. What a relief, we had a place to stay! We gratefully took them up on their offer. After dinner we were both so tired that we wanted to crawl in the tent and go to sleep, but there was a problem. We were going to be setting up the tent right outside the window that the customers looked out of. We really didn't want our little squatter's quarters to be the customer's entertainment for the evening. We decided to wait to put up the tent until the place was getting ready to close. But customers kept coming. We split a dessert, and tried to make it last as we waited. By 7:00 pm I was nodding off as I wrote in my journal. How I longed to just climb in that tent, read until it was too dark, close my eyes and hope that we would be warm enough, as the night temperatures dropped, to get some sleep. The bags were supposed to be good to 50 degrees, but the low was expected to be 43 degrees.

Finally, everyone left the restaurant, and we raced behind it to put the tent up while we still had some daylight. Just as we got everything organized and laid ourselves down on our wafer thin mats, a battalion of birds came at our bikes in force. It was like a bird playground as they flapped from bike to bike and squawked away relentlessly. My mind flashed back to a night we had with birds (kias) in New Zealand many years before, when the determined scoundrels left everything on our roof rack in tatters. We kept checking on these noisy Wyoming birds, until it was too dark to see, and they didn't seem to be doing any damage, but just loved jumping from bike to bike and circling the tent and overall raising a ruckus. We tried scaring them off, but they were not to be dissuaded. We gave up and settled in to listen to them flop, flap, flopping around us. Who knows what they were thinking in those little heads of theirs, but they kept real busy.

We started out the night with a couple of layers of clothes on and squirmed into our fleece bags. It didn't take long before we both started sweating. So we layered down and tried to get comfortable. About every hour I would get cold and drag another piece of clothing over and put it on. I added socks, and leg and arm warmers, extra pants layers, another shirt, etc. Each time I would be warm for awhile and then start all over again. The temperature just kept dropping. Each time I added more clothing it was harder to squirm back into the bag, which unbeknownst to me was shedding little red fleece balls that clung tenaciously all over all my layers. When I got up in the morning it looked like all my clothes had caught the measles. By 4:00 am I had put on every bit of clothing I had brought on the trip, and still wasn't warm. Not a comfortable night. By 5:00 am we were both up, ate our protein bars, packed the tent and were off.

It was cold. Really COLD! My one layer of gloves wasn't doing the trick so I drug out my Kitchen and Household Big Job Gloves, and Bryon even wore his green horticulture gloves for awhile. We had brought those gloves in the event of cold rain, but it was just so cold, we figured they would be of some help in keeping us warm. I woke up with a runny nose and never really felt totally awake. It was hard work just to keep moving, and I had to do that to keep from freezing. We had icy headwinds all morning, and I don't remember feeling more tired on the whole trip. However, later the winds shifted. We had made reservations at a Bed and Breakfast at a place called the Early Ranch, and we actually thought about canceling them because in the afternoon we got some wonderful tail winds and thought it was only about 20 miles further to get to Dubois. Those tail winds are something we love to take advantage of. But in the end, I was just too pooped, so we took the turn-off to this B&B, not knowing, really, what was in store.

The gravel road to the B&B quickly began to deteriorate and was very hard to ride with our thinnish tires, and all our bags. It went down, down, down the hill to the river below, and had nasty patches of fine dust, that conspired to topple us. I thought it would be hard to walk my bike back out on this road in the morning, let alone ride out. I was getting worried. Since I was the one who had researched and booked this place, I was feeling responsible. We passed one unattractive "homestead" and it was good to see that the *Early*

Ranch signs didn't point to it. Finally we came around a corner, over a ridge and spread out below us was a very old homestead—a gorgeous piece of real estate, right on the Wind River, with utterly fantastic badland-type hills as a backdrop. The life giving water in the Wind River created a luscious green strip through the browness that was everywhere else in the landscape. We were impressed. This place was awesome.

The owner of the place appeared in a golf cart, piled us in it, and immediately our reverie wilted under a barrage of rants about how bad the last group of cyclists had been. She went on and on about the miscreants on bikes, and we were—well—overwhelmed. At any rate, after we promised to be good cyclists and not wreck the cabin, we had a good chat with Ruth and she showed us to our nicely arranged, old west style log cabin. It was very pleasantly appointed inside and outside had a porch and comfy chairs overlooking the Wind River. Wonderful.

After we showered, napped, and ate the crackers, peanut butter and spam we had packed for dinner, we were treated to the thundering return of horses from the pasture to the corral. Four or five border collies and a beagle (who thought he was a border collie) helped, while Wayne (Ruth's husband) drove the whole menagerie toward the corral with his 4 wheeler. Apparently this was a nightly ritual and great entertainment for us.

Roundup at the Early Ranch, Wyoming

Ruth invited us to have a beer with them down at the corral. Since we have never yet refused such an offer, we happily joined the family there. The corral had stalls and storage rooms and a wonderful big covered porch where we sat with their daughter Julie and watched the show as it unfolded. Wayne was training a Tennessee Walker colt, and was working to teach the animal to bow down and roll over and lay down. It was quite an energetic undertaking, not unlike a wrestling match, but picture, if you will, a man and a horse wrestling. The horse wanted NOT to do what Wayne wanted him to do, but Wayne just kept at it, never losing his temper, until it looked like they were both bushed. The mother of the colt didn't help matters as she was very distressed, loudly vocal and persistent, which kept the colt in a jitter the whole time. Finally the colt laid down and stayed there until commanded to rise and was promptly rewarded with praise, oats and kindly pats. Anyone who has ever tried to train an animal would have related to that moment. But we soon realized that the show had only just begun, down at the Early corral.

The Early Ranch was also breeding horses and that turns out to be more of a complicated process than you would think. First of all, a suitable candidate from all those available had to be selected. Above all else, it seemed, she needed to be receptive to Sam, the *ever ready* stallion. He seemed to have no favorites, he was just READY. I was not sure how they knew which lady was the one for Sam, but eventually one was decided upon. Sam put on quite the show indeed. The energetic and amorous Sam bellowed and prodded and stomped the ground with passion, sending clouds of dust high into the air, before settling down to the business at hand. He was quite a guy, that Sam. You just never know, at the end of the day, what new sights and sounds you might experience. Talk about unconventional happy hours.

There were about six duplex log cabins on the ranch, and what appeared to be the original log farmhouse, converted into a lodge. They book a lot of retreats and family reunions, and cater to a "Western Experience" complete with trail rides and rafting the Wind River, etc. They also fit in folks like us, when they have room between groups. They were solidly booked for the next 30 days; we had luckily timed it just right.

We retired to our porch and watched the river, horses and dogs, as the evening sun danced across the water and set on the hills. Before dark the sky turned dramatic on us and featured a wondrous thunder and lightning display. It was the kind of storm that you don't want in the summer in the dry country, because it starts fires and has no rain in it.

The breakfast part of our B & B, was cooked in the morning by Wayne, in the Big House, and enjoyed by his family as well. We all sat together and talked while we ate. They are living out a dream, with this ranch, in such an awesome setting. We wished them well, and much to our delight, Wayne tossed our bikes in his truck and took us up the steep road back to the highway. The whole experience sure beat all to heck a night at any motel!

June 21st

We left home April 21st—so we have been on the bikes and on the road for two months now, and what's really great is that we are still excited about what's next. Yesterday and today have been beautiful. Today we rode along the Wind River and through the beautiful Red Rock formations that make this stretch of road awe-inspiring. It was a glorious morning, made more wonderful by the lack of wind and heat. We breezed the 20 miles into Dubois, almost effortlessly, and marveled at the scenery the entire way. Bryon sent this email home:

Climbing the Mountain

If you have read the excellent book, "Into Thin Air," you know how to climb Mt. Everest. Well for the last week I've seen the similarities as we have approached the Continental Divide. Our pass is about 9600 feet and everyone has been warning and wailing on about how difficult it is. (Mind you, these alarmists are not real bikers, but just horrified lay persons who don't ride.) Well, we have been approaching in Stages somewhat akin to Everest Climbers. Riverton was base camp and about 4700 feet. Then we climbed up to about 5600 feet and camped out. Last night we spent on a dude ranch and acclimated (while having a great time). Today we reached Dubois (Camp 4). Tomorrow we will arise at dawn and attempt an assault on Togwotee Pass, which will then drop us down into Teton National Park. There is much anxiety in camp tonight as it's a 2700 foot climb in the next 30 miles. Can we do it? What will the weather bring? Will there be bears?

Wish us luck! In MANY ways this will be the high point of our adventure.

And thanks again for the many emails.

Wyoming is a beautiful state!

—Bryon

We had the good fortune to meet another touring cyclist, on the route to Dubois, a very nice fellow, riding solo, who was camping and had the least amount of stuff of any camping cyclists we have ever seen. He just had panniers on the back with one side for tent, bag and mat, and the other side for clothes and all the rest. He had one other bag up front and it was small. He had only a titch more stuff than we did. But even he admitted that once the mosquitoes are out in force, and again when he hits the humid states, he will abandon camping and stay in motels. He had just come over the pass we were headed for, so we enjoyed his take on it. He recommended some roads in the Park, that he thought were terrific and worth a little extra effort to see.

Our new friend was doing the Adventure Cycle Route and had encountered many cyclists along its roads. I thought it was very interesting though, what he said just before we parted ways, "It's been really nice to talk to you two. You are so upbeat and so obviously enjoying your trip. Almost everyone I've encountered so far on this trip has been non-stop complaining about the hills and how much work it all is." He thought it was because they all carried too much stuff, which is part of it I'm sure. But the other part is that the Adventure Cycle Route is for really tough, fit people. It goes to more of the beautiful places, but it is a whole lot more work. It really does depend on what you want out of the trip you take, and what we wanted was to cross the country by bicycle, as direct as we could, with as few hills as possible.

It really perks us up, though, when we meet other cyclists, and we were in high spirits as we rode on toward Dubois until, just a few moments later, when the mosquitoes all of a sudden arrived with a vengeance, much to our dismay. Swat, swat, swat, scratch, say bad words, swat, swat, swat, itch, say more bad words.)

We found a little log cabin, right in the center of Dubois, which is a pretty authentic out-west town. The cabin had a little porch and was close to all the shops. Very pleasant and relaxing. We took in the ambience of Dubois, some of which you might classify as rowdy, (even tacky):

We're in the WILD WEST now—Dubois, Wyoming

We packed up all our gear and pronounced ourselves being, "...as ready as we ever will be." We were at 6,900 feet and would be going to about 9,600 feet tomorrow.

190

The Big Day

I didn't sleep very well last night due to a combination of anticipation, anxiety, and the weather. Mostly I stayed awake listening to the thunder and watching the lightning light up our room periodically. But there was very little rain.

We were on the road by 6:15 am and started meeting more cyclists as we labored along. First of all, a fellow from Manchester, England joined us for a few cranks of the wheels. He was camping across the country and had heaps and piles of stuff affixed to every possible spot on his bike, but still he could ride circles around us. Bryon emailed this account:

> When the weary bikers last wrote, we were approaching the Continental Divide. That approach had begun in Davenport, Iowa as we crossed the Mississippi, and was it ever a long, uphill battle. Dubois, Wyoming was the base camp for our final assault. I didn't sleep well that night, as that White Wall of the West sat out there on our path. We were lucky to have good weather and began the climb early. The first ten miles were just a gradual climb, highlighted by The Guy from Manchester. As we were cranking slowly uphill this Brit just appeared next to us on his bike and cheerfully greeted us with what a wonderful trip across the USA he was having. I was cranking up and down through the gears as he never shifted and just chatted and chatted, amusing us with his stories. I not only did not respond but could not respond much, as I was a-huffin and a-puffin along, screaming for oxygen. After about 15 minutes, Mr. Manchester shot off like he was on a motorcycle. What a numbing reminder of how we are the two slowest riders on the road.
> —Bryon

It took us a while to catch our breath after Mr. Manchester. But it was a cool day, which was terrific. After 10 miles or so the road began to go seriously UPHILL, and was a GOOD WORKOUT. A younger couple caught us and they, like most of the cyclists we meet now, were taking the Adventure Cycle Route and were heading to Yellowstone, when we're heading to Idaho. They had started their trip in Virginia, and were headed to Astoria, Oregon. They left 3 weeks after us and caught us already, doing 80+ miles a day. It is good to see more people headed East to West though, like us. We aren't the only ones to pick this direction.

The climb continued, rising toward Togwotee Pass, and we were caught once again, but this time by the "Lawrence of Arabia" of cycling. He was doing the Mountain Bike Route with a behemoth metal steed equipped with massive tires and an enormous Mad Max style trailer. He was loaded down like a hay truck. But, get this, he too came from behind and passed us. The route he was taking took him to out of the way places, where he couldn't always get provisions, including water. He had to carry, at all times, enough food and water for 4 days. My big regret of the trip is that I didn't get the camera out and take a picture of this "Lawrence of Mountain Cycling." He had a piece of cloth attached to his helmet to keep the sun off the back and sides of his neck, and he had a long sleeved, white, desert shirt. His hair was wild, like a man who had just come out of a month in the Sahara without a bath. He had big headlights on the front of his bike, and when Bryon asked him if he rode at night, he replied, "No, but I might need to." We wondered what else he might have in his trailer, should he need them, a few roadside bombs perhaps? He seemed a nice guy, but needless to say, eccentric. Then he too, took off and left us in the dust. The ride though, was pretty enough to take our minds off of our sadly lacking mph's. We were treated to gorgeous stone peaks off to the north, and little lakes here and there. We had some lightning and thunder but no real rain as we approached the pass. Bryon continued his email:

We managed to put our heads down and grind the hours away at 3mph. Sheryl was just fantastic. What a woman! I've had some allergy/breathing trouble and pushed my bike about 200 yards in the early afternoon as the combination of allergy and altitude got the best of me, but that girl just cranked on and on. At about 2:00 pm we rounded a curve to the most stunningly beautiful little green sign you ever saw. It said, it announced, it SHOUTED, "Continental Divide—Elevation 9658." We both had tears in our eyes to realize we had done it. What a great moment in this ride. What a great marriage. What a great moment in this life.

At long last—The Continental Divide

We just wallowed in pride and satisfaction, not to mention the fact that it was now DOWNHILL to Oregon! We were reminded of that by the second loveliest sign of the trip. It said, "Use low gears, 6% downhill next 17 miles."

We soared!

Our bikes soared, our hearts soared, our spirits soared!

We only covered 10 of those miles before the weather got ugly and we stopped for the night.

—Bryon

After we crested the divide, we were soon treated to our first glimpse of the Tetons. It was hazy—as though there was just too much moisture in the air. Nevertheless the view was impressive. We stopped and put on all of our leg and arm warmers, vests, rain coats, etc., and headed down the much earned 6% downhill. It was cold, but we had enough layers on that it was no problem. The first hotel we hit after the Pass, at 3:00 pm was still 8 miles from the place we had booked to stay. But we hadn't eaten since 6:00 am and were famished. We celebrated with a big late-lunch of ribs and a prime rib sandwich. Oh my, that hit the spot. We had burned a lot of calories. After lunch we went out to the bikes just in time to watch a storm race in. There was not only thunder and lightning but heaps of rain and hail too. It lasted over half an hour and we thought about heading out, but the road was terribly sloshy-wet and we knew we would get sprayed with water the whole way, from our own tires and those of passing vehicles, and it was very cold. We opted to stay where we were, and called to cancel the other accommodation. That turned out to be a good decision, as soon the rain started up again.

So there we were in a $103.00 a night "Resort Hotel." Sometimes you get your money's worth and sometimes you don't. In this case, we didn't feel very satisfied. Lots of pricier hotels have coffee pots in the room, and really nice continental breakfasts, but not this one. They wanted you to have to go to the restaurant and buy a cup of coffee from them (and pay them again for breakfast). I guess that's OK with some people, but we really enjoy getting up in the morning and having a cup of coffee in our room, before we venture out. I also like to make a cup of decaf, or herbal tea in my room before going to bed. No luck on that either. It just wasn't very inviting.

We were both exhausted from all the effort it took today. It was a good thing that this day had come relatively late in our trip. You could say we had reached a sort of battle hardened state. If we had faced all that exertion, cold weather conditions, and wind at the beginning of the trip, we might not have been able to get over that pass. It might have been so miserable that it could have ended our trip. But now that this last Big Goal was accomplished, it was kind of an odd feeling.

To be sure, we will enjoy the rest of the downhill and riding through Grand Teton National Park, especially if we get some pretty weather. But beyond that, there really isn't a lot we are specifically looking forward to in Idaho. So we are in a kind of unexpected mental mood right now, a little blip on the emotional roller coaster of riding bikes across the continent.

Nevertheless, we faded off to sleep with a smile on our faces realizing that we had accomplished the biggest goal of the trip. We rode our bikes across the Rocky Mountains.

The Tetons

Wow! What a morning. No regrets on deciding to stay up on the mountain. What we have seen this morning as we descended toward the Hatchet Motel/ Restaurant has been the jewel of the trip. It has been a clear, cold and beautiful morning. We bundled up and basically coasted the 8 miles to the Hatchet. The Tetons were majestic in the clear blue morning sky. We flew down the mountain and every corner we zoomed around, gave us a new view of these awesome mountains. As we coasted down the mountainside, admiring the Tetons, emotions overcame us both, and tears welled up. This was a grander, more magnificent reward than we could ever have imagined. Bryon's email paints the picture with these words:

> The morning was GLORIOUS! We started the blue skied descent when around the first corner swept the Grand Tetons.
> Breathtaking.
> It was one of THOSE moments in life when you just want to sing. Wow, what a morning. We were on top of the world, and zoomed down the mountainside toward Teton National Park, where we spent the day under the most glorious mountains you ever saw.
> Yes.
> Sunday was the highlight of this trip and somehow all those rains, winds, and uphill grinds just evaporated in the grandeur of the Tetons.
> —Bryon

The Grand Tetons, Wyoming

The Tetons were our companions the rest of the day, but we could see clouds rolling in and we wanted to see as much of the park as possible before the clouds engulfed the mountain tops. We were keenly aware that the two previous days had been soggy with rain, and we felt so lucky to have had such a wonderful clear morning, and headed with haste into the National Park. We looped around Jackson Lake and then took the road to Jenny Lake. The

Tetons from that road were just magnificent as it took us right along the base of the mountains. We tried in vane at every possible store to buy a panoramic camera, but no luck. What a shame, because what we saw that morning had to be some of the most panoramic of places in the country. (We could not believe they didn't sell those cameras!)

The wild flowers were out in passionate profusion. Yellows, purples, lavenders, whites, and pinks carpeted the landscape.

> We rode on into Jackson, one of the most fun little towns on the trip, and are having a layover day to just soak in the glory. Then it's DOWNHILL (famous last words) to Idaho and after that—on to Oregon!
>
> Keep those emails coming, we love um.
>
> —Bryon

Jackson Hole, Wyoming was named after a guy called Jackson (duh) and the whole area use to be called Jackson's Hole (I wouldn't want to be a Jr. High School teacher telling that name to her class). The old timers apparently referred to any little spot surrounded by mountains, as a *hole*. After awhile *Jackson's Hole* got shortened to *Jackson Hole,* and it truly is surrounded by mountains, every which way you look, but not just any mountains, these are MOUNTAINS! So the area is called Jackson Hole, but the town is known simply as Jackson, Wyoming.

We found a motel that had a bunch of old log cabins built back in the days of yore. We had trees all around us, and a shaded porch with chairs and a table at which we sat, soaking in the view of the ski slopes of Snow King, which rise up right out of the town. They were lushly green. In Jackson we had our pick of bars and restaurants and both we chose were great fun. They were one of-a-kinds, with heaps of quirky character.

The layover day was a real luxury, as there was no rush to get up. Coffee was on at the office and we kept going back for additional cups for 2 hours, as we lazed around and read, journaled, and relaxed. The rest of the morning was spent with mundane chores like mailing Bryon's rain pants home, getting hair cuts (I was starting to look almost as wild as *Lawrence of Mountainbiking*), buying T-shirts, and doing emails. After that we became tourists and just wandered around Jackson. We took in all the Art Galleries, and my-oh-my, do they ever have Art Galleries! What incredible talent was gathered there in Jackson. The oil and water color work was so distinctive, unlike any we had seen before, and the bronzes were equally interesting. Also there was some crazy-neat stuff like a whole shop where everything, from chandeliers to tables and chairs, was made out of antlers, horns and bones.

Out on the streets of Jackson we stumbled across a fairly lame *shoot-out,* staged near the central park, and then headed to the gem of the evening, a dinner theater production of *Oklahoma.* The acting and singing were of exceptionally high caliber, for such a small town. This layover day was making us feel like we were on vacation again, like we were playing hooky from work.

In the morning we followed the Snake River out of Jackson Hole and with whoops of joy discovered a paved bike trail that we hadn't heard about, which went on for close to 15 miles. Happy Days.

Mike Reynolds told us that there would be some hills to climb after Alpine Junction, but even knowing that, we found them to be a hard slog. It was pretty country though with trees, lakes and the river. However, at one point we were so hot and tired that when we spotted a shady spot on a gravel turnout, we raced each other for it. Luckily there was enough room for us both and we stretched out for a rest. It was amazing how comfortable we were on that gravel. When you are as hot, sweaty, and tired as that, comfort is easily found. Next to me were what appeared to be deer turds, but I didn't care, they didn't smell. After 10 minutes of shut-eye we felt revived and headed on to encounter a van that was pulling a trailer laden down with every imaginable sort of bike ever built. The family, all of them sore and tired, had just finished packing all their bikes back on the trailer after their day of riding in the heat. Among their collection was a bike that you pedaled with your hands, for a member of their group who couldn't pedal with her feet. They also had a tandem that was half hand-pedal and half recumbent. They had upright bikes and a regular recumbent or two. As we chatted with this lot, out of the blue, I screamed in terror and threw my sunglasses on the ground. Everyone went mute and gaped with open mouths, while I stammered around trying to explain. A HUGE spider had crawled inside my sunglasses and was filling up one lens right next to my right eyeball. I totally lost it. It took me awhile to calm down, but when I did, I figured the thing had found its way onto, or into my clothing or helmet whilst I had lain in the gravel back there, and it had only just worked its way to my eyeball.

Chapter Nine

Idaho & Oregon

Just a little ways out of Alpine Junction, Wyoming, we hit the *Welcome to Idaho* sign. It was the last of the *foreign* states we would cross, and it was a near delirious moment as we realized that the very next welcome sign would be for our home state of Oregon.

Irwin, Idaho was our next stopping place, and our motel had fresh paint and new carpets, but the place still needed some work. The front door to our room wouldn't close unless you lifted it up by the door knob an inch or two as you closed it. The TV had a remote but NO channels. We killed 6 spiders inside the room in the first 20 minutes of arrival. (What is it about spiders in this neck of the woods?) The saving grace is that we have some chairs outside to sit on and watch the world go by and the sun go down. (I think I have mentioned this topic of chairs being outside before. On this bike ride, I have really grown to prize this little luxury. After riding a bike all day, I don't want to then sit inside a hotel room, but am often so tired I don't really want to do much of anything. So a nice view, from a comfortable perch outside is just right.) At 8:00 pm it was a pleasant temperature, even though it had gotten into the 90's during the day.

When Bryon tried to get these reservations in Irwin, he called a lodge that was on the internet. For only $500.00 a night we could have stayed with them. We biked by another exclusive lodge on the way, and we can only imagine the price per night there. It looked like really upscale FLY FISHING LODGES and GUEST RANCHES, and only expensive new homes were along this river.

Our aged, but getting upgraded, motel had an upscale Log Cabin Restaurant next door, which seemed to have a pretty good business, but too pricey for us.

June Something?

I'm losing track of the days here, but yesterday we headed out at daybreak in order to reach Idaho Falls by early afternoon. After leaving our companion the Snake River, we climbed up to a plateau and caught a great tailwind for most of the day. The plateau was green, fertile farming country. We sailed along, whooping it up like rodeo riders, and energized to the tips of our sprockets. It's a good thing we had the wind, because there wasn't much else for visitors to get excited about out here in rural Idaho. We lived off rat holed candy and power bars, until we finally made Idaho Falls around 1:30. What? You say, "Only wimps and cyclist wannabes stop at 1:30." You would be right on that. But we were also shocked to the core when a couple of salads came to $20.00! City prices were something we were no longer accustomed to.

We used the afternoon to run some errands, one of which was mailing Bryon's gum drop red fleece vest home. I was still too afraid to part with mine. I hate being cold. But cold we weren't. It was really HOT! We talked to some used car salesmen who told us that it was 101 degrees. We were both out of reading material, so we rode around in this blast furnace called Idaho Falls till we found a book store and each bought a book. Then we sniffed out the Motel 6 and were elated to find it had a pool that was open! We hadn't had a pool the whole trip and this was gonna be a treat. And oh, I almost forgot, there was also this bit of *news from the road* from Bryon:

My good news today is that we didn't get arrested.

It seems that today's tailwind brought me more than speed.

This afternoon I was leading as usual and sailing along at quite a nice clip when I was hit by a lightning bolt on my upper leg, high on my inside upper leg. It was really up there, all too close to a special area where no guy ever wants to get struck by lightning.

It appears that my riding shorts have a tight layer of undergarment and then baggy legs overall. These baggy legs act as an air scoop and it seems that they had sucked up a bee which thought it would be cute to sting the begeezes out of me WAY up there. It sure felt like lightning at first, as I had no warning at all of this disaster. I started screaming and slid to a halt while yelling to Sheryl for assistance, still not sure what had happened to me other than this sudden explosion in my groin area. I could not see up these baggy shorts, but was dancing around the road, slapping at my thigh, still trying to determine the cause of my disaster when my dear wife arrived to save me. She got down on her knees and looked up my shorts. (Hey, she was trying to be nice!) She couldn't see anything so she stuck her hands up my shorts, as the astonished traffic began to slow and gawk at surely what must have appeared to be the lewdest act ever witnessed on a public highway in Idaho. While kneeling, she just kept feeling around and peeking up my shorts till she found the squished culprit. She removed it, stood up and regained her/our dignity much to the disappointment of the passersby's. We were just thankful the Sheriff didn't drive by.

June 27th

Last night Bryon and I sat down together and figured out each remaining day of the trip and made motel reservations all the way home. There are so few motels across Idaho and Oregon on our route that we needed to have firm reservations the whole way. If everything went well, we figured we could make it to Klamath Falls in time to meet our July 4th deadline.

What a Difference a Day Makes could be our theme song though, once again. We started out at dark thirty, to avoid the heat, and had to dig around and find our little blinking red lights for the backs of our bikes. Then we began to climb, nothing really steep mind you, but just a continual climb most of the day. The shoulder deteriorated and became hard to ride, it took a lot of effort and the traffic didn't help because it kept us on the ragged shoulder, all day long. The temperature started rising and by the time we reached about half way to Arco, we were going through our water so fast it was scary and this was to be a 70 mile day, IN THE HEAT! We kept thinking that there would be a farmhouse or a rest area, or something where we could get water, but there wasn't a blessed thing except hot dry nothingness sprinkled in with rocks, dirt, and some scraggly tufts of near dead vegetation.

But we spotted 2 UPS trucks along with their drivers, stopped along the road like a little brown oasis in the desert. I had never been so happy to see the UPS! We stood in the shade created by their trucks, and explained our plight. They were kind enough to pour what was left of the contents from their own personal water bottles, which they were drinking out of, into our empty ones. (I thought for a moment about the danger of catching something from them, should they be getting sick and didn't know it. However, they looked healthy enough, so what the heck? We gladly and thankfully took their water. But, just to be on the safe side, I put my bottle with their water in a bag, and decided I would only use it when every other drop of water I had was gone. I am such a wus about germs.)

The two men then told us about a little rest stop down the road a few more miles, where they thought we could use a toilet and get some water. We were really happy to get that information and headed off feeling less apprehensive about the day. The first place we spotted turned out to be a secure entrance to an extensive HIGH SECURITY facility run by the Idaho National Engineering and Environmental Lab (and managed by the US Department of Energy) way out in these woo woos of Idaho. Makes you wonder what is going on at this facility, doesn't it? I wondered, so I looked it up. From their web site I learned that the secretive place is supposedly committed to providing international nuclear leadership for the 21st Century, developing and demonstrating compelling national security technologies. (They have HUGE buses with darkened windows, which all look the same and have the facility's name on the side. We had about ten of them go by us at one point. A LOT of people work at this top secret place. At least we were assuming that people were in the buses, but we couldn't really see inside them, so who knows?) Associated with this highly secret place is also the ICP (Idaho Cleanup Project) which I guess is supposed to clean up all the bad messes made whilst the "developing and demonstrating" goes on. Sounds like a heck of a place to work, huh?

There was a little cement building at the road block entrance to the area and the guard let us each drink about a gallon of nice cold water and refill our water bottles. They let us come inside for a minute and, alas, it was air conditioned! Ah, it was heaven to us. But we could feel we really weren't supposed to linger there, so we went back outside into that relentless sun and stood shoulder to shoulder in the only shade we could find, that of a power pole, while we washed down an energy bar with the life giving water. I think I am getting tired of energy bars though, sometimes I gag on them.

This is desolate country. There is NOTHING out here. Not only are there no ranches, or homes, or businesses, or water, but there is NO shade! No trees, just low sagebrush type shrubs, and nothing much else. No shade means no stopping, because standing in the baking sun isn't exactly recuperative. There is just the SUN and the HEAT. It was a very long day. Some days of this journey have been like a vacation, some more like a forced march; and this one fell squarely in the forced march column.

We stopped many miles down the road at an actual rest area that had POTABLE water (lots of them don't). Bryon quickly laid down on a picnic table that was partially shaded. I found one too, and laid down, only to notice that it felt kind of sticky. Just as I began to register this, Bryon lifted his weary head and said, "I think that table was just painted." I pried myself off the thing as gingerly as I could, and sure enough, under closer inspection, there was a sign on a wall that had "Wet Paint" penciled on a piece of card board that was the same color as the wall it was stuck on. *Great*, I thought, *a camouflaged sign. Just my luck.* After surveying the damage, I found the only paint that had stuck to anything was on my helmet and my shoes, so it could have been worse. Wha*t else is going to happen on this infernally long, hot day?* I asked myself. Then we got back on the bikes and headed out once again onto the sizzling, frying pan of a road.

Today tried my patience, more than a couple of times. But one moment in particular tested me as no other has on this trip, and I'm sorry to say, I cracked under the strain. The thermo-blast that called itself a headwind was punishing us something fierce as we climbed a moderate incline on this blistering day. Once again, no shade anywhere, so we stopped on the shoulder to get a drink of water and the flies that had been pestering us for a couple of hours began to swarm like wasps on dead meat. I could not bear standing there being molested by those flies. Flies in my eyes, flies in my ears, flies in my nose, flies in my mouth—I was in NO MOOD for it. It was the last straw. Bryon, unaware of my mood, suggested we stand there and rest for awhile longer. I turned to him, and in a voice he had never heard before, I growled in a menacing, low, deep-throated way, reminiscent of someone possessed, "KEEP MOVING, JUST—KEEP—MOVING." I was not in a healthy state of mind, and I think I may have actually scared Bryon a little. It kind of surprised me how foul my mood had become. Dehydration? Sunstroke? Heatstroke? Exhaustion? Senility? Could have been all the above. But I know this much, it was 70 miles of riding that I won't forget anytime soon.

As we headed out along that road, barely fast enough to discourage the flies, we cranked by the entrance to the "Worlds First Nuclear Reactor" which is now on the National Historic Places Register. In 1951 the experimental breeder reactor (EBR-1), produced the world's first usable amount of electric power from nuclear energy, lighting up 4 light bulbs. The next day it produced enough electricity to power the entire EBR-1. It would have been interesting to see, but I just wanted to survive the day, to get to Arco and find an air conditioned motel room.

We thought ARCO was maybe an acronym for Atomic Regulatory Commission, or something, but can't verify that. One report I read seemed to suggest it was named after some guy with the last name of Arco. Not far from Arco there is a place on the map listed as Atomic City. This is quite the area. Lots of history and lots of secrecy (maybe radiation too, for all I know: maybe we'll start to glow in the dark).

As we rode into the town, a sign boasted that Arco was the, "First City to be lit by Atomic Power." That is a pretty unique claim to fame. But they also have the dubious honor of being, *the only city I have ever seen which totally defaced and rendered ugly its signature backdrop hillside of knock-down beautiful diagonally uplifted rock.* It must have been a gorgeous jewel for the city at one time, before the 1920's when they started carving and painting the year of each graduating class into the gorgeous rock. And these people knew how to carve BIG numbers, and still do. The people of Arco even erected a little sign explaining all the numbers. I guess they got tired of everyone asking them why the hillside was so massively disfigured.

After recovering in our air conditioned room, we set out to find somewhere to eat. We found a curious looking joint, an old house with a scraggly, neglected lawn, and some plastic furniture strewn around. There was a sign up that read, "All You Can Eat Ribs, Thursday—Saturday $9.99." When we heard that a group of 27 cyclists from "Affordable Cycle Tours' was coming there for dinner we thought that must be a good sign. But, in all the confusion they sort of forgot about us and when they finally got around to us, they were very, very slow to refill our plates with the all-you-can-eat-ribs, and just as slow to refill our water glasses. Then the rains came so we left. By the time we got back to the room I could tell Bryon was feeling "off." He seemed lethargic. But we had ridden 70 miles, with lots of uphill, in the heat and we were really not in the kind of shape where that's an easy day.

We were in bed by 8:30pm. As I began to drift off, I could hear his innards a-rumblin. Sure enough, he was up all night with something, maybe food poisoning (he thought it was the ribs), maybe the flu, maybe something he caught from the UPS guy's water bottle? We were supposed to be up at 5:00am and on our way, but he was so sick that there was no way that was going to happen. He had what felt like a low-grade temperature and couldn't keep any food down.

While Bryon tried to get some sleep, I went to a phone and tried to call to reschedule the motels across the rest of Idaho and Oregon. The first one I called in Carey couldn't fit us in, as they were completely full until after July 4th. The owner was really happy that we called, because she had no way to contact us, and as it turned out, she had "given" our room to some construction workers anyway. *OH great, isn't that just special?* I trooped off to the library to research any possible leads, motels, B & B's, whatever I could find, alternate routes even. I was not sure what we were going to be able to arrange, but our original goal was to ride across the country from New

York to Oregon, and that remained the goal. Maybe we could make it to Klamath Falls, but it was looking ever more doubtful; we'd just have to see what happened. I would be very happy if we managed to make it to Oregon, period.

We ended up staying 3 grueling nights in that tiny little room at the Lost River Motel in Arco, bumping into our bikes all night, and getting truly sick of the whole confinement. I was unable to line up hotels on the original route, because construction workers had gobbled them all up. On the alternative route we were going to have to ride 80-85 miles, in fierce headwinds, with lots of hills in the first half, and the scorching heat the rest of the day. It would be a dawn to dusk (or later) day for us. If we were both in terrific health, it would have been a huge challenge. Who knows how long it would take for Bryon to be well enough to tackle that. So we made the decision that we would find some kind of motorized transport. We didn't want to spend one more night in Arco, and we were running out of time. When I asked our motel manager about buses, there weren't any—but she volunteered that her husband loved to drive and he would take us the 80 miles to Shoshone, where I had managed to make a reservation for us.

The winds had been howling all day and appropriately, there was a hang gliding contest on in the Arco area. I wondered how bad the winds would have to get before they would call off a hang gliding contest? I was glad I wasn't out in those winds trying to cycle, though. They were NOT blowing westward!

On Saturday evening I went to the motel office to pay for that night and the manager's husband was there so I said, more rhetorically than anything, "So, we're still on for a lift to Shoshone tomorrow?"

He threw me for a loop when he replied, "Well, I don't know, I just noticed that I have a flat tire—I don't know if I can fix it…so I just don't know…it's not my fault."

Oh, boy, this was familiar to me. I had been a drop-out prevention counselor for a year once, and I felt now, talking to our "driver" that I was looking into the eyes of one of those kids I had worked with. Their problem solving skills had never gotten adequately developed, nor did their confidence to try to solve problems—they just tended to give up, saying, "It's not my fault." They also had a hard time being proud of their achievements. If you worked with a kid to help him learn the materials for a test, he couldn't see that his hard work had paid off. If he got an "A," he would say, "The test was easy." It was hard to get the point across to these kids, that they could actually make a difference in the outcomes of things, by their actions. If they did poorly, "It's not my fault." And if they did well it was, "I got lucky." So I began to problem solve with this young fellow. Finally we decided the tire was full enough that in the morning we would drive to a gas station and pump it up. If it wouldn't hold air, we would get it fixed. This was solvable. So, I went away feeling we were both of the same mind.

We were just about ready for bed, when the fellow came down to our room because he was afraid the bikes wouldn't fit in his trunk. We convinced him we could take the wheels off and they would fit in his trunk. Finally he said we would leave at 2:00pm the next day, Sunday. Sounded good to us. We were agreeable to anything at this point. Just get us out of Arco. (Not that Arco is a bad place, but if you have ever been there, 3 days is more than enough time for most visitors, especially those on bikes.)

We were just about asleep when we got a phone call from him and he decided it would be too hot to leave that late in the day (his car had no air conditioner) so we would leave at 7:00am. *Better yet*, as far as we were concerned.

At 7:00am we were all packed and ready to go, when we got another phone call that he'd overslept his alarm, but would be there shortly. When he finally did arrive, he had two really low tires. We pointed this out to him and he said, "That one too?"

We managed to get all the bike parts in his trunk except one bike wheel, which we put in a yard bag and I carried it on my lap in the back seat. We had all our bags piled up between us in the back seat, and the husband and wife team from the Lost River Motel sat up front. It turned into a very sweet trip with these two young people. They were hard workers, and doing a good job managing the motel. Before settling in Arco, they had been in Idaho Falls for awhile but he needed to leave there because he was always having problems, "...they have more cops there than anywhere in the country and I just kept getting into trouble." He didn't elaborate, and we didn't ask, but he was happy with Arco because there weren't so many opportunities to get into trouble, and there weren't so many cops. Everyone must know everyone else in a little town like Arco, and maybe they cut each other more slack, because they understand each others short comings. These two kids were just so genuine we couldn't help but like them both. We were very grateful for their kindness. When we got to Shoshone, they insisted that all they wanted was gas money, but Bryon would have none of that and gave them a bill that had them both grinning from ear to ear, and that was a fitting end to the Arco chapter.

Bryon was still running a fever on the morning we left Arco, and he slept off and on the rest of the day, in our room at the Governor's Mansion Bed and Breakfast in Shoshone. Our room was spacious and the breakfast was excellent, this place was a bargain. I then made reservations for a motel that was only about 20 miles away, in Gooding for the next night, because I didn't know how good Bryon would be feeling.

By the time we rolled into Gooding the next day, Bryon was on the mend, so I canceled the reservation and made one in Glenns Ferry. We didn't know that the winds were going to come up so HARD, but we made it there. More importantly, Bryon was feeling SO much better.

We had been crossing the Snake River off and on today, and now and again for the past few riding days. The beautiful "spreads" along the river transformed the sagebrush country into an exclamation of green.

In my notes I had written that Shoshone is in the middle of the "Miracle Valley," and just looking at the map, you get an understanding for how unique the surrounding area is. The Sawtooth Mountains and Sun Valley are only about 100 miles to the north, with the Sawtooth Scenic Byway beginning in Shoshone and heading North on highway 75 toward Sun Valley and through the Sawtooths all the way to Stanley.

The Snake River with all its beauty is the center for wild whitewater rafting possibilities, there are many rivers and streams for fishing, and we've been hearing about the Shoshone Ice Caves, where the ice never melts and folks ice skate even in the summer! In the old days, because of these caves, Shoshone was one of the few places within hundreds of miles, where you could get a cold beer in the summer. Discovered in 1880, the 40 foot high lava tube cave is 110 feet underground and close to 1,700 feet long. Water seeping in from a nearby river freezes and creates ice that averages sixteen feet thick. There are fossil beds in the area, more caves, and springs, and interesting rock formations, so there is plenty to do in this area.

Following Bryon today, as we cranked along, I could see that the three days free from riding had helped his "hamburger buns," as much as they had helped his temperature and other symptoms. For the first time since the start of our trip, he was sitting square on his seat, and pumping his legs straight up and down. I yelled up to him, "How are you doing?"

He yelled back, "It's like I've got a new butt!"

At Glenns Ferry we followed our motel lady's very good advice and headed to the Winery Restaurant. On the way there we biked over to the river and saw the area where the Oregon Trail Wagon Trains had forded the Snake River. There was an island in the river there, which must have been a main reason they crossed at this point, but it was a dangerous and risky maneuver. A smart fellow by the name of Glenn decided the ferry business would be a good thing to get into and voilá, the Oregon Trail gained a ferry crossing, and the town of Glenns Ferry was born. A railroad came and the town boomed, then it left and the town struggled. But no one was struggling at the Winery Restaurant. It was a gorgeous setting with golf course, vineyards, winery, wine tasting and restaurant all bundled together. We liked their wines and had a bottle of one of their reds with dinner. (It was only $9.00, can't beat that.) If I hadn't been on a bike I would have bought a case of the stuff.

July 2ⁿᵈ
We did nothing but climb, climb, climb, climb, climb, most of the morning on our way to Mountain Home, but the highlight of the day was at one point when we AT LAST passed the 3,000 mile mark! Oh, Happy days!

It was hard to believe that we had actually pedaled these bicycles 3,000 miles and now were only about a scant 100 miles from Oregon. I thought, *"NOTHING can stop us now!"* (Famous last words again, as it was to turn out.)

The news for the weather was: record heat for the next 4 days. We started our clothes-washing-by-hand ritual again and washed all our dirty, smelly stuff. As I watched Bryon laboring to clean his padded riding shorts it hit me that I only had to wash my light weight running shorts since the recumbent rider doesn't have to have padded shorts. (They dry really fast, too.) Just one more nice bonus for recumbent riders.

However the sun is harder on the recumbent rider's legs. My body kept screaming at me to *get out of the sun*, but I couldn't. I kept reapplying the UV protection sunscreen to my legs constantly, and I was so greased up that I could probably have been squirted across into Oregon.

July 3ʳᵈ
The end of the trip was at hand; we figured we would have just about enough time left to get as far as Juntura, Oregon but all of our motel reservations got thrown off with Bryon's illness, so even if we could have

pedaled further, we would have no place to stay. (We mailed our one-night camping stuff home long ago.) It was just as well because our good friend Barbara Stout, from Ashland, Oregon was nutty enough to volunteer to come pick us up in Juntura, and take us home.

(We added a few new items today, to our "Road Bounty" list for the trip. I was pleased to find a lovely big carabiner attached to a rope. It was a real trophy. Bryon found a substantial tow hook. It never ceases to amaze us, all the stuff we find along the road. Today we could, if we wanted, be the proud owners of a couple of nice, new beach towels, and a pillow case not to mention a couple pairs of gloves, a usable frying pan, a shirt, a flower pot, a sweatshirt, and two road kill owls, one of which was in beautiful condition, though entirely expired.)

Our plan was to ride as far past Boise, Idaho as we could stand in the heat. That way our ride the next day would be shorter and we could get off the road earlier on the 4th of July. Bicycling the roads on holidays is scary; just too many drunks and otherwise impaired folks driving heavy vehicles around.

Boise, Idaho

Boise was an attractive State Capitol/College Town with a river running through it, lots of trees, and a mountain to admire. I sat in the grass, under the shade of some trees at the Boise Library while Bryon wrote an email to all of our friends inviting them to join us for Pizza on our deck at home, and celebrate the completion of The Ride. We had everything mapped out, and just hoped that we would have no illnesses, or bike troubles on this last leg of the trip. (Ha!)

Before we left Boise I had had two flat tires in short order and before we got to the Oregon State Line, I was sick and getting sicker with a temperature, headache and nausea.

The front tube was beyond repair, so we had to use the only spare tube I had in my bags to fix it. Bryon put the tube in the tire and then bicycled it over to a gas station to make sure it would hold air. When he got back, put the tire on the bike and I climbed on—guess what? The back tire was really low, though not completely flat. What fun. I felt really bad for Bryon as he worked on the flats in the heat, but at least he found a shady spot to set up shop. I had to head off on foot to try and find spare inner tubes to stock up on, but the 20x1.35 was hard to locate. (All I wanted to do was crawl up in the fetal position and go to sleep.) Most stores carry 20x1.75 but not 20x1.35. And then, Bryon had to stop in the middle of everything, because he broke his glasses and had to head off to Target for new ones. Not a fun time. (But we were glad these flats happened in a city where we could re-supply.)

I stopped writing in my journal at this point, I was feeling too sick to be bothered. Bryon was left to fill in the final accounts of our trip:

Leaving hot sweltering Boise was NOT fun. After the miles and miles of desolation, we now were confronted by urban riding at rush hour with no (or little) shoulders. It was time to call it a day but there just were no motels on the road we chose to head ever westward. Traffic whizzed by at arms length. The thermometer continued to climb and sweat was matting our hair and running down into our eyes. It was one of those nasty moments you occasionally encounter in cycling when you just wish it was all over. As we approached the town of Meridian we finally spotted a rather upscale convenience store/gas station. Our Oasis.

We dismounted our now filthy bikes and stumbled into this delightfully air-conditioned refuge. Sheryl looked awful. Her lovely silver hair was wadded up and sticking to her face. Road grime and stinky sweat covered her sun burned face and arms. They should have thrown her out. I guess the reason they didn't was that I looked worse. I was wheezing and puffing and drinking down mouthful after mouthful from their icy water fountain when I looked up to see behind the counter the worlds most ditzy, blond, 17 year old high school drop out. She chewed her gum, scratched her parts, and stared at me like I was from Mars. I tried to work up a smile. Finally she managed an utterance, "Whered ja come from"? I heaved a sweaty sigh and mumbled, "New York City." Her eyes widened, she looked at our road weary bikes, my bedraggled wife, and finally the stinking, sweating, overweight guy who was drinking her water and she said, "No you didn't."

That night in Meridian held all kinds of anticipation; after all we were only 42 miles from Oregon. Could it really be that we would pull this off tomorrow? Sleep did not come easy for me that night, as I was excited. It didn't come easy for Sheryl, as now it was her turn to be sick. And just when we could almost see Oregon!

Sheryl toughed it out that morning and mounted her reliable red recumbent, and we pedaled west. We were back to croplands and we just slowly pushed west at a rate she could maintain. When we got to Parma it was time for lunch. Oregon was now just a very few miles off and Sheryl was willing to soldier on. We pushed on up highway 20 until we saw this beautiful left turn and the sign to Nyssa, Oregon. We made the turn and began to gather speed as we headed down a gentle slope to the Snake River which is the line between Oregon and Idaho at this point. There it was! WELCOME TO OREGON. We had done it. Perhaps you have never seen grownups kissing a sign but had you been on that bridge over the Snake River that day you would have come across quite a scene. We were hoopin' and hollerin' and jumping all around. It was delicious.

After over 3,000 miles, with 64 riding days (74 days total,) we finally made it to Oregon! July 4, 2002

It was also hot. And now that the adrenalin was shot, poor Sheryl just wanted to lie down and sleep. I didn't think there was any hope of her grinding out the last 13 miles to Ontario, as it was now the heat of the day, something over 100F. We rode into town and found the main gas station. Out in this country everybody drives a pickup, so I reasoned that anyone heading in the direction of Ontario would be a likely ride for our bikes and us, after all, we had ridden all this way to Oregon!

Country folks are friendly and helpful. Usually. I repeatedly explained our predicament and had one refusal after another. Finally I resorted to offering to pay for the gas to fill their tank. Nope. Sorry Mister. Not Today. It made me feel next to useless to not be able to find a way to get Sheryl to Ontario with a fever raging and a worn out body. Finally she lifted her head and said, "Let's ride."

What a sad, slow ride, to end our magnificent adventure. We stopped every time there was shade and let her rest. Finally about 4pm we rolled into Ontario and found a nice cool air-conditioned motel.

It was only too obvious that there was no way we were going to ride across the heat of Oregon while Sheryl was so sick and friends and relatives would soon be gathering on our deck to help us celebrate so the next morning I rented a vehicle and drove us home while Sheryl slept.

Afterword

It is the year 2007 now, almost five years since we started our ride. I was sick when we began and sick when we finished. But in between I lived an adventure that no amount of telling can re-capture. This is not the caliber of adventure you read about from those cyclists who have faced much greater obstacles, more challenging terrain, and went at a much faster pace, pulled a much heavier load and did it with far greater toughness and personal physical fitness. But this has been an ADVENTURE unlike any other of my life, and it was more interesting than I could have ever imagined. I am 60 years old now, and I don't think I will ever again do such a long bike ride. Some things are just "oncers." We continue to ride around the Klamath Basin, and Bryon and I take our bikes with us whenever we think we'll have a chance to ride them, wherever we travel. But we're not planning the next big road trip.

I did recently purchase a used foldable recumbent that fits in a suitcase, and I love it (A Bike Friday Recumbent called a SatRday). Bryon and I joined friends the previous summer and biked from Vienna to Prague. Since I couldn't find any way to rent a recumbent over there, I bought this suitcase bike. This past summer we joined the same friends and biked the Loire Valley in France. After that Bryon and I headed to the Netherlands and on our own biked the 400 kilometer Old Zuiderzee Route. I hope to put a lot of overseas miles on this SatRday as the years go by.

My biggest regret of the ride was when I got home and weighed in. I started off the trip at 146 pounds, I rode my bicycle over 3,124 miles in 64 days of actual riding. 46% of those days were into headwinds, and only 28% had tailwinds. I was sure I must have lost some significant weight and was anxious to find out how much I had lost. So I got on the scales with anticipation of a wonderfully low number appearing. I was dumbfounded to see that I weighed exactly 146 pounds, the same as when I started.

The thing I understand the least, regarding this whole process though, has to do with trying to write this trip up in book form. It has taken me over twenty times longer to write this story than it did to ride it. That has been a real eye opener to me and one which continues to make no sense.

I read somewhere, that the main thing that sets octogenarians apart from the rest of us, who die sooner, was that their overriding feeling about their life was that it had been an adventure. I like that. The adventure can take many roads, for sure, but constants in all adventures are not knowing what the outcome will be, and growing, learning, adjusting, overcoming obstacles, and appreciating along the way.

What I learned to appreciate the most on this trip was my husband. He not only did all the organizing, all the planning and all the navigating, but he waited patiently for me at the top of every hill. There is not one other person in the world that I could have done this ride with. I am now a new grandmother, and when I look back on this quixotic bicycle episode from my life I can hardly believe it actually happened. It was a Grand Adventure.

—**Sheryl Van Fleet**